D1603735

For Annelies

Donna Bunting Flake

The
Haunted Life
of
Lura

Donna Bunting Flake

simply francis publishing company

North Carolina

Library of Congress Control Number: 2022906049
ISBN: 978-1-63062-038-7 (paperback)
ISBN: 978-1-63062-039-4 (e-book)
Printed in the United States of America
Cover and Interior Design: Christy King Meares

For information about this title or to order books and/or electronic media, contact the publisher:

simply francis publishing company
P.O. Box 329, Wrightsville Beach, NC 28480
www.simplyfrancispublishing.com
simplyfrancispublishing@gmail.com

DEDICATION

I dedicate this book to my beloved Mama who died in early 2021. She instilled a love of literature and reading in me as a child. Mama cheered me on and provided suggestions and enhancements when I first began writing *The Haunted Life of Lura*. She must be looking down with a big smile on her face now that the work is complete.

CAST OF CHARACTERS

Lura Kennedy Davis – main character and wife of Tom Davis

<u>**Lura's parents:**</u>
Jackson Kennedy – father
Aila Kennedy – mother

<u>**Lura's Paternal grandparents:**</u>
Stuart John Kennedy – grandfather
Marette Kennedy – grandmother

<u>**Lura's siblings:**</u>
Laurence Kennedy – Lura's beloved younger brother, best friend
Josephine Kennedy – Lura's older sister
Maggie Kennedy – Lura's oldest sister
Murdock Kennedy – Lura's older brother
Angus Kennedy – Lura's oldest brother
Joseph Kennedy – Lura's older Brother
Louis Kennedy – Lura's younger brother
Cecil Kennedy – Lura's youngest brother

<u>**Lura's husband and his family:**</u>
Tom Davis – Lura's husband, father of Matilda Davis Aasen
Matilda Davis – Tom and Rita Davis' daughter, Lura's stepdaughter
Gay Aasen – Matilda Davis' daughter, Lura's step-granddaughter
Rita Gay Davis – first wife of Tom Davis, mother of Matilda
Stuart Davis – Tom's brother
Fanny Davis – Tom's sister-in-law and wife of Stuart Davis

Lura's extended family:

Wanda Kennedy – Laurence Kennedy's wife

Olivia Kennedy – Laurence and Wanda Kennedy's daughter and Lura's niece

Buddy Blue – Lura's nephew and genealogist

Special Friend:

Earl Brown – African American friend and servant of Lura

Friends at Brenau College:

Agnes Galloway – Lura's childhood friend, Brenau College roommate, and ghost

Louise McLeod – Lura's college roommate

Secondary Characters

Duncan McMillan - Lura's lawyer

Meg McGinnis - Neighbor of Wanda Kennedy

Elsie Everette - Lura's distant cousin who helped Matilda

CONTENTS

LIST OF IMAGES

KENNEDY FAMILY

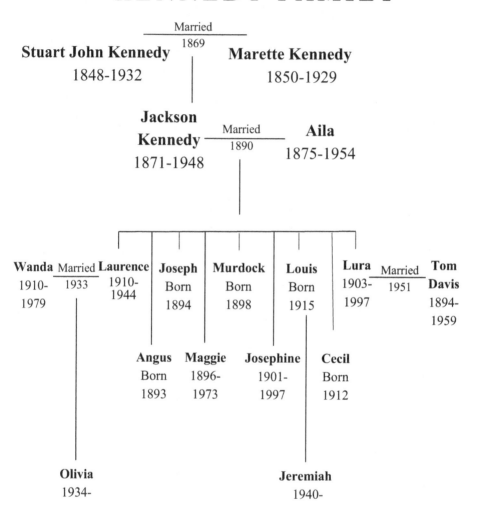

Married 1869

Stuart John Kennedy
1848-1932

Marette Kennedy
1850-1929

Jackson Kennedy
1871-1948

Married 1890

Aila
1875-1954

Wanda
1910-1979

Married 1933

Laurence
1910-1944

Joseph
Born 1894

Murdock
Born 1898

Louis
Born 1915

Lura
1903-1997

Married 1951

Tom Davis
1894-1959

Angus
Born 1893

Maggie
1896-1973

Josephine
1901-1997

Cecil
Born 1912

Olivia
1934-

Jeremiah
1940-

DAVIS FAMILY

FIRST MARRIAGE

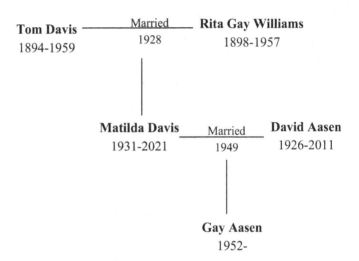

Tom Davis ——— Married ——— **Rita Gay Williams**
1894-1959   1928   1898-1957

Matilda Davis ——— Married ——— **David Aasen**
1931-2021   1949   1926-2011

Gay Aasen
1952-

SECOND MARRIAGE

Tom Davis ——— Married ——— **Lura Kennedy**
1894-1959   1951   1903-1997

PROLOGUE

Lura woke up with dread, knowing full well how this day would end. As quietly as humanly possible, she got out of her warm bed-she must not wake up Tom. She stood motionless looking at her seventy-year-old husband with regret. Lura retched, tasting the bitter bile throughout her mouth, but she forced it back down, knowing vomiting now would immediately alarm Tom and her plan would be delayed. The floorboards squeaked as she walked across the floor, and as she closed the bedroom door it creaked like a ghost was in the house.

Her shoulders slumped and her face was a picture of grief as she entered her living room. Upon seeing Sally, her beloved cocker spaniel, Lura's spirits lifted. Sally's tail wagged rapidly and Lura noticed Sally's happy grin, a trick that cocker spaniels alone in the canine world display. Sally obviously wanted Lura to pet her. Lura sank down on the floor, looked lovingly into Sally's brown eyes, and put her arms gently around Sally. Anguished tears fell from Lura's eyes onto Sally's back. She whispered loving words to Sally. Sally began to whimper softly and put her moist nose on Lura's arm over and over. Lura hugged Sally tighter and buried her face in Sally's beautiful coat. Lura breathed in the slightly "doggie" smell of Sally and remembered the dogs she had owned over her life, and how much she loved them and how she loved them more than most people. Lura thought of one little stray she found twenty years ago. This canine became her beloved Rose-her coat was black, white, and gray. Lura stood up from the floor and put her arms on the back of the desk chair, bent over, and put her hands on her face. She slowly sat down in the chair. Feeling regret for her marriage, she glanced at her bedroom door.

Sally persistently pawed Lura's leg and began to whine. Knowing Sally would not quit, Lura picked Sally up, gave her a hug, took her to the laundry room, placed Sally on her doggie blanket, closed the door, and returned to the living room.

Lura sat at the desk and began thinking about her deceased parents. She began an internal dialog with her papa first.

Papa, you played a big part in bringing me to this point by your selfishness, arrogance, and pride. You committed a crime so horrible that you were sent to prison for twenty years. When you escaped you chose to see our family hardly ever. Your behavior resulted in isolating me and my siblings from others. We all became accustomed to distancing ourselves from others and this has harmed me for my whole life. Even though I admire you for becoming a good person in the end, I was forever harmed by what you did early in your life.

Lura's eyes filled with tears as she reflected on her mother, Aila. She spoke a silent soliloquy to her mother.

Mama, you tried to be a good mother, but you had so much anger towards Papa that it spilled over to how you treated your children. After he committed murder, you were always mean to him and took every opportunity to say dirty things to him. Your children witnessed this negative behavior repeatedly, and it made us live in hell.

Lura reluctantly opened the drawer of Tom's rolltop desk and sat looking at the two things in the drawer-a fancy bottle of Shalimar perfume and a thirty-two caliber Smith & Wesson revolver. She was perplexed how her bottle of perfume got into this drawer. She was about to reach for the gun, then reconsidered and picked up the perfume. She opened the bottle and breathed deeply, smelling the exotic medley of aromas. Under normal circumstances she would have delighted in the sweet smell. Lura thought of having worn Shalimar on her honeymoon and how this scent always made her happy, till now. Lura put the Shalimar bottle back in the drawer.

Just then she heard the laughter of neighborhood children as they ran across her front lawn. She thought, "how could they be happy when there is no happiness in me at all?" Lura bit her lip till her mouth tasted the distinctive taste of her own blood. She sat with her hands in her lap, staring at the gun in the drawer and was so scared of what was to come that she almost stopped breathing. Sweat broke out on her skin, mostly on the back of her neck and on her scalp. She gathered all the courage she could find and reached for the gun. It was heavier than she expected. It was slippery and smelled of cleaning oil. She pointed it at her left temple.

"No, Lura, No!" yelled Tom, his voice frantic. He grabbed the gun. They struggled.

BANG!

CHAPTER 1

Lura's Young Life

1903-1915

Grandpapa Kennedy roared, "Lura where are you wee lass? We can't begin the storytelling without you, little darling."

Seven-year-old Lura with long red hair and unusually light blue eyes ran into the huge cozy living room and took a seat directly in front of her grandpapa. The room was filled to the brim with Lura's siblings, parents, cousins, aunts, uncles, and grandparents, all of whom were descendants of Scottish Highlanders. The faces of the children looked eager and happy because they knew their grandpapa was going to tell them stories. Liking audience participation, Grandpapa was already deciding which of his progeny to involve in the stories.

Grandpapa said, "Who can tell us how we came to live here in Quewhiffle, North Carolina?"

Sixteen hands went up in the air and several little boys jumped up and down pleaded, "Ask me, ask me."

Grandpapa Kennedy took several moments looking around at potential children to answer the questions. He had a special affection for shy and introverted Lura. He wanted her to become more outgoing, so he looked directly at her and said, "You can tell us the answer."

Lura hesitated at first then said, "We came here from Scotland a long time ago."

1

Grandpapa said, "That's right Lura. You gave a good answer. Now, who can tell me more of why our ancestors left Scotland?"

Lura's older brother, Angus, a slender boy with a head full of black hair, and the promise of a black beard someday spoke up. "Our people came here from the Scottish Highlands beginning in the 1740s because the English treated us like dogs. They wouldn't let us wear the tartan, speak Gaelic, or sing our Scottish songs. They even stopped us from raising our Scottish flag."

Then 17-year-old Bruce interrupted Angus and said, "Let *me* tell you how it really was."

People in the room knew Bruce was a know-it-all, and they hated for him to begin talking because he would never stop unless someone interrupted him. He was extremely intelligent in book learning, but his social skills were sorely lacking. Behind his back people called him 'the walking encyclopedia.' Grandpapa knew he could cut Bruce's story short, but he decided to let Bruce be in the limelight for a little while.

Bruce proudly spoke up. "In the 1700s, over 5,000 Scottish men, women, and children left Scotland due to the intense persecution by the English. After the Battle of Culloden, the Kennedy Clan lands became property of the English government, and their houses and cattle were destroyed. The evil English forbade Scottish customs and Scottish artifacts. If a Scotsman was caught wearing a tartan or flying the Scottish flag, he could be imprisoned or even hanged. Thousands of our dear Scottish brethren came here to the New World to live where they could have the freedom to practice Scottish customs. Most of them sailed to the New World, entering at the port of Wilmington, North Carolina. Then they traveled by shallow boat up the Cape Fear River to Cross Creek, today people call it Fayetteville. Our close Kennedy relatives came here to Quewhiffle, and other Scots

2

established towns and communities in this area-Aberdeen to our west, Inverness to the northwest, and Raeford southeast of here. There is even Scotland County to our southwest."

Grandpapa interrupted Bruce by saying, "Thank you Bruce, but now I want to ask the young ones their opinions."

Turning around and facing the fireplace, Grandpapa reverently lifted an old wooden box from the mantle. He carefully placed the box on his lap, and said, "Who can tell me what's in this box?"

Marcellus, Lura's six-year-old cousin lifted his hand and said, "I know. It's a hat with red hair inside."

Grandpapa slowly opened the lid and took out a flat knitted green plaid hat with a frayed pompom on top. Grandpapa turned the hat inside out and there sewed to the underside of the pompom was a thick and long lock of red hair.

As he softly stroked the long lock of ginger-red hair, Grandpapa said, "Look here Marcellus, you are absolutely right about the red hair. Do you know who this hair belonged to?"

Marcellus shook his head to indicate he did not know.

Grandpapa reverently stroked the ginger hair for a full minute to build suspense, and then continued, "This hat belonged to my great grandpapa, Jimmy Kennedy, and this is his very own hair. Marcellus, come here and touch his hair."

Marcellus walked up to Grandpapa and timidly put his hand on the hair. "The hair feels like my mama's hair."

Grandpapa said, "I want everyone in this room to have an appreciation of and affection for our ancestor, Jimmy Kennedy. He fought for Scottish independence in 1746 at Culloden. He was captured, put in prison, and given the choice of being hanged, or going to the New World.

3

"Marcellus, which do you think Jimmy picked, to be hanged or to come to America?" asked Grandpapa.

With a confident smile on his face Marcellus said, "To come here."

Grandpapa replied, "Yes, you are right Marcellus. Jimmy Kennedy was a smart man, so he chose to come to America. Jimmy and all the other Scottish prisoners coming to America had to sign an oath to the King of England. When the Revolutionary War broke out between America and England, Jimmy's sympathy and love were with America and not England. He remembered he had made an oath of loyalty to the British King, and he knew he must not break it. To not break his promise, he moved to Cuba temporarily during the war, then returned here to Quewhiffle. Remember children, if you make an oath, you must always keep it, no matter what. That is how our Scottish Highlander ancestors lived their lives, and how we must live our lives today."

At this point in the storytelling, Grandpapa took a swig of whiskey, and said to his attentive audience, "That delicious drink gives me the strength I need to demonstrate the Kennedy war cry. Do you want to hear it?"

Grandpapa stood up, stretched his arms above him, breathed in a huge breath of air to get ready for his war cry performance. He began a screech that turned into a heart piercing howl that lasted almost a full minute, until he was totally out of breath. His cry sounded as if he said, "Arureekzeepuz." The deafening cry from Grandpapa made the men jump, the ladies scream, and the children try to match his incredibly loud war cry. The noise in the room was deafening once again. Then everyone fell over laughing.

The kids and parents alike yelled, "More stories, and more War Cries."

Then the singing and the bagpipe playing began and this went on till the wee hours of the morning. With the sound of several bagpipes blasting in her ears, Lura still managed to fall asleep against the chest of her grandmother. Lura was taken home and put in her own bed by her papa. She slept soundly and awoke the next morning thinking of the fun she had at the party last night. She loved the singing, bagpipe playing, and storytelling. She loved being a member of this loving community.

Lura's grandpapa, Stuart John Kennedy, was a County Commissioner, a Deacon and founding member of the Sandy Grove Presbyterian Church of Quewhiffle, and a wealthy pillar of the community. He and his wife, Marette, were born before the Civil War and were staunch Democrats. Their big house was just a ten-minute walk down the Old Chicken Road, from the house belonging to their son, Lura's papa.

Lura's grandpapa was different from her papa. Her grandpapa was kind, fun, entertaining, and he could be trusted to do the honorable thing. Lura always felt loved and completely comfortable with her grandpapa.

Lura's own papa often perplexed her with his behavior. When Jackson Kennedy was good, he was incredibly good, but when he was bad, he was horrible!

One of Lura's favorite memories of him was when she got into a tickling contest with him and her brothers and sisters. They all rolled around on the front lawn until they were breathless. He knew exactly when to stop tickling them, and when to let the children pin him down on the ground and tickle him non-stop. They played like that until her mama called them to the porch for watermelon and lemonade. Lura understood

5

these good times and basked in the happy times spent with her papa. She was much closer to her playful and affectionate papa than her temperamental mother.

At other times, Lura's papa thoroughly confused or embarrassed her. She remembered one time when she went with him into Raeford to buy some things at the general store. She was already a bit worried because she smelled whiskey on her papa's breath. Normally the storekeeper would serve customers in the order they came into the store. Jackson said to the frail elderly man who was the next customer to be served, "I need to get my groceries first. I'm in a big hurry."

The elderly man timidly and almost silently responded, "I'm in a hurry, too."

Jackson, with a look of exasperation, shoved the man and caused him to fall and spill a barrel of peas all over the floor. Then with a look of arrogance and superiority on his face, he moved up to the counter and handed his shopping list to the shopkeeper. He looked at the old man struggling to get up and whispered under his breath, "Poor white trash."

Lura was humiliated and worried that if he did this to an old man, what would he do to others who crossed him?

Then she remembered what happened at the house raising bee when she heard the new widow in town tell her neighbor, "I sure do like that handsome, tall, brown-eyed Jackson Kennedy. He could charm any lady without even trying. He makes me have butterflies!"

The widow's friend said, "Hush your mouth! Goodness gracious, don't you get mixed up with that Jackson Kennedy. First, he has eight kids and a pregnant wife who would have a conniption fit if she heard that you were saying these things. Second, he is a hot-headed Scot who is easy to anger. He has gotten in trouble numerous times, but his wealthy father always gets him out of trouble. Once, Jackson threw eggs at the buggy of a boy who had gained the affections of his girlfriend. He's also been in trouble for public drunkenness."

The widow said, "I didn't even know he was married. He has been flirting with me ever since I arrived today. Well, I swear, I am going to leave him alone. What in tarnation was I thinking!"

What Lura and other people did not know was that her Papa often questioned his own behavior. The night of the house raising bee when Jackson finally went to bed, he thought about his behavior that day. He knew he acted inappropriately forward with the pretty widow. He often acted this way to women when his wife was not there. He remembered what he learned in church and Sunday School, and he knew God would not like him acting like that. Jackson believed in God and wanted to do what was right, but so often his own libido or his Scottish highland temper got between him and God.

Lura also questioned her Papa's behavior to the woman at the house raising bee. She felt bad that her Papa liked talking and touching ladies other than her mother.

She knew he was often angry and would sometimes hit her or her Mama or her brothers and sisters. But now others were noticing bad things about her Papa. She sometimes pondered these things in her bed at night, and this made her worry for hours rather than fall asleep.

Lura had heard stories of the courtship of her parents. She heard that when her papa was courting her mother, that he often told her that she was as pretty as a speckled puppy, and that he loved her better than any other girl in the world. Whenever her papa would say this, her mother would hug and kiss her papa and say,

"Darn tootin,' now gimme some more sugah."

People told Lura that the day her parents got married, her mother was over the moon in love with him. Her parents had nine children in quick succession, and Lura was the sixth in line.

As a young child Lura felt secure that her parents loved each other and loved her and her brothers and sisters. Lura's early childhood was happy. She and her siblings spent almost all their free time playing together, or with the multitude of Scottish cousins in Quewhiffle.

Lura liked to tell jokes and recite rhymes and poems. She remembered one of the first times she recited a poem in public. It was at her seventh birthday party held at her grandparent's house. Six cousins had already recited poems. Lura stepped up and said,

"I have memorized a poem and I want to recite it for you."

Lura's Grandpapa lifted her up on a chair and she timidly began to recite the poem.

Wee Willie Winkie runs through the town,
Upstairs and downstairs in his nightgown.
Rapping at the window, crying through the lock.
Are the children in their beds?
Now it's eight o'clock.

After she finished, Lura received enthusiastic applause and a warm hug from her grandpapa. She was pleased with herself.

Lura Kennedy was born March 11, 1903, into a well-to-do family in south-central North Carolina in a tiny community known as Quewhiffle. Known as 'the sandhills,' this land was the perfect environment for growing immense forests of longleaf pines and loblolly pines. These trees, used for harvesting pitch and sap, could make a person rich in the turpentine business. As the entrepreneurial Kennedy's turpentine business prospered, they bought more land with each succeeding generation.

When Lura was seven-years-old, her baby brother, Laurence, was born and she adored him. The affection Lura had for Laurence changed her in a big way. Rather than go outside and play, she spent most of her free time with Laurence. She loved to put her finger beside Laurence's hand, and he would then wrap his tiny fist around her finger. When Laurence turned six-months-old, she loved to hold him in her lap and say, "You are the most beautiful baby in Quewhiffle, AND in North Carolina, AND in America! You are the sweetest baby I ever saw." She talked to him in baby talk tones of excitement and exuberance. He would respond with a huge toothless grin and make sounds like he was trying to talk, but he only made sounds of squeals and soft shrieks. She would kiss him on his right cheek, then his left cheek, then his right cheek until baby Laurence used his chubby baby hand to push her away, as he had reached his limit for kisses at the moment.

Lura knew that there would never be a person as precious to her in the entire world as her dear Laurence. She vowed to do all she could do to keep him happy and safe as long as she lived.

When Laurence turned two, Lura's mother had another baby, and he was named Cecil. Shortly after the birth of the new baby, she whispered to Laurence, "I am your mother now." She was so glad there was a new baby in the house because she knew her mother would focus her attention on the new baby, and this allowed her to have more time with Laurence.

Lura enjoyed school and made good grades. One day at recess, she overheard her teacher talking to a new teacher at school.

"I have taught all the Kennedy children, but Lura is the smartest of all. She won the spelling bee last week and is a quick reader. I am honored to have this gifted child in my class."

Not knowing which child the teacher was describing, the new teacher looked around at all the students on the playground, and asked, "Which one is she?"

"Lura is the pretty girl with red hair holding hands with your student, Agnes Galloway," said Lura's teacher.

Hearing these comments made Lura so happy that she skipped all the way home from school and went straight to find Laurence and to tell him what her teacher had said.

Lura's whole life turned upside down and inside out during the summer before she turned nine-years-old. To Lura it felt like there was an earthquake that tilted the platform her life was built upon. She learned of the change in her life at breakfast one morning when everyone in her family was at the kitchen table except her Papa.

Lura casually asked her family, "Where's Papa?" The younger children just kept eating their oatmeal, but the older ones looked at Lura's mother with looks of anguish and anxiety. Maggie, her older sister, burst out crying and ran from the table. Seeing her older siblings behave like this made Lura scared. No one answered her question, and this made her even more fearful.

Lura thought to herself, *did he die and they are not telling me?*

This time Lura looked directly into her mother's eyes and in a louder voice said, "Where is Papa?"

Squirming in her seat, Lura's mother replied angrily, "You don't have to yell Lura. I heard you the first time. Your Papa left."

Lura said, "Where did he go?"

With a beet red face, her mother replied, "I will tell you later when you are older. Now eat your breakfast and don't ask me about your Papa again."

Lura, like Maggie, burst out crying and ran to her room. Lura tried to talk to Maggie to find out what happened to their Papa. Maggie said she did not know, but Lura could tell she did know and was not telling.

As the days went by following this 'earthquake,' she constantly thought about her Papa's sudden and unexplained departure. She was sure her mother knew what was going on. Lura felt that her older brothers also knew what happened to her Papa. Lura was angry that no one would tell her where he was. She heard bits and pieces of conversations mentioning lawyer, court, police, but she never knew enough to put the story together. The sudden and inexplicable disappearance of him made Lura sad much of the time. She began to spend much of her time alone or just with Laurence.

What Lura did not know was that her mother told her older siblings and all their relatives *not* to tell Lura and her younger siblings the true facts of Jackson's disappearance. Everyone was afraid of Aila's wrath, and everyone knew that telling the younger children would result in Aila's intense hate and vengeance.

Christmas 1912 came and went, and he did not come home. She had prayed and hoped he would come for Christmas, after all, he was always there at Christmas.

On the day after Christmas, Lura could not stand being ignorant of his disappearance any longer.

She came into the kitchen where her mother was washing the dishes and said, "Mama, I have to know what happened to Papa."

"I thank you kindly not to ask me again, or I will slap the mess out of you. I'll tell you when you are old enough to understand, now, do not ask me again."

Lura left the kitchen and went into the living room. She sat down with Laurence to play with his new train set and she tried to get her mind off her papa, to no avail. After playing with Laurence for a couple of hours, she decided to ask her mother again and explain why it was so important for her to know. She came into the kitchen and found her mother with hands and arms covered in flour, as she was making biscuits.

"Mama, I must know what happened to Papa," she said.

Without even thinking, her mother slapped Lura hard, leaving a red handprint partially covered by flour on Lura's cheek. Lura's lower lip started to quiver, and tears stung her eyes.

"I warned you, Lura. If you ask me again, I will slap you again," said her mother.

She quickly ran from the kitchen to cry in privacy. As she cried, she thought about her papa's disappearance and reasoned that if he could disappear, then Laurence or any of her brothers or sisters, or even she could disappear. She began to worry this might happen to Laurence, so she stayed even closer to him and checked on him when he slept. She got more worried that terrible things might happen to members of her own family, and this caused insomnia, and more worrying, particularly in the wee hours of the morning. For her, this was a vicious circle of worry. On a night one month after Christmas at three o'clock in the morning, she began screaming in her sleep and it awakened everyone. Her mama and her siblings ran to her bed, and her mother spoke to her and gently shook her shoulder to wake her up. Finally, she woke up, but she was still shaking and crying.

"I dreamed Laurence disappeared, just like Papa did, and no one could find him," she wept.

Lura did not mention her papa's disappearance anymore. She just kept her worry bottled up inside. The Christmases of 1913, 1914, and 1915 came and went and she still did not know what had happened to her papa.

The home of Lura and her family in Quewhiffle

Appears courtesy of Fort Bragg Cultural Resources Management Program

CHAPTER 2
Temporary Tranquility
1916

After several years of not seeing her Papa, Lura almost ceased to think about him. She needed to put him out of her mind to some degree in order to not go crazy, and to seek any kind of contentment. She began to concentrate on things other than his disappearance. Lura found some joy in everyday activities, in Laurence, and in her friends.

As the dawn broke in the sandhills of North Carolina on January 5, 1916, a light layer of frost covered the ground and rooftops. But by lunchtime, the tiny ice crystals had evaporated with the warming rays of the brilliant sun. This was one of those longed for gold and silver days when the air is cool, but the sun's hot rays warmed every living creature. Although this day began like any other mild January day, something would happen this night to change the trajectory of the lives of twelve-year-old Lura and her family forever.

Not knowing this was to be her last afternoon of simple childhood fun, Lura eagerly welcomed her friend Agnes to her house. Lura admired Agnes Galloway's long brown pigtail braids which hung down to her waist. Like Lura, Agnes was also of Scottish ancestry, and her family lived in Quewhiffle.

Both Agnes and Lura loved to recite nursery rhymes. Agnes liked to sing and play the piano, and Lura liked to sing Scottish songs. This afternoon the two girls sat in Lura's living room on the piano bench as Agnes played. The two girls sang Agnes' favorite song, *A Highland Lad*. After singing for an hour, the two girls went to the front porch and sat on the old porch swing. They swung as high as they could make the swing go. They looked at each other, Agnes nodded, and this was their special cue to begin saying their favorite nursery rhyme in perfect unison.

Hey Diddle Diddle
The Cat and the Fiddle
The Cow jumped over the Moon.
The little dog laughed to see such fun, and
The dish ran away with the spoon.

They continued swinging in silence until they began to feel sleepy from the regular creaking of the swing, and the warmth of the sunshine on their backs.

Lura's mother asked Lura and Agnes, "Would you take this bag of roasted peanuts to your grandparents? Grandpapa said he had a hankering for them just the other day."

"Yes ma'am," Lura answered.

The girls walked down the dusty Old Chicken Road which divided the community of Quewhiffle in half. Lura toted the bag of treats for her Grandpapa. The road was bordered with longleaf pines. Lura loved to smell the fragrant scent of the trees. She wished the honeysuckle were blooming because one of her favorite pastimes in the summer and autumn was to pick the flower, put the stamen in her mouth, and savor the sweet taste of the honeysuckle.

"Lura, I am fixing to tell you something, but you must cross your heart and hope to die if you tell anyone."

Lura obediently made a cross over her heart and responded. "I cross my heart and hope to die."

"My Mama got arrested and they took her to a jail in Fayetteville," whispered Agnes, even though there was no one nearby to hear her.

"I cannot imagine that your kind and sweet Mama could do anything to get her taken to jail. What happened?" asked a horrified Lura.

"Thank Goodness Mama only got a warning and was released from jail when my Papa came to pick her up later that same day. Mama has strong beliefs about women being allowed to vote. I feel the same way. Lura, have you heard of the Suffrage Movement?" she asked.

"No. What's that?" asked Lura.

"Giving women the right to vote in elections. Many women march and hold signs in their hands to protest that women cannot vote in elections now. Mama was at a meeting of the Fayetteville Suffragette Committee when the police barged in."

"Heavens to Betsy, Agnes, your Mama's got gumption! That sounds so scary," exclaimed Lura.

"Well, most men do not want women to get the right to vote." Agnes paused and then continued. "Mama told me that sometimes when women are arrested for protesting, that they are forced to stay in jail a long time, and they refuse to eat anything. It's called a hunger strike."

"What's a hunger strike?" asked Lura.

"Here's how a hunger strike works. A woman is taken to jail for protesting because she cannot vote in elections. The woman decides she will starve herself to death to get publicity for her mission. Newspaper reporters come to the jail and take pictures of the poor skin and bones lady. The newspapers publish articles and pictures of the victim. The publicity causes the public to feel sorry for the Suffragettes.

But sometimes the prison guards stop the hunger strike by forcing food into the woman prisoner. The guards stick a dirty tube down the prisoner's throat, all the way to her stomach. Then horrible rotten liquid food is poured into the tube."

"Mama told me this has happened to several of the ladies she knows. Mama also said that two women were killed when this was done to them because the prison guard poked the tube into their windpipes."

"Agnes, that's horrible. I never heard anything like that in my life! How could that go on here in America?"

"Well, it's not easy being a woman," said Agnes.

"You know, I believe women should have the right to vote, just like your Mama," said Lura.

The girls walked along the road in silence for a while, as they had exhausted the topic of suffrage for the moment. Soon the stately home of Lura's grandparents, Stuart and Marette Kennedy, came into view. Lura felt proud of the prosperity of her family.

In the front yard were thirteen-year-old Earl Brown, who was tall and muscular, with light brown skin, and Earl's kind Papa, Gabriel, who was a giant of a man with skin as deep brown as the mahogany furniture inside Lura's house. Earl and Gabriel were busy painting her grandmother's fence. Gabriel Brown had worked for the Kennedy family all his life, just like his father and grandfather before him. Lura recalled that in one of her grandpapa's stories he talked about Gabriel's grandfather, Stuart Brown, who was a slave. Thinking of that gave her the shivers, because she could not imagine something so horrible as slavery.

Lura also felt sad that even in this day and time many townspeople treated Earl and others of his race poorly. One vivid memory from a long time ago was the time Lura went to town

17

with her Papa, and she heard a man say some horrible words to Earl for no reason at all. Lura wanted to shout at the man to stop him talking like that to Earl, but she was afraid. Lura always liked Earl.

"Miss Agnes, I hear your family is moving to Kinston soon. We're gonna miss you," said Gabriel.

"We are going to miss living here in Quewhiffle, and miss all our friends here," Agnes replied.

As Agnes and Gabriel talked, Lura thought the streaks of white paint on Earl's face and arms looked strange against his brown skin.

"Earl, I hear you have a birthday next week. Happy birthday!" said Lura.

"Thank you, Miss Lura," said Earl with his eyes looking down to the ground.

"Happy birthday, Earl," said Agnes with a bright smile.

Earl did not know what to say. His Papa had always warned him about being careful with white girls and white women because you might get in trouble if you said or did the wrong thing. Even at his immature age, he knew he had to be careful.

"Everyone in Quewhiffle is going to miss you, Miss Agnes," said Earl.

"Don't you two girls stand there till the cows come home. Come on up on the porch, so I can give you both a hug," said Lura's impatient grandmother.

She stood up from the rocking chair where she had been shelling peas, held out her arms, and hugged both girls. Lura's grandmother's huge drooping, pendulous breasts pressed into the chests of Agnes and Lura. "I see you two have newly budding ninny bugs, so you are both growing up my sweeties!"

18

Lura blushed noticeably, but Agnes looked perplexed because she did not understand. Lura happily sat down on her grandmother's lap and gave her another hug. Grandmother Kennedy whispered in Lura's ear, "Hey Diddle Diddle...." Grandmother Kennedy taught that nursery rhyme to Lura when she was a tiny girl, and they both loved it. Grandmother Kennedy even made Lura a cross stitch sampler of the nursery rhyme, and Lura treasured it.

"Agnes, you have grown taller since I last saw you. Are you still wanting to be a famous singer and pianist?" asked Grandmother Kennedy.

"Yes ma'am. I am taking both voice and piano lessons every week. My teacher tells me I am getting better fast," Agnes said shyly.

"That's mighty good sugar. Sometimes you must sing for me. I'm not a singer, but I am a good storyteller. Lura's grandpapa and I often compete to see who can tell the best story. Sometimes at a party when we both want to tell stories, he says to me, "You hold back and let me do all the storytelling today.""

But then I put him in his place by telling him, "I am free, white, and over twenty-one, and I can do exactly what I want to do."

Then Grandmother Kennedy smiled mischievously and said, "Lura, who do you think is best at storytelling, me or your grandpapa?"

Lura just shrugged her shoulders indicating she could not decide. Grandmother Kennedy swiftly changed the subject. "Did I ever tell you girls about the day Sherman's army came through Quewhiffle in the War of Northern Aggression?" She did not wait for an answer and just continued.

"Sherman's army began walking on our land at sunrise, and after dinner, they were still walking on our property. We sold all our valuables except our silver just to keep food on our table. But we still had our silver flatware, and I didn't want Sherman to take it. We got old granny to sit on top of two shabby quilts that covered the silver. When two of Sherman's officers came into our house to look around for anything of value, they looked through the entire house, but thankfully they did not ask old feeble granny to move. So, that is why we still have our silver today."

Lura handed the bag of peanuts to her grandmother and said, "These are for y'all." Her grandmother glanced at the sky and said, "You two should hurry home. I can smell the rain coming, and the sky is getting dark in the east. Y'all run home lickety split, little darlings."

The girls started home immediately. When they had been walking in a hurry for about five minutes, Agnes said, "What in the world are ninny bugs?"

"That's what my grandmother calls nipples on a girl child before she gets breasts. Once your ninny bugs get even a little bit big, they are no longer called ninny bugs. I remember my grandmother giving me a bath as a young child, and she would say, *wash your ninny bugs.*"

Agnes started to laugh and then Lura joined her. They laughed so hard that tears rolled down their faces and their sides ached.

"Since we are on the topic, your grandmother has the biggest breasts of anyone I ever saw," giggled Agnes.

Lura could barely speak because she was laughing so hard, but she said in halting phrases, "My mama told me that she saw my grandmother throw one of her breasts over her shoulder a few years ago."

At that the girls could not contain their mirth, and first Lura fell on the ground laughing, and then Agnes did the same. Both girls were laying in the dirt road on their backs howling with laughter until the raindrops started to pelt them. Then they were up in a flash running to Lura's house as fast as their skinny legs would take them.

As Agnes and Lura neared Lura's house, they noticed the pungent smell of freshly cooked collards. Agnes and Lura came inside and sat down at the table with the rest of the family.

Maggie, Lura's contrary older sister, said, "You two are dripping wet from the rain. I'm not going to sit beside you and get wet too."

Lura's mother did not seem to notice the girls were wet. "Agnes, I am glad you could come for a visit. I know your family is getting ready to move away, and we will miss you," said Lura's mother.

"Mama, why do we have to have boiled eggs, collards, and spoon bread three days this week? If I had my druthers, I would have steak, fried chicken, and biscuits," said Maggie.

Lura's mother Aila, spoke slowly, drawing out her words as most southerners are wont to do. "Well Maggie, you ain't getting steak, fried chicken, and biscuits tonight. I am too tired to make that kind of dinner. It's your Papa's fault that I'm exhausted almost all the time. He left me to take care of everything. He got us into this mess. I cook, grow vegetables, can the vegetables, clean the house, and manage you children. Do you realize how humiliating it is for me to have to do everything myself without the help of a husband?"

Agnes and Lura did not say anything, they just rolled their eyes at each other because they did not like the food either. Aila grew furious that her children did not speak up and agree with her. Aila looked like the epitome of authority standing at the head of the table with her hands on her ample hips.

Standing there, Aila took a moment to reflect on her life, and the reality of her life made her feel wretched. Her discontent became clearly visible as her shoulders slumped, her chin quivered, and big tears fell onto her blouse.

"You kids can eat or not eat. I don't care," Aila said in a quiet but controlled voice, trying to recapture some of her composure.

"Maggie and Josephine, you two wash the dishes and clean up, and if the kitchen is not clean in the morning, I will yank a knot in both of you." Then Aila turned from the table and left the room quickly. Lura noticed the familiar sound of her mother's stomping feet going up the stairs, and the sound of her mother slamming shut her bedroom door. The door slamming shut made the house shake a little and caused a cool draft to enter the screen door on the front of the house.

Everyone remained at the table just looking at each other. The Kennedy children had become accustomed to angry outbursts from their mother. Agnes' lower lip started to quiver, and tears formed in her eyes. She did not want to have to go home now since her family's upcoming move would not allow her to see Lura much in the future.

"Lura, do I need to skedaddle now?" Agnes asked, looking terribly upset.

"Heck no, Agnes. This type of thing happens all the time," smiled Lura.

Lura and Agnes abandoned their unappealing dinner and went upstairs to the bedroom Lura shared with her two sisters.

"Collards are really bad for your voice I hear," laughed Agnes with a mischievous smile on her face. Then Lura laughed too. Lura knew her sisters would not come to their shared bedroom

22

till late in the evening, as first they had to wash the dishes, and then they would sit on the front porch in hopes that some of the local boys might stop by.

Lura and Agnes entered the girls' pale-yellow bedroom. Josephine, Maggie and Lura shared this room. Each had her own single bed. The room looked cozy with its oval braided rug and large fireplace.

Lura eagerly closed the door behind them and was happy to have some privacy.

"I am going to tell you another secret, but you must cross your heart and hope to die if you tell anyone this," whispered Agnes. She paused then continued. "I know I'm not supposed to like Negro boys, but I have a soft spot in my heart for Earl. He is smart and kind and, in many ways, so much superior to all the other boys I know. If things were different, I would like to be his girlfriend," confessed Agnes.

"You are full of secrets, but my lips are sealed," said Lura.

Then Agnes and Lura began to play their favorite game, "Pretend." They had played this game since they were little girls. They pretended to be various people in a big made-up family named the Staffords. The Stafford family members often performed in operas and displayed conflict and jealousy in their relationships. Both girls liked to pretend they were in love with the main character in the game, the dashingly handsome young man, Norman Stafford. Little did the girls know that this name would come back to haunt them in years to come.

Lura and Agnes had been playing "Pretend" for about one hour when they were interrupted by a loud scream and the noise of something heavy hitting the floor downstairs.

CHAPTER 3

He Returns

1916

Fearing something horrible had happened, Lura and Agnes ran down the wooden staircase as quickly as humanly possible. Lura tripped on the last stair and fell partially on top of her mother who was already sprawled on the floor at the bottom of the staircase. To Lura's utter amazement, her Papa was there bending over both. Just then all Lura's brothers and sisters arrived at the bottom of the stairs. Six-year-old Laurence began to cry since both his sister and his mother looked like they were hurt. Lura reacted by instinct, stood up quickly, held Laurence and comforted him. Lura's Papa motioned for everyone to step back, and he gently shook Aila's shoulder and spoke to her.

"Aila, honey, are you alright?"

Aila's eyelids fluttered, and she began to move. Lura's Papa helped her to stand up, but being dazed, she completely ignored everyone around her for a few moments. Then with an angry and disgusted look on her face she said, "Jackson Kennedy, what the hell are you doing here?"

Jackson replied with a weak smile, cowering a bit, "Aila, I just wanted to pay a little visit and see you and our family."

Aila's brain began working at full speed as she considered what needed to be done to keep everyone safe. She thought to herself,

What the hell is happening? God, he's an escaped convict and I MUST not get into legal trouble. How can Jackson DARE walk into this house like he deserves to be here? I feel my legs trembling and I sure don't want to fall and faint again. Hell, Agnes is here. I must make her leave. We must pull those window shades down.

Aila with a fake sweet smile on her face looked at Agnes, grasped the girl's upper arm, and began leading her to the front door as she said, "You go on home now sweetheart. But don't you tell your parents, or anyone on earth that you saw my husband tonight. Agnes, I promise if you tell anyone, I will personally WRING YOUR NECK!"

Tears formed in Agnes' eyes for the second time that night. She meekly lowered her eyelids and said in a timid voice, "I won't tell." Then she turned and trembled slightly, walked out the front door with the screen door banging behind her.

As soon as the door closed, Aila whispered, "Quick, lower the window shades and dim the kerosene lamps."

The two oldest boys jumped to do this quickly – they also feared that someone could easily walk by the house and see their Papa. As they did this, the rest of the children were either shaking, crying, or holding onto one another. They were frightened because they did not understand what was going on.

"All of you go to your rooms now and go to bed. Your Papa and I have a lot to talk about."

None of the children protested because they could feel the tremendous tension in the air. Also, they knew they might be slapped if they did not obey quickly. They were amazed that neither of their parents told them why their Papa had appeared tonight after having been gone for so long. They felt they needed an answer, but they were too afraid to speak.

25

All the children walked slowly upstairs in silence and got into their beds. Laurence walked by the room he shared with his brothers and went into the girls' room and sat on Lura's bed. Lura held Laurence, sang quiet songs to him, and comforted him. The older children tried to listen to catch a bit of the conversation between their parents, but they only heard a few words.

Back downstairs, an angry Aila and Jackson were sitting on opposite ends of the sofa.

"Where in God's name have you been since you escaped from prison? Do you know something Jackson? You ruined my life when you committed murder. How dare you come to *my home* as if you still live here?"

"Aila, please calm down and let's talk all of this through. It has been awfully hard for me too, although I know I made all of this happen."

Aila sat with her arms tightly clutched across her chest, and Jackson sat with his body turned towards Aila in a hopeful posture.

"I love you Aila and I have always loved you. I thought of you every day I was away and wanted to contact you and hold you so much, but I was afraid of being captured and sent back to prison."

"I do not love you and I will never love you again. Do you ever think about the harm you have caused me and our family?" said Aila.

"I think about that, Aila," said Jackson in a pitiful voice. The room became silent for a few minutes.

"After you escaped from prison, the police came to see if you were hiding here. They warned me not to let you stay here. You knew enough not to come here then. Now, tell me exactly, what happened since you escaped from prison, and why you are here now?"

Jackson took a deep breath and began his saga. "Two of my fellow inmates were nice guys. Joe Peacock, Tom Smith, and I became friends. When we escaped Joe had three years left on his sentence for theft, and Tom had eight years left for Second Degree Murder."

Jackson paused, then continued. "All three of us were called 'long-termers.' It was Joe's idea to try to escape. It was December 21, 1914, and I had been in prison for one and a half years. Joe, Tom, and I were out with about thirty other inmates working on a farm and the guard was not paying attention to any of us. We knew from previous experience that this guard did not care if he did a good job. We three had been planning to escape whenever the circumstances were in our favor, and this was the ideal time. So, we signaled to each other that we would make our escape now and meet behind the barn which was twenty feet away. It was as simple as walking a few feet away from the rest of the inmates who could see what we were doing, and they were happy for us – they smiled and nodded and made hand signals of good luck."

"This sounds crazy, Jackson."

"Joe told us that his uncle's farm was close to the place where we escaped, so we went there. We were running some of the time and walking some of the time. When we got there an hour later, Joe's uncle hugged him and Joe explained what was happening. We went into the house and saw his ten children who looked grubby, skinny, and tired. I was sad to see that these children had to take turns eating their soup because they only had three spoons. There was a shabby looking Christmas tree in the corner of the living room and no gifts were under the tree, even though it was four days before Christmas. Despite Joe's uncle being poor, he gave us clothes and food and a small amount of money to get away. We were all enormously grateful."

Aila listened in disbelief.

"We left Joe's uncle's place and then we split up in Halifax. At the train yard, I saw two hobos. I asked them which train would take me to Jacksonville, Florida. One of them replied, 'Today is your lucky day because there is a train sitting on the track up ahead and it's leaving for Jacksonville in thirty minutes. We are going to take it, too.'"

"We located this train and found an open car, and all three of us jumped in. I asked them if they traveled on trains a lot. The shorter hobo with a patch over his eye said to me, 'We take trains all over the county like this.' Then he pulled a deck of cards out of his pocket, and we played poker until the train started moving. I told them that I did not have any money to place bets, and the hobos laughed saying neither did they."

"Why are you telling me this, Jackson?" asked Aila impatiently.

"I tell you Aila, that night on the train was one of the coldest times in my life. The only thing that made it just a little bit better was that my two new friends kept me entertained by telling me the signs they leave for others of their wandering lifestyle. These signs could indicate who might provide free food, or who might have dangerous dogs, or who might give them a place to stay. When our train pulled into Jacksonville, the hobos told me they would ask around to learn when the next train to Pensacola was. I was lucky because the Pensacola train was already on the track and was scheduled to leave in fifteen minutes. So, I said goodbye, found an empty train car as before, and jumped inside. Eight hours later the train pulled into Pensacola. I jumped off and walked the last fifty miles to Destin. It took me three days to get there."

"I remember that my Mama's cousin, Charlie, lived in Destin," said Aila.

"Charlie always liked me, and I thought he would help me since I was in a pinch. But he was in a bad state when I got there. He said he had cancer and that his wife died last year. He said it was sad that they never had children. Charlie was always the most independent Scot that I knew. He lived life his way. He was one to defy authority and to value kin more than anything else. That's why I went there, plus he worked in the turpentine business."

"What does that have to do with anything?" said Aila, angrily.

"Charlie said he was happy for me to live with him. He said I could help to take care of him, and he could take care of me. It was easy for him to put in a good word to his friends in the turpentine business that I needed a job. I knew that my experience helping my Papa with his turpentine business since I was knee-high to a grasshopper would help me get a job. I also decided I needed a new name."

"I can't wait to hear this. Are you crazy?"

"I picked the name 'James B. Davis,' but asked people to call me J. B. I stayed with Charlie till four days ago when he died. Before he died, he told me to open a dresser drawer and take out a bag, the bag was stuffed full of cash. He told me to stay with him till he kicked the bucket, and then to leave immediately and begin a new life in another place. So, I did what he told me. It's just a coincidence that Charlie died on January 1, and I was able to arrive here four days later on my 45th birthday. I saved every penny I could from working to give to you and the kids," he said. Jackson took out a bag and removed a wad of cash.

Jackson explained, "Aila, here is $2,631 from Charlie, and another $329 from my earnings."

Aila's mouth dropped open and she opened her eyes wide in astonishment.

"Well, I declare Jackson! Happy Birthday," said Aila in a soft voice as she took the money and started counting it.

"I know my Papa has given you money to run the household these past few years, and from this point forward it will be much better for you and for us, for me to give you the money you need."

Aila continued to stare at the money.

"Aila, I know all of this is hard, but I can make good money and bring it home to you and the kids once or twice a year. This way we could at least have some happiness and the financial needs of our home could be met. I would much rather live a normal life, but at this point, this option seems all that I can do."

"Jackson, I think that is what you should do," said Aila in a voice that was much friendlier than when he first arrived.

"Aila, there is another particularly important thing you and the children must do for this to work."

"And what might that be?" asked Aila sarcastically.

"No one outside of you, our kids, or my parents should EVER learn that I come to visit my family. I need you to strictly enforce this rule. I know it will be hard for all of you. The reason for this is because you will never know when I might show up here in Quewhiffle. If you had a group of people at our house, and I walked into the gathering, inevitably someone would report me to the police."

"It will be fairly easy for me. I do not like to be in large crowds and if I see people at all, I always prefer being with people one on one, or in a small group. In reality, I prefer my own company and I do not like to invite people over to my house. On the other hand, this is going to be ridiculously hard on our kids who have friends over to our house all the time." Aila paused then continued. "I will enforce this rule, but it's not going to be easy."

"Thank you, Aila."

"Jackson, you can sleep here on the sofa. You know where the sheets, pillows, and blankets are. We can talk more in the morning. I'm exhausted," Aila said as she stood up and went upstairs to her bedroom.

When Lura woke up the next morning, the first thing she noticed was the wonderful smell of bacon cooking mingled with the fragrant smell of homemade biscuits baking. Lura's mother had not made biscuits in a while, so Lura knew this was a good sign that Mama was happy again.

Lura jumped out of bed and ran downstairs, and there at the bottom of the staircase was her Papa with arms wide. He gave her a big hug, then picked her up and swung her around, so her legs flew out making a circle. This simple act by Lura's Papa made her feel more secure and more loved than she had felt since he left three years ago. At this moment, Lura was the happiest girl in the world. For years, she had wondered if her Papa was dead, or if he had abandoned her and run away to start a new life with a new family. However, with this hug and her Papa's obvious love for her, she knew everything was going to be all right.

Lura watched with joy as she saw her Papa embrace each of her brothers and sisters as they came down the stairs. Her 23-year-old brother, Angus, and her 21-year-old brother, Joseph, looked a little embarrassed, but they still enjoyed their Papa's affection. As Lura watched her Papa, she noticed how he looked now that it had been such a long time. Being twelve-years-old, Lura felt grown up compared to her nine-year-old self when her

Papa had disappeared. Today she noticed that her Papa was quite handsome, with a head full of chestnut brown hair slightly peppered with gray. He was muscular, tall, tanned, and had a beautiful smile. As much as she wanted to hear what had happened to him with every fiber of her being, she also had much to tell him about her own life.

"Y'all are forgetting something," said Jackson as everyone began to pile food on their plates. Knowing their Papa wanted them to say grace, the children put down their spoons and bowed their heads for Jackson's prayer which he said in Gaelic. What Jackson did not know was that this was the first prayer said out loud in his house since he had gone to prison. After the prayer, everyone began eating the delicious breakfast. Jackson had not eaten homemade biscuits for a long time, and as he tasted the flaky delicious, sweet hot biscuit slathered in butter, a huge smile of delight and intense satisfaction appeared on his face.

Just then there was a knock at the door. The older siblings, Aila, and Jackson froze in their seats and became pale. Sweat broke out on the necks of both Aila and Jackson. To say they were scared to death is an understatement. Aila pointed to Jackson indicating he should leave the room, and he went into the hallway immediately. Only then did Aila haltingly pull the window shade aside just an inch to see who had knocked at the door.

She was relieved to see it was the ever so loyal Gabriel and his son, Earl. She knew they would not tell anyone that Jackson was visiting, but she still wanted to be careful and not let them see Jackson.

She quickly recalled that a few days ago, she had asked them to come over and fix a broken window. Aila opened the door, stepped outside, and closed the door behind her.

"Sorry Gabriel, but this turns out not to be a good day for you to repair that window. I will call you next week."

Gabriel nodded and turned to walk home with Earl at his side. Aila returned to the kitchen table.

"After I leave, tell Gabriel and Earl what happened to me and that I will come home from time to time. Warn them not to tell anyone else. I know I can trust them even better than most of my family," said Jackson to Aila.

Aila nodded in affirmation. After this interruption, all the children began querying Jackson with questions about his long absence. They wanted to know why he went away and what he was doing.

Although it was not true, Jackson explained to his children that because their family needed more money than he could make in Quewhiffle, he had been working in different towns to try out his earning potential.

Jackson said in a matter-of-fact way, "I made a lot of money in Destin, Florida until things dried up there. I am thinking of trying Alabama, as the turpentine industry is growing there like a wildfire in a starved forest. It is essential that I travel for work so you children can have the good things you need in life. Even when I go away for a different job, you can always count on me to return. I promise you that!"

Lura's heart sunk when she learned he was going to leave again. She said, "Papa, we want you here with us all the time. Please don't go again."

The younger children all echoed Lura's pleading that he not leave them again. The older children knew the truth and did not say anything.

Then Jackson did something that seemed strange to Aila and the children. He walked over to the bookshelf and picked up the large family Bible and returned to the table holding it to his chest. This action made all the children stop eating and look at their Papa expectantly.

"I have something to tell you that is important," said Jackson.

"I cannot tell you why, but you must tell *No One* that I came home, and that you saw me. Do not even mention my name to a single living soul. I have had some bad things happen to me in my life, so for now you must not tell anyone I was here. If you tell anyone, then I could get into terrible trouble and then bad things will happen to me. I know you do not want bad things to happen to your Papa. Will each of you take an oath on this Bible that you will not tell anyone that you saw me?"

Each of the children willingly took this oath with his hand on the Bible. "I swear an oath that I will not tell anyone that my Papa came to Quewhiffle." Finally, Jackson walked over to Cecil in his highchair, put his face near Cecil's face.

"Cecil, would you do something for your Papa who loves you so much? Would you promise not to tell anyone that I came for a visit and that you saw me?"

Four-year-old Cecil, who was small for his age, was frightened of this man he did not know. When Jackson put his face near Cecil's face, he pulled his little body and head as far as possible to the back of his chair in his attempt to get away from the stranger. His eyes opened wide, his lower lip quivered, and tears spilled down his cheeks.

Aila realizing that Cecil was frightened, nudged Jackson aside and knelt beside him and put her face near her son's face, "Be a good little boy and say you will not tell anyone you saw your Papa." Aila smiled at him, and nodded her head up and down, so her young son would know what to do. Cecil stared at his Papa and for a minute he did not say anything or nod his head. Finally, he nodded his head like his Mama did.

After the oaths were made by all the children, everyone other than the parents seemed perplexed and worried about what just happened. They just sat there in silence with saucer eyes looking at each other and their parents.

Jackson attempted to lighten the dark and perplexed mood in the house by asking his children what was new in their lives. He remembered all that the children told him and recalled it in the months to come when he was once again far away from them.

CHAPTER 4

Revelations

1918

Dear Mama, I know you are going to get me a birthday gift, but this year I want something different for my 15th birthday. I want your birthday gift to me to be this: We sit down together, and you tell me all the details of why my Papa left us and why he does not live with us now.

Your loving daughter, Lura

Lura placed this note in her mother's bedroom on the marble topped dresser.

After giving Lura's request much consideration, Aila decided to honor Lura's special birthday wish. About ten in the morning on Lura's birthday, they went into Aila's bedroom, sat down in the two comfortable chairs, and Aila began.

"Lura, what I am going to tell you will shock you. I will tell you all that I know. Different people told me different portions of what I will tell you. I think you have heard stories about your Papa being a bit of a troublemaker as a teenager. He got into fist fights and drank a lot. Because your Grandpapa believed 'boys will be boys' he used his prominence and his money to get your Papa out of trouble. He reasoned that your Papa would grow out of this juvenile behavior. Most men who were feisty in their younger years would have mellowed by the time they were forty-one, but this was not the case for your Papa."

She paused, took a deep breath, and continued. "I will tell you what happened. I have memorized much of this, so if it sounds like I am not showing much emotion, it is just because my emotions have become deadened with the horror of it all. On a hot Saturday night in August 1912, your Papa went to the saloon in Raeford with two other men from Quewhiffle. Many friends of mine who were there told me about the evening. They said your Papa and his friends drank whiskey, told stories, sang songs, told bawdy jokes, and laughed until the bar owner kicked them out about midnight." Aila stopped and took a deep breath.

"Your Papa was thoroughly enjoying himself and he did not want to stop partying. He was obviously much more drunk than his two friends. The three men came out of the saloon and continued their loud singing. They had just finished singing all the stanzas of *A Highland Lad* as the new Raeford Chief of Police, P. C. Oakes, walked up to them. Chief Oakes told them that he could hear their drunken singing from two blocks away, and that people were complaining of the noise.

"Chief Oakes told them to stop singing, go home, and go to bed. The two friends stopped singing, but your Papa said, 'Let's try a different song,' and he started to sing *The Merry Muses of Caledonia*, at the top of his lungs. I always hated that song! Chief Oakes realized that he was being tested by this loud drunken bully. In a much more authoritative voice, Chief Oakes said, 'Go home now Jackson! You are disturbing the peace.'

"Your Papa was stumbling and staggering around and replied in a slurred belligerent voice, 'My favorite Scottish song is this one, *Once I lay with another man's wife*... Do you sing that in the shower Chief Oakes? Here is how it goes...' I am told your Papa sang it as if he was almost in a drunken stupor.

"Chief Oakes calmly told him that he was being arrested for public drunkenness and disturbing the peace. Then the Chief roughly put handcuffs on your Papa who was obviously boiling with rage.

"Jackson silently vowed to get even with the police chief. Chief Oakes put him in jail. Being locked up made your Papa furious. He was only able to refrain from uttering incriminating threats to Chief Oakes by the skin of his teeth. He was bailed out of jail by your Grandpa."

Aila took a deep breath, and Lura used this break to react.

"Mama, I saw Papa do some mean things in his life, but I never saw him act like this. Grandpapa should not have catered to him like he did."

"After the arrest, your Papa and Chief Oakes saw each other from a distance a few times. On each of these occasions, your Papa immediately began singing Scottish songs loudly, and in an angry intonation. Chief Oakes soon realized he had a powerful enemy. Your Papa delighted in thinking of all the ways he could harm the Chief. Soon he came up with a plan." Aila stopped, drank some water, then continued.

"Lura, what I will tell you next is the worst part of all. On Saturday, August 31, 1912, your Papa, and your brother Murdock, took the family buggy to downtown Raeford to spend the day. Murdock was excited because he knew that Saturday was the day everyone went to town to shop, to run errands, and to socialize. Your Papa gave Murdock money and told him to go to the general store and buy candy and enjoy his day. Your Papa spent the next few hours drinking whiskey at the saloon and socializing with friends.

"At 3:30, he left the saloon to look for Murdock. He found him at the stable with his friends. Your Papa pulled money out of his pocket along with a grocery list and gave it to Murdock. Your papa told Murdock, 'You run to the shops and get everything on this list then take it to your Mama, lickety-split. You can get a ride home with our neighbor Steve who is also headed home in an hour or two. I have to do some business before I go home, so I will need the buggy.' Murdock replied, 'Yes, Sir,' and then he jumped up and headed to the general store. Your Papa knew Murdock would do exactly what he was asked to do, so he had no concern that Murdock would remain in Raeford to be a witness to that night's planned evil deed.

"Your Papa went back to the saloon and continued drinking for two more hours. When he left the saloon, he was staggering, and he smelled of whiskey. He was under the influence of alcohol, but he had kept himself sober enough to be in control of his actions. I was told he also had a look of determination and hate on his face.

"He staggered through the narrow alleyway between the McKeithan Market and N.S. Blue Store on Main Street. He walked up to his horse and buggy, stumbled as he got in his buggy, and removed his gun from underneath the blankets. He drove the buggy down Main Street – all the while shooting randomly into the crowd. Six men and two women were hit by bullets, but thank God, all survived."

Lura interrupted sobbing, "This cannot be my loving Papa. I know he could never do anything so evil and vile as this. Mama, I never heard of this type of behavior by a civilized person. My Papa must be a beast. I feel like I am hearing this about another person and not my own flesh and blood."

Lura's mother said, "Do you want to hear the rest of the story?"

With her eyes full of tears, Lura nodded her head to indicate yes.

Her mother continued. "Chief Oakes was two blocks away and he came running towards the noise of the gunfire to investigate. Your Papa jumped out of the buggy and hid behind his horse and wagon. He waited for Chief Oakes to appear. Chief Oakes came into view and was looking around trying to figure where the gun was fired from a few minutes ago. Before Chief Oakes noticed anything amiss, your Papa fired his gun two times, hitting the Chief in the chest and the head. Chief Oakes with a look of astonishment, fell to his knees. The townspeople were trying to help Chief Oakes, and he was heard to say. 'I think he killed me,' and in ten minutes, Chief Oakes was dead."

Lura jumped out of her chair and screamed "No! No! Not my Papa. I cannot take it in. I cannot believe it. I know he did things that were bad when I was younger, but never anything like premeditated cold-blooded murder. How could someone who is my own Papa commit this atrocity?"

"Lura, the fact of the matter is that your papa DID all these things. He is a beast. Let me tell you what happened after he shot Chief Oakes. He knew that unless he acted fast, he would be captured. He yelled out to the crowd, 'If any of you come after me, I will blow you away.' He jumped in his buggy and whipping the horse, rode away at breakneck speed.

"The county Sheriff was notified, and he and two deputies came to investigate the crime scene. Afterwards the Sheriff and his deputies came to our house to look for your Papa. They knocked on our door and I opened the door, with you and the other younger children standing beside me. The Sheriff asked me where your Papa was. I told him that earlier he was in Raeford, but he missed supper, and now I did not know where he was.

They asked me to step outside and talk to them. Suspecting something sinister, I asked Maggie to take you and the younger children upstairs to the girls' room, and to put all of you to bed."

Lura looked on with disbelief and fear as her mother continued the tale. Lura wanted to scream or lash out at what she was learning. But all she did was sit still as tears fell down her face.

Lura's mother continued. "I followed the men out to the front porch and closed the door behind me. At this point I was trembling, and my heart was beating so fast that I thought it might burst. Thoughts of what trouble your Papa had gotten into flew through my mind. The Sheriff asked me questions about what he was doing earlier in the day. By then Maggie came onto the porch, stood beside me, and held my hand. Then the Sheriff told us what your Papa had done. I collapsed and Maggie began to cry. The Sheriff caught me and lifted me onto one of the rocking chairs. Maggie and I were both in shock and we sat on the front porch with the Sheriff and his deputies for hours - just waiting for your Papa to return home. Most of the time we sat in ominous silence, and I pondered possible outcomes for this tragedy. I was furious with your Papa and my love and my sympathy for him just vanished-that very night. Maggie continued to hold my hand and comfort me." Aila stopped to breathe then continued.

"It was not till midnight that your Papa's horse and buggy came into the yard with him and Grandpapa inside. The Sheriff walked up to the buggy and spoke to your Papa. Just then the Sheriff noticed that Jackson was trying to take a gun out of his pocket. The Sheriff shot your Papa in the leg to stop him. He yelled out in pain and started cussing. The Sheriff arrested him,

41

got a physician to bind up his wounds, and took him to jail." Aila reflected then continued.

"In the next several days, your Grandpapa hired fifteen of the best lawyers in the state for your Papa's defense. I was glad your Grandpapa took charge because I was too depressed to take any action at all. I could not even take care of you children. It felt like your Papa had killed me, and I was so fearful for the future of our family, and absolutely humiliated that my husband would do something so stupid and evil.

"His trial began on May 15, 1913, nine months after the murder. I attended the trial. The evidence was clear and incriminating against him. The testimony from Chief Oakes' son, H.U. Oakes was particularly powerful. He said when his father was murdered his mother was eight months pregnant with twin baby girls. The twins were born one month after his mother became a widow, and then his mother died two months later from a broken heart. At that point, the baby twin girls became orphans. This was a tragedy that never should have happened. After his testimony half of the people on the jury had tears in their eyes."

Lura was shaking but let her mother continue, because she had wanted to know exactly what happened for so long.

"Although our Scottish kinsmen continued to be supportive to our family, most of the locals thought that your Papa should be charged with first degree murder and die in the electric chair. Since your Papa planned Oakes' murder in advance, technically it was premeditated. In the end, your Papa was charged with second degree murder and sentenced to twenty years in prison with no parole.

"I was absolutely devastated and furious. I was so harmed emotionally that for years I could not give you and your brothers and sisters the care, love, and affection y'all needed. I know for a long-time you children just had to do the best you could do. I was thankful that my older children helped the younger ones, and I am forever thankful that you looked out for Laurence so well Lura. I know all my children suffered from my lack of affection and love, but probably you suffered the most. Lura, you were just at the age when you needed me so much. I know that before your Papa was taken to prison, he was your best friend and your play buddy." Aila sobbed and wiped a tear from her eye. "I did not see your Papa after the trial. I never saw him again until he appeared unexpectedly at our house in January 1916. I did not visit your Papa in prison."

In a soft voice, Lura spoke up. "What happened to Papa after the trial?"

"After the trial, he was imprisoned at Caledonia Prison Farm in Halifax. It is a medium security prison mainly for inmates serving a life sentence. He escaped on December 21, 1914, having only served one and a half years of his twenty-year sentence. Then he went to the Florida panhandle to work in the turpentine business and stayed with our relative Charlie McNeill until Charlie died of cancer. He then came here to Quewhiffle for a brief visit with us."

Lura interrupted saying, "I remember this visit as if it were yesterday. He took the Bible and made each of us swear we would not tell anyone we saw him. At the time I could not understand why he would ask this of us."

Lura's mother continued, "It was his first visit to our house since he was arrested for killing Chief Oakes and seeing him in our home was such a surprise that I fainted. When he left us, he went to Sylacauga, Alabama, because Sylacauga had the perfect climate and soil for growing longleaf pines for the lumber and turpentine business. He is living there now, and his business is prospering. He brings money home to us from time to time. He goes by the alias, James B. Davis, but he is usually called J. B."

Aila and Lura sat in silence for a few moments.

Aila finally asked, "Lura, do you see why I did not tell you and the younger children why your Papa went away? How could I possibly tell this to his babies? I had to go around town telling people NOT to tell my children the circumstances of the murder. The townspeople knew that they would have my wrath if I found out that they told the gory story to my babies."

For the first time Aila noticed that Lura had tears running down her cheeks and said sympathetically, "I am sorry Lura. Do you want to go to your room and lay down for a while? I know this is a lot to take in at one time. Then you could come back later and ask me any questions you want."

In a voice with intermittent sniffles, Lura said, "Yes, I will do that and come back later."

Lura left the room and closed the door behind her. She went and asked Laurence to sit with her for a while and that made her feel better. Lura turned all that happened over in her heart and in the end, she could not fathom why her Papa behaved that way. Later that night before she went to sleep, she returned to her mother's room and knocked on the door.

Aila opened the door and let her in. "What is it Lura?"

"Thanks for telling me everything about Papa. I can't think of questions now, but I might in the future."

Aila said, "Is there anything I can do to help you feel better? Maybe you want to go somewhere with a friend or do something different to distract yourself from this dreadful story."

Despite feeling overwhelmed and greatly saddened by all she just learned about her Papa, Lura felt this was her one opportunity to convince her mother to say yes to something her mother would not usually permit. "I heard there's a women's suffrage gathering in Fayetteville next week. Could I go to that?" asked Lura.

Of course, Lura did not mention to her mother the possible dangers from attending a meeting for suffragettes, such as imprisonment or tube feeding those imprisoned women on hunger strikes. Aila looked at Lura for a long time and Lura really thought she was going to say no.

"Lura, you seem a lot more grown up now that you are fifteen. It is fine with me for you to go," Aila said.

Lura was looking forward to the gathering, even as she tried to come to terms with the horrible deeds committed by her Papa. That very night Lura sat down and wrote Agnes a twenty page letter detailing all she learned about her Papa, and about the upcoming meeting in Fayetteville. Writing the letter helped Lura to digest the facts she had learned this day.

CHAPTER 5
Quewhiffle to Southern Pines
1919-1920

Quewhiffle would soon be no more. This was because the land that was once known as Quewhiffle would be encompassed by the new military facility to be named Camp Bragg.

When the U. S. declared war on Germany on April 6, 1917, there was an urgent need for trained soldiers to fight the war. To train the soldiers, the U. S. Government purchased property in and around Quewhiffle to create a center to train soldiers for the war.

Lura's mother, Aila Kennedy, her grand-parents, Stuart and Marette Kennedy, and everyone else in their beloved hometown were forced to sell their property to the government. Lura's family did not like this ultimatum one bit. The people of Scottish descent felt as though the U.S. Government was a "Yankee Institution" dictating how Southerners should live. There were legal battles between the Quewhiffle residents and the Government, and the Government always won. All the landowners in Quewhiffle were forced to sell their land. They were paid between $20 an acre, down to ninety-seven cents per acre.

The planned training facility was to include all of Quewhiffle and much of the adjacent land. It was to be twenty-four miles east to west, and 7.5 miles north to south, and it was to be named Camp Bragg. The word "Camp" was used since the government planned for the military establishment to be a temporary training facility.

Aila, Stuart John Kennedy, and about 170 other families living in Quewhiffle and adjacent land began selling their property and relocating in 1919.

Many Quewhiffle inhabitants tried to resist this mandatory take-over of their property. Among those who resisted the take-over the most strongly were the members of Sandy Grove Presbyterian Church. Stuart John Kennedy, being a deacon at the church, was particularly vocal in his resistance. If a landowner would not accept the amount of money offered to buy the land, condemnation proceedings began, and the land was taken away under the laws of eminent domain.

A handful of families caused Camp Bragg Administrators frustration and difficulty because they would repeatedly return to Camp Bragg after the Government made them leave. After these few families returned to Camp Bragg ten times, the Camp administrators unofficially decided to just look the other way until these individuals died out. Camp Bragg became permanently established on Sept. 30, 1922, and thus the name was changed from Camp Bragg to Fort Bragg.

Stuart John Kennedy was devastated at having to leave his beloved Quewhiffle. There were two things that made the move slightly less painful. One factor that pleased Stuart was that the Government allowed Sandy Grove Presbyterian Church and its cemetery to remain intact, even though almost all the other structures on the new military base were demolished. This allowed Stuart Kennedy to return to the Sandy Grove Church, to visit the cemetery, to sit in the church pews, and to attend occasional church reunions. Another factor that helped Stuart

Kennedy adjust to the move to Raeford was that Gabriel Brown and his family decided to move to Raeford also.

Aila Kennedy had mixed feelings about selling her land in Quewhiffle. On the one hand, moving away from Quewhiffle would provide her and her family more privacy than continuing to live beside those who knew all about Jackson's crime, imprisonment, and prison escape. On the other hand, it was hard to leave the house where her children were born and the land where she grew up. In 1921, Aila sold over 5,000 acres of her land in Quewhiffle to the Government. All the Quewhiffle citizens had to decide where to relocate. Most of them chose to move to Raeford which is thirteen miles to the southeast of Quewhiffle. In 1919, Raeford had a population of 1,235. Aila chose a different place. She chose to move her family twelve miles to the northwest of Quewhiffle, to the fashionable golf resort town of Southern Pines which had a population of 734. Aila did this because she was seeking privacy, and because she believed the people of Southern Pines were of a higher social class than the people of Raeford.

Aila was also delighted that with the sale of her land, she was richer than she ever imagined she would be. Not only did she have money to buy a big house, but she also had a huge amount of money to keep for a rainy day. Aila and her children moved to Southern Pines in May 1920. For Lura, moving to Southern Pines was exciting but also sad. She missed her early childhood friends in Quewhiffle, but she did not miss her life there after her Papa committed murder. Her life in Quewhiffle was harmed insurmountably by his actions. Once they moved to Southern Pines, Lura enjoyed helping her mother decorate the big new bungalow.

There was another big event later in the Summer of 1920 that pleased Lura immeasurably. On August 26, 1920, the 19th Amendment giving women the right to vote was ratified. Lura had been following the heroic efforts and humiliation of women trying to obtain the right to vote. Lura strongly believed that women were equal to men in every way except for physical strength. Because Lura lived in a small rural southern town, her opportunities for standing up for Women's Suffrage had been limited to showing up and marching in protests in nearby Fayetteville, writing letters of support, and talking to people at school. Lura felt that this was a victory that she shared with women throughout the U.S.

CHAPTER 6
God's Timing
1916-1923

Jackson came to the decision that he could and must change his personality and the way he behaved. He knew he had to figure out how to change, and what his life should be like afterwards.

After he left Quewhiffle, he went to Sylacauga, Alabama because it was known for excellent trees and a superb climate for the turpentine business. After he arrived in Sylacauga, he took time to reconsider his life. He deeply regretted his hot-headed arrogance that propelled him to kill Chief Oakes. When he committed murder, he felt invincible and immune to consequences, but soon afterwards, he bitterly learned that there were horrible ramifications for his actions.

He bought fifty acres of land near Sylacauga to begin a turpentine business. He needed to hire an overseer to begin the business, but he wanted to be extremely careful in his selection.

He went to the hardware store, the barber shop, and the local Presbyterian church to ask around for the name of an excellent potential overseer. He heard the same name over and over, Allen Jenkins. At the hardware store, Jackson learned that Allen had lost his job at a local factory that closed the previous month. The following Sunday, Jackson decided to go to the local Presbyterian Church. To his astonishment, the person teaching the Adult Sunday School class turned out to be Allen Jenkins. As he taught the class on the topic *God's Timing*, Jackson began to perceive

Allen's fine character and integrity. Jackson was impressed. He felt it was God and fate that brought Allen Jenkins to him. He hired Allen Jenkins on the steps of the church that very day. They worked closely together to begin the business.

Allen was the type of man who influenced people not by his words, but by his actions. He personified kindness, generosity, and humility. He was satisfied with his lot in life-his modest house, his lovely wife, and his children. He always helped friends and neighbors and those in need, even if it meant taking money out of his own pocket. He and his wife, Gail, put aside money specifically for the purpose of helping others. When they got married, they decided to budget money to help others. This decision made both happy. As Jackson watched Allen over the months, he wanted to know his secret for a happy life.

One day after the two men had worked together for five months, Jackson asked his overseer what his secret to a happy life was. Allen smiled and said, "Be happy with your lot in life, help others, love others, love your family, be humble, be caring and follow the teachings of Jesus and put Him first." Allen Jenkins served as a role model to Jackson, and this helped him to change his life.

The event that cemented Jackson's determination to change his life was a sermon at the Presbyterian Church which spoke to him in the deepest crevices of his heart. This sermon was about how any man can change his life, his attitude, and his frame of mind by simply seeking to be a better person and asking for God's help. The sermon pointed out that every person has fallen short of the commandment to love your fellow man. The minister quoted the Bible scripture in Matthew 19:26. that read, "With God all things are possible." He pondered his eagerness to take these Bible truths to heart. Surely, he had heard the same thing growing up in Quewhiffle. He reasoned that now was just his time to change.

Jackson decided he wanted to abandon his shallow, arrogant, selfish, and angry life as it had never really brought him any true happiness or contentment. He wanted to be like his new friend Allen and follow the teachings of Jesus.

After these life altering decisions, Jackson, alias James B. Davis, worked hard to help the needy and distressed in Sylacauga. He became known as the guy who always put out a helping hand.

Jackson bought a bicycle for the son of one of his employees who could not afford to pay for this luxury. That boy was so appreciative that he strived to become like the kind man who gave him the wonderful gift. The boy asked to come to the mill to personally thank Jackson. Jackson not only let him come to the mill, but he also took him to three ball games and to church four times.

One of his employees at the turpentine mill became sick with cancer and was scared that his family would become destitute. Jackson went to see the man in the hospital and promised him that he would continue to receive his salary for the rest of his life, even if he never worked another day. He became a regular visitor in the home of his former employee and helped the family with paying for medicines, buying clothes for the children, and providing money for Christmas gifts for the entire family. Jackson was warmly welcomed into the man's home, and he spent many hours sitting beside the bed of his terminally ill friend, sharing stories, and getting to know him. The man asked Jackson to sing Scottish songs, as Jackson had become known for this. Jackson softly sang, *I Love a Lassie-A Bonnie Highland Lassie*, and *A Highland Lad*.

When the man was dying, Jackson was there with the family. The family told him that their father could no longer speak because he was too weak, but he could hear others speak to him. Jackson wanted to say something profound and meaningful to his friend, but he found this difficult.

At first, he talked to his friend about inconsequential things like the weather and the news, but then he realized this was his last opportunity to talk to his friend, so he said, "You have been a great father and husband. You have worked so hard your entire life. I want you to know I admire you. I love you and I know you love me, too."

To his great surprise the dying man whispered, "Yes."

This brought tears to Jackson's eyes and immense joy to his heart.

Jackson became a valued and respected citizen of the town. Everyone spoke warmly of him. He joined the Masons and the First Presbyterian Church where he made frequent large donations. To Jackson's great surprise, his Sunday School class gave him a medal for generosity and kindness, something he would have never received in a thousand years in Quewhiffle.

Jackson's original plan had been to move from place to place every two years to lessen the chance of being recaptured and sent back to prison. He made a life altering decision. The friendship and peace he felt so keenly in Sylacauga made him want to remain in Sylacauga, so he abandoned his plans to move from place to place. The happiness he felt there outweighed the risk of being taken back to prison.

He bought a large two-story sprawling house in the center of the town, and frequently had friends over to visit. People in Sylacauga kept asking about his family, and he told them that his wife, Timberland Davis, an alias, had an extremely sick mother in the mountains of North Carolina, and she spent nearly all her time with her. His friends begged to meet his wife.

On Jackson's next trip to visit his family in North Carolina, he told Aila that he wanted her to come to Sylacauga for one month and pretend to be Timberland Davis, the loving wife of J. B. Davis. He explained she did not have to treat him any differently than usual when they were alone. He told Aila that her doing this would help him be more convincing to the people in Sylacauga. Jackson also told Lura and her siblings that their mother's other name would be Timberland, and they thought this was a strange name and questioned their Papa about his choice of a name. But Jackson would not budge in his decision that the name would be Timberland. Lura reasoned it had something to do with her Papa being in the turpentine business and working with timber.

Aila gave this a lot of thought. She could see no reason why she should be part of this charade. Why should she go there to make his lie, his pretense more convincing? Yet she was also intrigued. Was all this true? Has he really reformed? Was he really living a good and sober life? Who were these people who seemed to admire him? This is not the man she had lived with. Aila could not believe that this utterly selfish boorish aggressive drinking bully was now asking her to help him make his lie appear true.

But then Aila looked at the idea another way. He was now paying all the expenses for her and her children. When Jackson first went to prison, Aila had to ask her father-in-law for money, and this humiliated her. Also, now Jackson was more pleasant to have around. She reasoned that if she did cooperate, she could find out how genuine his new character really was, and just for a little while she could forget the murder, the escape, his drinking, his previous bullying, and abusive behavior. If she went to Sylacauga, she could hold her head up high and be somebody in society. His part of the deal would be to accept that there would be no reconciliation, that he could never be forgiven, and in private, they would remain distant. Aila thought that the idea of meeting people who might be interested in her was frightening, but this time she would not be hiding the embarrassing parts of her life. Aila knew she could not do this alone and if she came, then Lura would have to come with her. To Jackson's surprise and delight, Aila agreed to come to Sylacauga, but only on the condition that she would bring Lura along. Jackson eagerly agreed to this. Aila reminded Jackson she was still mad as hell with him and all he had done. She told him again that she would never forgive him. She reminded him not to expect any hanky panky. Then she told Jackson that she was not doing this for him; she was doing it for herself. She promised to play her role perfectly.

Aila had a tough time convincing Lura to come with her. At first, Lura said no. But Aila told Lura it would mean so much if Lura came along, it might be fun, and it surely would be an adventure. Finally, Aila won Lura over to her way of thinking.

As Aila and Lura took the train to Sylacauga, they could not believe they were going to Alabama to play the roles of their lives. With trepidation, Aila tried to look at this trip as an actress playing the role of a totally different person. In this new role, Aila would be free to meet new people and be a bit outgoing. Both Aila and Lura wanted to feel excitement and happiness again, even if it was in an acting role. Lura, who was shy and introverted knew she would need to pretend to be outgoing to survive this experience. Both were a bit nervous but exhilarated at all that lay ahead.

The night Aila and Lura arrived in Sylacauga, Jackson gave a big reception at his magnificent new home in honor of his wife and daughter. Aila was amazed at the popularity of her husband, and how much the people in Sylacauga loved him. When the doorbell began ringing and people started filling up the huge parlor, Jackson would walk up to his friends and shake their hands or give them a hug. All the people attending were happy. Jackson seemed to be a completely different man in Sylacauga from the one at home. After the party had been going on for about an hour, Aila spoke to Jackson saying she needed to go to bed as she had a headache. Jackson was disappointed that Aila left, but he was delighted at how much fun Lura seemed to be having.

Of those Lura met this first evening, Lura particularly liked Camilla Reid, the town librarian, and Gail Jenkins, the wife of her Papa's overseer, Allen Jenkins. Lura liked Gail's sweetness, kindness, and intelligence. Lura admired Camilla's keen intelligence and the way she would mention authors and characters from Greek mythology in ordinary conversation. Lura also admired Camilla's striking long red hair, her tall stature, her slimness, and her impeccable manners. Lura was happy to learn that Camilla and Gail were best friends and often had outings together. Camilla suggested that Lura and her mother join her and Gail for a tour of Camilla's library, and a visit to the ice cream parlor the next day. Lura eagerly agreed.

Lura thought, 'This is how life would be if I did not have to hide from others at home.'

At the end of the party, Lura went to her mother's room to check on her. When Lura entered, her mother was sitting up in bed reading a book.

"Mama, I don't think you have a headache. You just wanted to get away from the party."

Aila smiled and said, "Saying you have a headache, Lura, can get you out of all sorts of events. Remember this when you need it. How was the rest of the party?"

"I met many nice people, all of whom had great praise for Papa. I spent most of my evening with Camilla Reid, the town librarian, and Gail Jenkins who is Papa's overseer's wife. They told me a lot about Sylacauga, and they asked us to spend tomorrow afternoon with them."

Aila did not mind meeting people in small groups, and she felt this might be interesting, so she readily agreed.

When Lura returned to her room, she gave this evening's events a lot of thought. She decided to try to enjoy her time in Sylacauga and not mourn and fret about the inadequacies and constraints of life at home. She said out loud to herself, "Carpe diem."

The next day, Lura and Aila walked from Jackson's home along beautiful tree lined streets to the public library, just two blocks away. Camilla and Gail were at the front door of the library to meet them, and Camilla gave them a tour. What Lura liked most about the library was that the expansive main reading room's domed ceiling contained literary quotes, names of famous authors, painters, playwrights, and actors. Camilla had planned the domed ceiling cleverly, even before the building was under construction. On the ceiling above the English literature section of books was the quote 'To Be or Not to Be.' The ceiling over the art books contained the names, Van Gogh, Michelangelo, and DaVinci. The ceiling over the law and legal books had paintings of famous judges. The ceiling itself looked like a magnificent work of art. Lura told Camilla how much she liked Camilla's creativity in planning and implementing this.

After the library tour, the four ladies went to the ice cream parlor. As they ate their delicious banana splits, sundaes, and ice cream concoctions, the four ladies talked easily. Camilla said that J. B. had made quite a name for himself in Sylacauga, and he was liked by all, that he was a kind person and a valued member of the town. Aila told Camilla and Gail that she was shy and that she often chose to be by herself rather than being with anyone but her family. Both Camilla and Gail said that was simply fine. Everyone should know their own preferences.

In the days to come, Lura joined Gail and Camilla on bicycle rides, book clubs, and country walks. They had lengthy discussions about how hard it was for women to win the right to vote and how much they relished their new right to vote now. They also helped Gail deliver meals to the poor. Aila only joined in with the bicycle riding. Camilla, Gail, and Lura enjoyed each other's company. Lura pondered the thought of inviting her new friends to Southern Pines because she wanted to extend the time they could spend together, but she quickly realized this could never happen.

Lura appreciated that her friends did not pry into her personal life. As Lura spent more time with her new friends, she thought of the ideas first put forth by Socrates:

Great minds discuss ideas.
Average minds discuss events,
Small minds discuss people.

Lura liked knowing that Camilla and Gail both had great minds, and that Camilla was not the only one with knowledge of the classics.

One evening when Lura, Aila, and Jackson were having a quiet evening, Jackson said, "I have been thinking. With all the money I am making here in Sylacauga and all the money we received for selling our land in Quewhiffle, I think we should build a new house in Raeford. It should be the finest house in the town. Even though I could not live there openly, I could visit in secret."

Aila, always liking to impress others, jumped at the idea. She certainly wanted a big new impressive house, but she wanted it to be built in Southern Pines rather than Raeford. Jackson reminded her that if her new house was the envy of the town, then it would be best if she already knew most of the people in the town. Aila considered this and decided that if she had the biggest house in town, it could be in either Southern Pines or Raeford. Lura had no real attachment to the Southern Pines house, so she felt fine about the idea. What she really liked was that building this new house and furnishing it would give her a chance to try out her new interest, interior decorating. So Lura went to get paper and pencils and the three of them began making plans and drawing several different possible house plans.

"I want a grand staircase and a front door with beveled glass. I want fifteen-foot ceilings and a music room," said Aila.

"I want a huge yard with an immense circular driveway in the front, and I want a covered entry on the side for our automobile," said Lura.

The three of them had a fun and productive evening, and Lura and Aila had their work cut out for them when they returned home.

Jackson also liked having Aila and Lura in Sylacauga with him. He often told Aila and Lura that they played their roles brilliantly, and he was proud of them. Aila realized that lately she had been happy in Jackson's company, but she still did not feel any love for him.

Due to the immense success of Aila and Lura's visit, Jackson decided to offer his two grown sons, Angus and Joseph, jobs at his turpentine business in Sylacauga. He wanted to do this because he often got lonely for his own family members. Also, if Angus and Joseph were living in Sylacauga, Jackson could keep an eye on them. Because Jackson knew how easy it was for him to go in the wrong direction in his life, he wanted to make sure these two sons made good and productive choices in life.

On Jackson's next visit to North Carolina, he made the job offer to Angus and Joseph, and his sons enthusiastically accepted. Both had heard remarkable stories from Lura about the reputation of their Papa in Sylacauga, about his beautiful house, and his interesting friends.

Jackson told his sons that the job offer was contingent upon two things:

1. His sons must use the last name "Kennedy", and

2. His sons must not let on to anyone that he was their Papa.

Once in Sylacauga, Angus and Joseph interviewed with Allen Jenkins for jobs at Jackson's turpentine mills. They both were hired and rented two rooms at Belle's Boarding house. Like their mother, Angus and Joseph were good actors and they treated their Papa as they would treat any other supervisor. Never once did they act like they were his sons. The brothers were happy in Sylacauga, particularly Angus. Angus wrote a letter to his mother and described his Sunday buffet lunch at the boarding house: southern fried chicken, butterbeans, black eyed peas, squash casserole, sweet potato soufflé, fried green tomatoes, hot biscuits, hushpuppies, creamed corn, peach cobbler, and a ten-layer chocolate cake. His letter said he was making good money at the turpentine mill, and that he had a girlfriend who worked at the local drugstore.

CHAPTER 7

Lura's first year at Brenau College
1926-1927

Dressed in a white cotton drop-waist blouse with a long navy tie, a navy-blue skirt that was mid-calf length, and a navy-blue cloche hat, Lura stepped off the train to begin college. Like most of the other students, Lura's hair was bobbed. Although she was twenty-three, she looked younger than most other students. Lura was the picture of a young 1920s college student.

Her mother accompanied her and helped her bring her luggage. A Brenau chauffeur took mother and daughter to the college entrance in a shiny new red Lincoln convertible.

On the short ride to the campus Aila said, "I am so glad we do not have to walk to the campus in this heat, Lura! It is hotter than blue blazes here."

Lura did not answer her mother because she was trying to see everything she could see. As the car turned a corner, the campus came into view.

"Look at that sign Mama," Lura said.

A huge yellow banner read, BRENAU WELCOMES STUDENTS TO THE 1926-1927 SCHOOL YEAR. Underneath the banner stood three attractive smiling college students greeting the newcomers and giving directions to the various dorms. Lura asked for directions to Bailey Hall. She was told that Bailey Hall would be easy to find because it was an extension of the largest and most beautiful building on campus, the auditorium. Lura and her mother walked toward the majestic auditorium, each carrying one suitcase. They loved their first look at Brenau. They entered Bailey Hall and went upstairs to room 401 on the fourth floor. Lura was excited to see the room where she would live for the next year. The walls of her room were light yellow, and the room contained two single beds, two desks-each with a bookshelf, two chests of drawers, a full length mirror, and a sink. The first thing Lura did was unpack her framed picture of her dear baby brother, Laurence.

"I am going to miss him every day. Please tell him to expect at least one letter a week from me, and he should send at least two letters to me weekly," Lura told her mother.

While Lura and Aila put the sheets and covers on her bed, Aila said, "Lura, I am sorry that you and Agnes could not be roommates together. I understand the college wants students to make new friends, so they discourage relatives or close friends from rooming together."

"That's Okay. Agnes' room is next door to my dorm room. I will share my room with Louise McLeod. Agnes was matched up with another music student for her roommate. I cannot wait to see Agnes again. Agnes chose to come to Brenau due to its excellent music program, and I chose to come here because Agnes would be here. Even though Agnes and I wrote letters regularly after she left Quewhiffle, we have so much to tell each other as college students. It surely has been a long time since we were childhood friends," Lura replied.

Aila continued helping Lura put away her fashionable 1920s wardrobe. Lura loved her new wardrobe, and she liked watching her mother unpack her new treasured things-four cloche hats, six beaded headbands, a long pearl necklace, six pairs of semi sheer hosiery, two pairs of kid gloves, a daring red flapper dress with beads, and eight silk dresses.

62

Lura and her mother left the dorm through the back entrance. Just outside, they sat down in a beautiful flower laden courtyard on an ornate stone bench. They ate their lunch which Aila brought with her on the train and enjoyed the babbling and rippling of the flowing water in the pristine white three- tiered fountain.

Aila knew that time was drawing near for her to take the train back home, but she felt reluctant to leave Brenau. Interestingly, Lura could not wait for her mother to leave so she could go back to her room and meet her roommate. Aila and Lura said their goodbyes quickly and both hurried to their respective destinations.

When Lura entered room 401 again, two young ladies were already there. Immediately Agnes and Lura hugged each other, and Agnes gave Lura "the look" and they proceeded to recite *Hey Diddle Diddle* like they had done so many times as children. After this, they fell into giggles and hugged again. Agnes and Lura commented how each had changed in the seven years since they had last seen each other.

"So, how is Earl?" asked Agnes.

"He's fine and quite grown up now," remarked Lura.

"Lura, here is your roommate. Let me introduce you to Louise McLeod," said Agnes.

Louise shook Lura's hand. "Nice to meet you."

Louise wore a forest green drop-waist silk dress that scandalously barely covered her knees, black sheer hose, T-strap black shoes, a forest-green ribbon around her neck, a long pearl necklace, and a forest-green cloche which perfectly framed Louise's natural blond curly hair, and her striking blue eyes. Lura perceived all of this about Louise immediately. Within a couple of minutes, Lura also decided that Louise was bold, modern, and from a wealthy family.

"Louise, I am so pleased to finally meet you, too! I enjoyed our correspondence over the summer," said Lura.

"Lura, it is my delight to meet you," said Louise as she looked at Agnes. "I just met Agnes and understand that you two were childhood friends. I am glad that her room is next door to ours. She just told me that unfortunately, her roommate cannot come to Brenau this semester, so Agnes is all by herself. I thought it would be great if you, Agnes, and I could be a happy trio and do things together."

Louise kindly reached for Agnes' hand and gave it a squeeze. Lura looked at Agnes for the first time with concentration. Agnes was the antithesis of Louise. Agnes seemed a bit old-fashioned with her muslin brown dress which covered more of her legs than was necessary. She wore a brown cloche, a short pearl necklace, and had medium bobbed brown hair, deep brown eyes, and a timid smile that revealed her gullibility.

Then Agnes spoke. "It is going to be great living next door to you two and doing things together. Thanks for treating me like a roommate. Would you two like to walk with me to see the campus? I particularly want to get a close look at the auditorium where I will spend so much time. I have come to Brenau to study piano and voice."

Both Lura and Louise said yes at the same moment, and then everyone laughed. Louise said, "Lura, tell us about you and your family."

Lura knew this was coming and dreaded talking about her family, but she had already decided exactly how to describe her family.

"I live in Raeford, which is near Fayetteville, North Carolina. I come from a large family of nine children, and I am the sixth in line. You may have noticed the picture I placed on my chest of drawers.

64

It is of my brother Laurence, who is sixteen. He and I are close, and I will miss him the most of anyone else while I'm here at Brenau."

Lura paused then continued, "I have not totally decided on my course of study here, but I think their program in Domestic Science includes studies in Interior Decorating. My Papa is in naval stores, and he travels with his job. Both of my parents are of Scottish ancestry. Lastly, I love animals, particularly dogs. I almost forgot to tell you that I am beginning college a bit later because for the last three years I have been home helping my mother with health problems."

Agnes remarked, "The last time I saw Laurence, he was knee high to a grasshopper. He seems quite grown up in this picture. I see he still has his golden curls."

Lura was so relieved that Agnes did not refer to Lura's family's scandal.

Agnes and Louise made a few nice comments about Lura's remarks. Then Lura asked Louise to tell them about her life.

Louise began, "I am also of Scottish ancestry and my father is the head minister of the largest Presbyterian Church in Richmond. Mama thrives on her work with the Colonial Dames, and both my parents love the social life in Richmond. I must admit the things I like to do are not compatible with being the daughter of a minister. I am eighteen, and I love to dance, go to parties, and flirt. I am not sure what my major will be in college. Oh, and don't you think it's strange for a girl who loves to flirt to go to college at an all-girls' college? My parents are the ones who decided I should attend a girl's college. Now Agnes, we need to hear from you."

Agnes took a deep breath and said, "I am twenty-two, and my father has been a Presbyterian minister in Kinston, North Carolina for the past six years. Before that, my family lived in Quewhiffle near Lura. I have a passion for music and want to be a pianist or a vocalist.

I have been practicing all my life and that is my dream." Agnes paused, then continued, "Let's go downstairs and see the inside of the auditorium, and then explore the rest of the campus."

The three girls agreed to go on a tour. First, they walked downstairs to the auditorium. When they entered, Agnes walked reverently to the space just before the stage. Both Lura and Louise felt Agnes looked a little strange. Agnes' eyes were sparkling unnaturally, and her mouth was open slightly. Agnes was awe-struck as she savored her first views of the overwhelmingly ornate auditorium. She stood there in silence gazing at the opulence, and she had a feeling in her bones that this place would always have a special meaning for her. She tried to take it all in, but the significance of the experience transcended her current understanding.

Agnes finally looked at Lura and Louise and was happy to see that they also looked suitably impressed. "Look at the size of this auditorium. It seats up to 1200 people. I particularly like the gold-leaf statues. Because I will be a voice and piano student, this auditorium will be MY place. I claim it as my own forever. I cannot wait to perform on that beautiful stage."

The girls then walked around the rest of the campus. Lura savored the beautiful grounds, the abundance of trees which provided ample shade, the flowers, and the architecture of the campus. Lura's heart was warmed by the beauty of this campus.

Louise pointed toward a stately huge live oak tree which had sturdy looking steps made of beautiful dark wood which led to a huge platform holding a treehouse high up in the tree.

"That's the cat's meow," said Louise. She was about to charge up the staircase, when she stopped to read these words on a tiny sign at the entrance:

'Class of 1905 gives this treehouse to Brenau College. It is the exclusive property of Seniors and may not be invaded by lower classmen. We hope that it offers a dignified and cool retreat whither the stately Seniors may withdraw from the noisy throng on the campus. Seniors, welcome to the 'Crow's Nest.'

The three girls walked in a loop around the entire campus. After a simple dinner at the dining room at the North Hall Dorm, the girls returned to their dorm and changed into evening attire, then walked to the Oriental Parlor for the new student reception. This expansive reception room contained much opulence; chairs that appeared to be from the English Tudor period, walls covered in paintings of colorful flamingos, and oriental rugs so thick that walking on them felt like floating. As soon as the girls entered the room, they could smell the delicious Swedish meatballs, freshly baked ham biscuits, and other aromas that they could not identify.

Louise delicately placed a lemon tart on her tiny China plate, then took a small bite. The flavor of the tart and sweet lemon in her mouth was the most delicious thing she ever tasted.

"Agnes and Lura, I feel I have spent time in this room before because it seems all so familiar," said Louise.

Soon Louise forgot about trying to figure out why the room reminded her of another place. She just enjoyed the events of the evening.

Louise wandered off from Lura and Agnes and introduced herself to several of the faculty, and some of her fellow freshmen. Lura and Agnes sat down in two comfortable seats, watched all the people, and rested a bit after their long walk in the afternoon. For the first part of the evening, Agnes and Lura stayed close together talking about childhood days in Quewhiffle. Agnes reached for Lura's hand.

"It is a dream come true to be here with you at Brenau. We had great times together as girls in Quewhiffle. But now Lura, it's time for us to step boldly forward and speak to our classmates."

Lura and Agnes mingled timidly with a few faculty members, but they could not help glancing at Louise who was making her way through the room with the poise and confidence of the belle of the ball. Soon Louise met the dashingly handsome Mr. Norman Stafford, one of the faculty of the School of Music. Louise found him to be intelligent, a great conversationalist, tall, with black hair and huge brown eyes. He looked to be about thirty-five-years-old. She had been talking with him for about five minutes when she thought of introducing him to Agnes. She gestured to get Agnes to notice her and come to meet Mr. Stafford. Louise was delighted to introduce the two to each other. She could tell that Agnes was impressed with him but felt shy. Mr. Stafford told Agnes that he had been assigned to work closely with her on her piano lessons. This made Agnes' day. The reception ended, and the girls returned to their dorm rooms and got ready for bed.

After turning the lights off and getting into their respective beds, Louise and Lura continued talking. "Lura, I figured out why the Oriental Parlor looked so familiar to me. It looks exactly like a room in the Whitehall Palace in London where I spent a lot of time."

"Louise, when did you spend a lot of time in England?" asked Lura.

Louise took a deep breath and began speaking,

"Lura, I do not know if you believe in reincarnation, but I do because I have lived it as vividly as I am in this room with you at this very moment. I remember one former life most of all. It was in 1533 when I lived in England and caught the attention and affection of Henry VIII. He met my sister, Mary Boleyn first, but he soon got tired of her and then he met me. I used all my techniques to make him love and lust for me. My methods worked and he was soon in love with me. I thought nothing could ever change his love and dedication to me.

"We lived at the Tudor Whitehall Palace which had more than 1500 rooms. We lived in the portion of the palace known as the York Place. One of the reception rooms at York Place looked so much like the Oriental Parlor which we visited earlier this evening," said Louise.

Lura thought, *She really believes she lived in Tudor England! I can't believe it. What else is she going to tell me, that she and Henry were able to develop wings and fly?*

"I loved my early years with Henry, but as you know, I had enemies who told him lies about me. Henry eventually turned against me and had me beheaded. I remember that day at the Tower of London much too vividly. In most reincarnations, a person does not have any physical characteristics of their former self, but from my birth, I had the scar from being beheaded. That is why you will never see me without a ribbon around my neck."

Lura thought, *Maybe one night when Louise is sleeping, I will remove her ribbon around her neck hiding her scar. What if there is no scar? But what if there really IS a scar? This is all too much!*

To Lura's delight, Louise continued, "I recall every detail of my time with my precious daughter, Elizabeth. I loved to have her with me as much as possible. Even though it was contrary to the royal customs, I often kept my baby with me on a small pillow beside me. Henry and the other royals were embarrassed by my display of affection. I loved that child with all my heart and being permanently separated from her was the hardest part of my execution."

Lura thought, *That baby was Queen Elizabeth I.*

Louise stopped talking, and the room was silent for few minutes.

Finally, Louise said, "Lura, what do you think of what I have told you?"

Lura was smiling broadly, and again she thought to herself. *How convenient that the darkness in our room prevents Louise from seeing my face. If it was daytime, my face would surely reveal my true feelings. I definitely do not believe her and I feel she just wants attention. But it will help me to let Louise think I believe her. That way when questions come up about my difficult family, I can always redirect the conversation to Louise's life with Henry.*

"Lura, have you fallen asleep?" asked Louise.

"Sorry, I was just thinking how to answer you. I've never given any thought to reincarnation, but your experiences are fascinating. I want to have lengthy conversations about this. But let's go to sleep now and start discussing this first thing in the morning. I am so tired now and I need to sleep."

Lura woke up the next morning early, but she lay in bed thinking about how exciting it was going to be to have Louise as her roommate and to have Agnes next door. She thought about questions she could ask Louise about Anne Boleyn. When Louise woke up, Lura started with the questions. Louise was alert and happy to talk as soon as she opened her eyes. Lura was delighted that her roommate was a morning person.

"Louise, I have some questions to ask you about your life in England in Tudor times. Tell me about the fabrics in the clothing in Tudor England," said Lura.

Louise began speaking enthusiastically, "We had beautiful colorful fabrics then. I remember my purple satin gown with sleeves embroidered with scenes of Henry's hunting party. I loved my black satin muffler with its pink taffeta lining. My yellow velvet gown and my orange velvet gown were two of my favorites. Our bed coverings were luxurious back then too. I recall one bed covering that was a dark russet color which was made of damask. I loved little Elizabeth's tiny bed with a covering made of damask fringed with Venetian gold and silver thread. It had a crimson satin cradle head.

Lura, I can go on and on, but let me think on this question and tell you more later."

"Yes, do think about the fabrics and tell me more later," Lura replied.

"Louise, I have some more questions on other topics. How often did you take a bath? How often did Henry bathe? Do you think Henry would have been totally satisfied with his first wife if she had produced a male heir? What kinds of gifts did Henry give you?"

As much as she tried to hide it, Lura could not resist a smile.

As the girls dressed, Lura kept asking questions about Henry, and Louise kept answering in amazing detail. Louise also offered fascinating tangential details, but those details were intriguing, too. Lura interrupted from time to time to clarify a point. Both Louise and Lura were thoroughly enjoying their conversation.

Then a startling idea came into Lura's mind, Louise *sounded like she really was a reincarnation of Anne Boleyn!*

Lura also felt thankful that whether or not Louise was a reincarnation, that she would surely be loads of fun and thoroughly entertaining.

By 8:45 in the morning all three girls went downstairs to the auditorium to attend Freshman Orientation. Louise could not take her eyes off the outfits of her fellow classmates. "These girls are dressed in the most fashionable fall outfits! They are the picture of perfection for 1926 college students. I am so glad I got a new wardrobe to come to college!" said Louise.

"I would like us to sit in the back row," said Lura.

"We don't want to do that, Lura. I want to clearly see the face of every speaker and I want them to see me, too. I want to sit in the first row," said Louise persuasively.

"Let's sit in the third row," compromiser Agnes chimed in, and so they did.

As they sat there waiting for the program to begin, Agnes had a relaxed opportunity to look carefully at the opulence of the auditorium. She knew from the Brenau reading materials which she received in the mail, that the auditorium was built about 1878 and it was one of the original buildings of the college. Her eyes scanned the enormity of the space. She loved the organs on either side of the stage and the number of pipes looked to be in the thousands! Agnes decided this definitely did not look like a college auditorium, but rather it had the appearance of an elegant European opera house.

The first speaker was Dr. Haywood Jefferson Pearce, President of Brenau College. In a warm and fatherly voice, Dr. Pearce began his welcoming comments. His comments lasted about fifteen minutes, but these are the words Lura remembers the best:

"My dear young ladies, welcome to Brenau College. The word 'Brenau' means 'Gold refined by Fire.' Our women's college prepares you to be agents of change in the world.

Here is what the Ideal Brenau Student strives to do:

- *To find satisfaction in being rather than in seeming*
- *To find joy in doing rather than in dreaming*
- *To be prepared for service thereby earning the right to be served*
- *To be pure in heart; vigorous in mind, discreet in action*
- *To love deeply, fear nothing, hate never*
- *To enjoy that freedom which comes from knowledge of the "Truth"*
- *To be modestly conscious of the limitations of human knowledge and serenely confident of the limitless reaches of human endeavor*

Lura felt in her heart that she wanted to be exactly like the ideal Brenau student. She had not yet verbalized her goals for her life, but

Dr. Pearce verbalized them for her today. Lura looked at Agnes, and both young women knew they were thinking the exact same thing! Both said a silent "YES!"

Dr. Pearce went on to introduce the Directors of each of the Departments in the school. When he introduced Miss Catherine Bright, Professor of Oratory, Louise whispered to Lura, "She is a great beauty."

When Mr. Norman Stafford was introduced, Louise gave him a big smile and Agnes blushed noticeably.

Dr. Pearce introduced Miss Eva Pearce who was the Dean of Students. She told the students the rules that must be obeyed at Brenau:

- Your day starts at 4:30 am.
- You need to wash up, dress, eat breakfast, clean your room for the daily inspection, and attend Chapel here in the auditorium before 9:30 a.m.
- Never leave campus without permission.
- Never walk on the streets of Gainesville without a chaperone.
- No gum chewing-if you are caught chewing gum, you cannot leave the campus for five weeks.
- No automobile riding with men-this results in immediate expulsion. You should be thankful because before 1920, girls were not allowed to speak to boys.
- All students must extinguish their lights at 10:30 p.m. when the light bell is sounded.

As Miss Pearce outlined the school's rules, Louise groaned, "This girl's school has more rules than Carter has pills. I know I am going to have a tough time with some of these rules."

Classes at Brenau started two days after Freshman Orientation. At the end of the first day of classes, Louise, Lura, and Agnes were eating dinner together and eagerly telling each other about their first day of classes.

"Lura, I'm glad we are in Mr. James Simmons' English Literature class together. He is going to have us read the Shakespearean play, Henry VIII, and write a paper about it. I can promise you that we are both going to get an A on our papers. I know every word of that play so well that I can recite the entire play at this very moment," said Louise confidently.

Agnes and Lura stared at each other in disbelief. "Okay Louise, begin the prologue," urged Lura.

Louise took a big breath and began speaking the words of the prologue with a late medieval English accent:

I come no more to make you laugh.
Things now that bear a weighty and a serious brow,
Sad, high, and working, full of state and woe.

Louise then switched to her normal Southern accent. "Now I am going to recite my favorite lines from this play which come from Act IV, Scene I. These words are spoken by a gentleman who was present at Anne Boleyn's coronation.

Her grace rose and with modest paces.
Came to the altar where she kneeled and saint-like
Cast her fair eyes to heaven and prayed devoutly.
Then rose again and bowed her to the people,
When by the Archbishop of Canterbury
She had all the royal makings of a queen...

Then Louise sighed and had a dreamy look on her face.

"That was so beautiful!" said Lura. She paused and then continued. "I want to tell you about my day. My Domestic Science classes will cover interior decorating, fabric selection, cooking, recipe alterations, and home management. Did you two know that Brenau is renowned as a pioneer in women's colleges for beginning this Domestic Science and Domestic Arts program? Brenau even has a model home on the campus, and each student in the Domestic Sciences major has to stay in the model home for two weeks to practice home management there."

"My turn now girls," said Agnes. "I was in seventh heaven to begin my music and piano course today. Mr. Stafford is a great teacher, and all the girls were flirting with him just a little. I must admit I was a little nervous to begin his class. I just have to constantly tell myself that I am a good pianist, and I will be successful in my musical future."

Louise gently took Agnes' hand. "Agnes, you are going to be the best pianist that ever lived! I know the Theatre and Drama Department is going to be the perfect major for me. Today we learned the plays that will be performed by Brenau students this year. They are:

- *Peg O' My Heart*
- *The Mirage*
- *The Bat*
- *Six Characters in Search of an Author*
- *Lysistrata*

"I never heard of any of those plays. What is *Lysistrata* about?" asked Agnes.

"You are never going to believe this," Louise replied. I thought Brenau was too old fashioned for *Lysistrata*. It's an ancient Greek comedy about a woman's mission to end the Peloponnesian War by getting all the women to deny the men sex until the war ends. Maybe I can play the lead role. The only problem with this play is that here at Brenau, females must play male roles. I would much rather perform this play with men acting the parts of men. You both must come to see it."

The happy trio shared experiences every day and became best friends. They relied on each other and delighted in their friendship.

Soon the autumn leaves began to fall and blanket the campus in beautiful shades of orange and red. All was well with Agnes, Lura, and Louise, and they felt exhilarated by college life and being in the bloom of youth. Agnes was totally immersed in her piano rehearsals and lessons. She already had a crush on Mr. Stafford who was a kind and encouraging piano teacher.

One night when Louise was away, and Lura and Agnes were studying together, they talked about Louise. "I have to tell you something Agnes. Louise believes she is a reincarnation of Anne Boleyn," said Lura. The two talked about this for a long time and Lura told Agnes many of the stories Louise had told her.

"I am not sure if reincarnation is possible. You know Lura, the universe holds secrets we can never imagine in this lifetime," said Agnes.

"Lura, I have something to tell you that you must never tell a living soul. Go ahead and cross your heart and hope to die."

Lura's eyes opened wide, and she became slightly alarmed but hid her emotion. "I promise not to tell anyone," as she made a cross across her chest with her fingers.

"You know that Earl and I were friends as children in Quewhiffle," Agnes began. "After my family moved away, Earl and I wrote letters to each other from time to time. I knew my parents would disown me if they knew I wrote letters to a Negro boy. I devised a plan to avoid them finding out and having a conniption fit.

76

I got my best friend at school to receive Earl's letters and then she would give them to me. I read them, memorized portions of them, then gave them back to my friend to keep for me in a secret place. Earl and I became quite good friends, and we shared our hopes and dreams in our letters. I am still corresponding with him and now he can send my letters here to me at Brenau. He does not use his name on the return address. You know how society is, they would never accept a Negro man and a white woman as a couple. So, Earl and I are careful not to let anyone know. I just wanted you to know about this. I know you and Earl are also friends."

"I have another confession," said Agnes.

"You're full of confessions today, Agnes," said Lura. "Do continue."

"Like you, I always felt close to your dear brother Laurence. Earlier this year, Laurence and I also began corresponding. He is a wonderful young man. Even though he is five years younger than me, I am starting to like him more and more. I also wanted you to know about this."

Lura was astounded at Agnes' two confessions, but she acted casual in her reaction to her. After she went to bed that night, she thought about what Agnes said for a long time.

Because Lura knew Agnes as a child, in general she knew more about what to expect from her than Louise. But the longer Lura and Louise roomed together, the more Lura liked Louise. What Lura had now with Louise and Agnes was harmony and friendship. Lura was not accustomed to harmony, but rather disharmony. For example, she was used to her older sister, Maggie, acting furious over something that was totally inconsequential. Lura had never lived with anyone with such a positive outlook as Louise. Louise was a fun roommate and kept Lura entertained by talking about her history. Lura never revealed she did not believe Louise. She thoroughly enjoyed coming up with questions for Louise about Henry. Lura became bolder in her questions as she got to know Louise better. Louise did not seem shy talking about sex or anatomy. Lura's most recent question to Louise was, "Could Henry fill up his codpiece in his suit of armor?"

Lura wrote weekly letters to Laurence telling him about her reincarnated roommate, about how Agnes had changed since Laurence last saw her, and what campus life was like. Lura could count on Laurence to always communicate with her. She received two letters each week from him. From Laurence's letters Lura learned of her mother's depression, that he joined the school choir, that he spent time with his grandparents, and that he liked to help his grandpapa with his turpentine business.

Lura noticed something about herself, too. She realized that she was becoming friendlier because she didn't have to hold potential friends at a distance as she did back home.

Lura's current separation from her mother due to college turned out to be a tremendous benefit to her. She felt happier than any time since she was a young child. The only negative for Lura was that she was separated from Laurence.

Every time Agnes went into the auditorium, she always thought to herself, this is my place. She wanted to perform there, and then go on to perform at various opera houses and concert halls around the world. She had a great yearning to be a famous musician, to receive flowers at performances, letters from secret admirers, and wonderful favorable reviews in all the newspapers. She felt sure all this would come in her future, but the first step would be to be the best performer in Brenau's opulent auditorium.

Agnes delighted and marveled at the music department's eight Steinway grand pianos, and at the ninety-five upright pianos, all of which were kept perfectly tuned. She loved the fact that the auditorium was built using opera floor plans, and that it contained seating for 1200 people. The stage was fifty feet wide and thirty-five feet deep.

Agnes was an excellent and accomplished piano student. Mr. Stafford told Agnes that she was the most talented piano student to attend Brenau in ten years, and that she would be a great pianist one day. At Mr. Stafford's request, Agnes played classical piano pieces at least once a month in the elegant and acoustically perfect auditorium to an audience of Brenau faculty and students. Every time Agnes went into the auditorium, she always thought to herself, this is my place.

By the end of Spring Semester 1927, all three girls were happy and thriving and they expected things to go this way until graduation day.

Each of the girls went home to their families for the summer. Lura was delighted to see Laurence but oh how she longed to return to Brenau. Lura yearned for the cooler air in the higher elevation of the foothills of the Georgia mountains. The girls wrote frequent letters to each other and relished their communication.

Lura at Brenau College
Courtesy of Brenau University, Director of Photography

CHAPTER 8
Brenau's Ghost

Finally, after waiting endless lazy scorching summer days, Lura returned to Brenau, and the first person she saw was Agnes.

Running up to her, Lura threw her arms around her friend saying, "Agnes, you're a welcome sight. I've missed you so much. There is no friend in Raeford that I care about even half as much as I care about you."

As expected, Agnes gave Lura "the look," and they began reciting their favorite nursery rhyme in perfect unison. Afterwards they laughed till tears of happiness and friendship came into their eyes.

Then Louise walked up and said, "Don't leave me out." The three young ladies hugged all together and were overflowing with happiness.

"Lura, I had forgotten how striking you look with your red hair and your pale blue eyes," said Louise. The three girls constantly interrupted each other because each had so much to tell. Lura and Louise perceived that Agnes was about to burst to tell them something.

"Agnes, go ahead and tell us what you are dying to say," urged Louise.

"Over the summer I wrote to Mr. Stafford asking for suggestions to improve my piano skills. He wrote me wonderful, detailed letters throughout the summer. Sometimes his letters talked about how he loved music, how he chose music for his career, how he envisioned his career unfolding. I am in love with him. I want the two of you to read his letters and give me your opinion on how he feels about me. I know I am going to tremble when I am in his company," said Agnes.

Both Lura and Louise feared that Agnes had heartbreak in her future.

"We are happy to read those letters, Agnes. But first I have news for the two of you. I am in love with a gorgeous and lovable man named Roger Stith. He also lives in Richmond and is twenty-years-old," said Louise as she clasped her hands and jumped up and down to display her enthusiasm.

Agnes and Lura asked all about Roger. Unfortunately, Lura did not have any love interest to reveal, and she felt a bit sad about that.

As promised, Agnes, Louise, and Lura stayed up extremely late on this first day back at college, and Louise read each of Mr. Stafford's letters to Agnes aloud. Agnes tried to interpret hidden meanings in the letters, but Louise and Lura pointed out the simple facts of the letters and said that the letters were about friendship and nothing more.

The classes began a couple of days after the girls arrived at Brenau. Lura enjoyed the courses she took, English, Math, Art, Music, and History. One day she entered the room she shared with Louise bursting with enthusiasm. "How about this Louise, in my history class, I was assigned to write a term paper on Henry VIII. You will help me, right? This is going to be the most fantastic term paper in the history of the school. With your help I can make it come to life."

"I would love to do that term paper with you. It will help me relive some of my past and I have so much to tell you," exclaimed Louise.

In the end, both Lura and Louise authored the paper together and earned an A+. Lura's history teacher told her it seemed like Lura was really living in Henry VIII's time because Lura's descriptions were vividly detailed and heartfelt.

On November 1, Louise broke one of Brenau's cardinal rules. Her boyfriend Roger came to Gainesville, and Louise snuck out of her dormitory and went to meet him. They went riding in his car and then went to dinner at the Dixie Hunt Dining Room. Louise, with her eternal optimism, knew she would not be caught. But Eva Pearce, Dean of Students, happened to go to dinner at the same restaurant and saw Louise with a man. Louise did not see the Dean of Students there. The next morning before chapel, Louise got a note to go to President Pearce's office.

As Louise walked to the President's office, her legs were shaking, her skin was pale, and her hands were freezing cold. She was worried to death that someone saw her last night with Roger.

She was quickly ushered into the President's office. President Pearce asked her to have a seat and Louise noticed that the Dean of Students was also in the room.

"Louise, you were seen with a man in a restaurant last night. That is a serious violation of our College Rules," said President Pearce.

Louise nodded her head nervously.

The Dean of Students then spoke. "Last night some friends and I went to the Dixie Hunt Dining Room for dinner. I was so surprised to see you there, and even more surprised to see you with a man. Can you tell me why you violated our college's rules with your behavior last night?"

"Miss Pearce and Dr. Pearce, I am so sorry I broke the school's rules. I am in love with Roger, and we plan to get married. He lives in Richmond, and he had the opportunity to see me briefly. He took me for a meal to the restaurant so we could talk, and then we came straight back to the campus, and I went alone into my dorm room. We needed a quiet and relaxed time to talk."

"According to the rules and regulations of Brenau College, you violated two rules which require immediate expulsion. Rule One is 'Clandestine meetings with men.' Rule Two is 'Any conduct which, in accordance with the standards prevailing in well-bred society, would render a student undesirable as a member of the college community marks that student as liable for expulsion.' Please call your family and ask them to come and take you home. Please leave as soon as possible, but certainly before 72 hours," said the Dean of Students.

Louise began crying. She could barely whisper, "Please give me another chance." She could no longer speak. She slid out of her chair onto the floor and laid in a fetal position hugging herself and sobbing. She knew she had brought this on herself.

Saying goodbye the next day to Louise was terribly hard for Lura and Agnes. Tears and promises of letters mingled with the hugs. The happy trio at Brenau was no more.

After Louise left, Agnes moved into Lura's room. This made life a little less lonely for the two friends. Lura really missed her Henry VIII conversations. Both Lura and Agnes were always happy to receive letters from Louise, and they usually came at least once a week.

Agnes often pondered her life. She was certainly Earl's good friend, and she deeply cared about him. Sometimes she would imagine how it would be to have him kiss her and how it would be to have him date her. But each time she pondered these things, she realized that this could never work, that society would ostracize her and probably severely injure or kill Earl if anything really happened between the two of them. In the end she felt she was protecting Earl.

Despite their age difference, Agnes also had feelings for Laurence, but recently when she received a letter from him, he told her about his first girlfriend. Because both Earl and Laurence were not available to Agnes, she turned increasingly to Mr. Stafford.

Each day Agnes began daydreaming about Mr. Stafford more. She knew she was starting to love him, but she did not feel that he felt the same way about her. Agnes continued with her piano performances in the auditorium to the delight of the student body and the faculty.

Over the Thanksgiving break, almost all the students went home, but Agnes stayed behind to work on Chopin's *Minute Waltz,* a complicated piano piece which she would perform on the last day of school before the Christmas Holiday began. It was highly unlikely that the school would have allowed Agnes to remain at Brenau unchaperoned during Thanksgiving break, but somehow the authorities overlooked Agnes' plan to say on campus. When Mr. Stafford learned that Agnes was going to remain on campus, he suspected that someone in the administration had granted permission for her to remain at the school. He asked Agnes if the two of them could practice the *Minute Waltz* together in the morning in the auditorium.

Mr. Stafford made plans to meet Agnes in the auditorium at 10 a.m. the day after Thanksgiving. During this rehearsal, as she was playing the Steinway, she felt Mr. Stafford's hand cover the top of her hand, and she stopped playing immediately. She thought he did that to make her stop playing because she had made a mistake in the music. Agnes looked at him and he looked at her and they both smiled. Then he shocked and thrilled Agnes by kissing her, tenderly and lovingly.

"You are so beautiful that I could not help kissing you."

Agnes took this to mean he wanted to marry her, and her heart was full of love for him.

85

At the end of the rehearsal he said, "I think you need to work harder on this piece. Let's meet here again tomorrow morning at ten o'clock so you can practice more."

Agnes, being so shy, smiled and nodded her head yes. She was too overcome with emotion to speak. In her naiveté, she believed he would declare his love for her and give her an engagement ring in the morning.

Agnes returned to her empty dorm and spent the afternoon and evening reading and rereading all his letters to her. She made elaborate plans in her head of what their wedding would be like, what their children would look like, and how it might be a little hard to be married if both were musicians. Still, this did not matter to her. She did not sleep a wink all night due to her anticipation of what would happen when they met again.

The next morning Agnes met Mr. Stafford as promised, but something seemed so different than the previous day in his demeanor. This alarmed Agnes and her piano playing reflected her worry. In the middle of the lesson, Mr. Stafford said they should talk. Agnes did not know whether to expect a ring or a scolding for poor playing.

"Agnes, I am so sorry I kissed you yesterday. I really should not have done that because I am engaged to be married on Christmas Day. Your beauty and your magnificent playing simply made me want to connect with you. I have been thinking all this over carefully. We should go back to the way we behaved before yesterday. I am so sorry Agnes."

Hot tears of humiliation filled Agnes' eyes and for a couple of minutes she could not even breathe. The shock of what he said paralyzed her so she could not move. Agnes felt like she was going to explode or disappear. Finally, after what seemed an eternity, but was only one minute, Agnes regained the ability to breathe and move.

She jumped up and ran out of the auditorium and to her room in Bailey Dorm. She shut the door, threw herself on her bed, sobbed, wailed, and bawled her heart out. Because everyone was on Thanksgiving break, no one heard her mournful crying. She spent the whole night sobbing and shaking from the sorrow. During the early hours of the morning, she pondered her life. Agnes felt she could not get over Mr. Stafford's rejection and still go on living. Agnes came up with a plan in which she would not have to face the reality of what happened with Mr. Stafford and the possibility of life as a spinster.

Early Sunday morning, she got out the letters Mr. Stafford had mailed to her and which she had preserved so carefully. She got out pen and paper and wrote a note to Lura.

"My dear friend Lura, I am heartbroken. The man I wanted to marry and grow old with has told me he is marrying someone else. Here are his letters for you to keep or destroy. I do not want the school authorities or the police to find them. Please explain what happened to Earl and Laurence and tell them I am sorry. Do you remember how I told you the auditorium was MY PLACE? It will always be my place because I am going to visit there after I die. I will also visit you from time to time if it is possible, as you have been a devoted friend to me since I was a little girl. Your forever friend, Agnes."

At 7 a.m. Agnes put her note to Lura and the letters from Mr. Stafford inside a large envelope, addressed the envelope to Lura, and dropped it in the dorm's mail slot. Agnes walked downstairs to the auditorium where she knew no one else would be this early in the morning. She looked at the Steinway piano in the center of the stage and decided to play one last time. She played Chopin's *Minute Waltz* impeccably and was pleased with her performance. Finding the piece of rope she had seen the day before on the stage floor, she picked it up, and then walked up the stairs to the balcony. As she created a noose in the rope and hooked it over a piece of metal protruding from the balcony, she tried to take her mind off what she was doing by whispering her and Lura's nursery rhyme from memory:

Hey Diddle Diddle... She continued whispering the nursery rhyme until the moment the rope became tight from the weight of her body and her neck broke. With her suicide, Agnes claimed the Auditorium as her own forever-and no one who attended Brenau would forget her.

Lura was home for the Thanksgiving holiday and had no inkling of Agnes' suicide. Her mother received a telephone call on Sunday afternoon from Dr. Pearce at Brenau who knew about the special bond between Agnes and Lura. He wanted Lura to learn what happened while she was still at home. Lura's mother told Laurence and the two of them decided to tell Lura together. When Laurence asked Lura to come and talk to him and their mother, Lura suspected something had happened to a family member.

Lura was seated with her mother beside her, and Laurence knelt in front of Lura and took both her hands in his large warm hands.

As he shook his head back and forth in sadness, he said, "I don't understand or know why, but our dear friend Agnes killed herself."

Lura screamed, "No, No! Not my Agnes. She was my friend for eternity. She loved me and I loved her. I cannot go on without her!"

Lura stayed home from school for a week to try to recover from the shock. Lura told Earl about Agnes' suicide and the two of them cried together.

Earl drove Lura and Laurence to Agnes' funeral which was the saddest event Lura ever witnessed. At the end of the graveside portion of the funeral, Agnes's mother came up to Lura and said, "She considered you her dearest friend in all the world. Lura, thanks for being so good to my poor daughter. I have one favor to ask of you. Can you introduce me to Earl? I know Agnes and Earl corresponded and she cared for him. It does not bother me one bit that he is a Negro. Agnes did not know that I knew of her friend Earl."

Earl was standing a little ways away from the other mourners. Lura walked up to Earl and asked him to come with her to meet Agnes' mother.

Not knowing what to expect, Lura said "Mrs. Galloway, this is Agnes' friend, Earl Brown." Agnes mother reached for Earl's hand, held it, and said, "I know Agnes was your friend and she cared for you. Thanks for being her friend and for holding her up in letters all those years."

Earl was so overcome with surprise and with grief that all he could do was let the tears fall from his eyes and whisper,

"Thank you, thank you."

Lura was depressed for a long time after Agnes died. Dr. Pearce frequently checked on Lura and invited her to tea along with a few female faculty members.

Even in her grief, Lura mustered enough strength to complete her studies at Brenau, and graduate.

Agnes' claim that her classmates would not forget her, and that Brenau's auditorium would be her special place, all came to fruition.

In the late spring, after Agnes' suicide, Lura came to the auditorium for a concert early one stormy evening. Lura arrived forty-five minutes before the performance so she could study for a test while sitting in one of the seats. Sometimes Lura sought out quiet places to study outside of her dorm room.

Lura had been alone in the silent auditorium for about five minutes when her eyes were drawn to the stage by a flickering blue light beside the bench in front of a huge Steinway piano. In the beginning, the light was faint, almost imperceptible, but it progressively became brighter until it transformed into Agnes standing there beside the piano bench looking straight at Lura. Even though the image of Agnes was slightly distorted, Lura knew exactly who it was.

Part of Lura wanted to rush to the stage and embrace her dear friend whom she missed dreadfully. However, Lura was frightened. She had never seen a ghost before. Lura was unable to move a muscle in her body due to her fear. She was both attracted to and terrorized by seeing Agnes' ghost. She could not move her body. Even her vocal cords were paralyzed. She tried to scream, but the only sound she was able to make was the faintest of whispers.

Then the electricity in the auditorium went out, as the storm was growing in severity. With no electricity in the building, the only thing visible was Agnes and the blue light around her.

The electricity was restored after a couple of minutes, and Lura heard the conversation of a group of girls entering the auditorium. When the electricity came back on, Agnes vanished. As soon as Lura was able to move, she rapidly left the auditorium and returned to her room. She pondered what happened in the auditorium, and recalled that in Agnes' suicide note, she told Lura she would try to visit Lura if it were possible. Now Lura knew it was possible.

Soon other classmates reported that from time to time, they would see a blue light on the stage, then the appearance of a young woman in a flowing white dress. Even though most of the Brenau students were afraid of Agnes' materializations, some bolder students and students who liked to dabble in the occult welcomed Agnes.

Agnes' apparition would always begin as a flickering blue light that would slowly come into focus as a young woman in an ankle length flowing white dress. She was sometimes glimpsed in the back of the stage in performances and was once or twice seen on the sidelines at musical performances.

One evening about a month before Lura graduated from Brenau, Agnes materialized in Lura's dorm room. Lura had prepared herself for this to happen one day. She reasoned that Agnes felt a bond to her and that she would not hurt her. Agnes just wanted to remain close to Lura. Agnes arrived as she had done before, starting as a flickering blue light, and transforming into the Agnes Lura knew. Agnes did not speak to Lura, she just stood there with sad eyes looking at Lura. Lura was not frightened this time, and she felt sure that Agnes wanted to visit Lura one last time in the dorm room where they shared so many happy memories.

Brenau College Auditorium
Courtesy of Brenau University, Director of Photography

CHAPTER 9
Lura Visits Sylacauga
1929

Upon her return to Raeford, the newly graduated Lura looked for jobs but there were no jobs to be found. So, she primarily stayed home with her mother, and spent time with Laurence. They had long conversations about Agnes trying to understand why such a bright talent ended her life. Laurence confided in Lura that he had developed feelings for Agnes, but he did not know how to express them in letters. Lura told Laurence that Agnes also had feelings for him, too, but unfortunately, Agnes did not live long enough to tell him that she deeply cared for him.

Soon another girl became Laurence's love interest. That girl was Wanda who had gone to school with Laurence since first grade. Laurence never noticed her when she was a skinny flat chested kid, but with Wanda's new womanly body, pretty face, and outgoing personality, he began to notice her and think of her continuously. Wanda made it a point to make Laurence notice her. She would seek him out for conversation, pat his shoulder, compliment him, and bring him homemade sweets she baked for him. They fell into the roles of boyfriend and girlfriend, as naturally as ducks glide into water.

Although satisfied that Laurence was happy with Wanda, Lura was just a little jealous. When Laurence and Wanda got married, Lura was happy to be the maid of honor. On Wanda and

Laurence's wedding day, Lura and Wanda were alone for a few minutes. Lura took that opportunity to talk to Wanda.

"You know that Laurence and I have always had a special bond. I am counting on you to be good to Laurence and to always take care of him. If anything ever happened to Laurence I just could not go on."

Beaming, Wanda assured her, "Lura, I promise you I will always take care of him."

By the time Lura had been home from Brenau for five months, she was thoroughly bored in Raeford once again. She recalled the wonderful time she had in Sylacauga and decided she would ask her Papa if she could go there for another visit. Sadly, for Lura, this trip to Sylacauga would prove to be vastly different from her previous trip.

Lura asked her mother if she wanted to go back to Sylacauga too, but Aila's health had been poor, so she declined. The real reason that Aila chose not to go is that she just did not want to be around Jackson and have to pretend that everything was fine in their relationship.

Sitting all alone in a closed train compartment intended for six people, Lura was about halfway between Raeford and Sylacauga when Lura stopped reading her *Life* magazine. She was distracted by a light in the seat across from her. The light became blue and looked hazy, and then transformed into the form of Agnes in a long white dress.

Agnes smiled at Lura and said in a whisper, "In a few months, your father will be free from prison and back home again with you." This comment from Agnes thoroughly confused Lura, as she knew that her Papa was in Sylacauga, and not in prison.

Then Agnes disappeared. Lura thought this comment from Agnes was strange. Thankfully, Agnes' materializations no longer frightened Lura, but rather seemed like a loving visit from her old friend. Lura noticed three differences between this visit and previous visits from Agnes. In this visit, Agnes smiled, was seated, and she spoke. Lura felt that this message from Agnes meant that her Papa was going to be pardoned, and that would be a good thing. Of course, to be pardoned, he had to be recaptured and sent back to prison.

When Lura's train arrived in Sylacauga, she was met by her Papa, town librarian Camilla Reid, overseer Allen Jenkins, and Allen's wife Gail. Lura hugged each one closely.

Wanting to be playful with words with her Sylacauga friends, Lura exclaimed, "I'm tickled pink to be here! Really, I'm in seventh heaven to see you again, but I must admit I'm plumb tuckered out."

"Could you be more explicit as to how happy you are Lura?" said Camilla to encourage her to continue the play on words.

"If I felt any happier, I'd drop my harp right through the clouds," said Lura with a broad smile and a sparkle in her eyes.

Lura's Papa played the game, too. "Lura, I'm as happy as a tick on a fat dog." Everyone burst into fits of laughter.

"We will take you to a new restaurant, but first I need to sign a couple of checks at my office," said Lura's Papa.

Lura's Papa and Allen took Lura's suitcases off the train and carried them to his huge Packard, followed by the ladies. Camilla and Gail competed to get information from Lura and tell her all their news. "Lura, you are now a college graduate! I am so proud of you. Tell me about Brenau," said Camilla.

Before Lura could say anything about Brenau, Gail rushed on, "Tomorrow afternoon we want to take you on a picnic. We can cycle there. I have made a fresh peach pie, potato salad, deviled eggs, and I bought a country ham."

The ladies talked enthusiastically about fun things they could do together. They threw out potential ideas for outings as the car arrived at J. B. Davis' main turpentine mill. They continued their banter as they walked into the turpentine mill and into the spacious office of J. B. Davis. They all sat down at a large conference table surrounded by comfortable chairs.

The ladies were still coming up with great ideas for outings when a strange man walked into the office.

"I am Dr. J. H. Norman, and I am here to take Jackson Kennedy, also known as J. B. Davis, back to prison."

"What in the world is going on?" asked a confused Allen Jenkins.

To everyone's great astonishment, J. B. Davis said, "I am Jackson Kennedy."

Lura began to cry, and was thinking, *Oh my God! Oh my God!!*

"No way J. B.! This must be a terrible jest, and I do not like it at all! I know you like to joke, but this is definitely not funny," said Allen.

Dr. Norman had deputies posted outside this office, and at the various exits of the turpentine mill, so he was not worried that Jackson would try to escape.

Dr. Norman explained, "This is not J.B. Davis. It is Jackson Kennedy who escaped from Caledonia Prison in North Carolina on December 22, 1914. He was serving a 20-year sentence for murdering a police officer, and he escaped after a year and a half. I am here to take him back to prison."

Jackson wanted no more lies. It was important to him that the people in this room also know that the brothers Allen Jenkins hired were actually his sons.

"What Dr. Norman said is true. It is all true. Also, I want you to know that the brothers we hired to work here, Angus and Joseph Kennedy, are also my sons."

Camilla, Gail, and Allen had a look of utter astonishment on their faces. Jackson's shoulders slumped, and he put his hands over his eyes and bowed his head. He sat like that for a long time, and no one spoke. When Jackson finally removed his hands from his face, he had a slight smile on his face. He did not look sad or bitter.

"I knew this could happen one day. In a way this is a kind of relief because I can stop putting effort into keeping up appearances. Over the years since my escape, I have contemplated surrendering myself so many times, but my liberty was too precious." Jackson paused, "Dr. Norman, could we stop in Birmingham on our way back to North Carolina? I need to visit with my lawyer there, and give my son, Angus, Power of Attorney. He needs this authority to manage the sale of my property here."

Dr. Norman agreed, then he handcuffed Jackson, making him wince.

"Is that really necessary?" asked Angus, but Dr. Norman did not reply.

When they all walked outside, Jackson saw *Caledonia Prison Farm* written on the side of the car. His eyes teared up, his shoulders drooped, and he looked like a broken man. There was a crowd of Jackson's employees gathered around the car, along with five reporters holding cameras. The reporters were busy snapping pictures and shouting questions which no one answered. As Dr. Norman walked beside his prisoner, Gail blew Jackson a kiss as she was holding hands with Camilla; both had tears in their eyes. Jackson's workers were visibly upset too, and they cried out to their caring boss.

"We care."

"Take care friend!"

"We will get this thing straightened out."

"God bless you J.B."

Lura thought to herself, *How could the reporters learn about this so soon? Probably someone overheard the conversation in Papa's office, and the news spread like wildfire. What is my mother going to say? This will humiliate our family all over again! There will be terrible publicity.*

The reporters started asking questions, but Jackson did not say a word to them.

"I need to talk seriously to my son, Angus, and my daughter, Lura. Can they ride with us as far as Birmingham?" asked Jackson.

Dr. Norman felt pity for Jackson and even though it was against the rules, he allowed Angus and Lura to ride with them. During the two-hour car ride, Jackson gave Angus instructions.

"Angus, sell my house in Sylacauga, as well as all the turpentine mills and give every one of my ninety-nine turpentine employees $100 as a gift. Give Allen Jenkins $500 as a gift," Jackson told him.

"Angus, you should call your mother and your grandparents and tell them what has happened before returning to Sylacauga. What else can you think of to do, son?" asked Jackson.

"We need to see about getting you pardoned. You have led an exemplary life for years in Sylacauga. That should count for something," said Angus with great emotion.

Lura, looking mournful, said to her Papa, "I am so sorry Papa. Your life in Sylacauga was happy and now it all seems like a fairytale."

After the tense and emotionally laden ride, the car stopped in front of Perry's law firm in the center of Birmingham, and everyone except for the driver went into the law office. The receptionist for Jackson's lawyer, Miss Smith, looked thoroughly confused as to why Jackson was handcuffed. She and Jackson knew each other from previous visits.

"What is going on?" asked Miss Smith.

"I am in a lot of trouble, and I need to see Julius immediately," Jackson replied.

Jackson told Julius all that had transpired and asked him to draw up a Power of Attorney for his son, Angus Kennedy. Julius got his office staff to prepare all the documents needed. When all the official work was completed, Julius reached out to shake hands with Jackson but then just hugged his friend because Jackson was handcuffed.

"This Power of Attorney I have given you, Angus, will be revoked as soon as I am released from prison."

When they exited the law firm, there were about twenty reporters trying to get near Jackson, but, as before, he would not speak to them. Angus said goodbye to his Papa and said that he would go to Sylacauga to sell the property, and then go to Raeford. Lura hugged her Papa goodbye. Angus got a taxi to take himself and Lura to the train station while Dr. Norman and Jackson got back in the prison car. They arrived at Caledonia Prison within five hours.

Lura was right in anticipating publicity. The newspapers all over the country reported these happenings with relish:

The Philadelphia Inquirer: Modern Jean Val Jean Back in Jail - *There was no more trusted citizen of Sylacauga than James B. Davis, ... a kind-eyed man of magisterial appearance and known by his friends as a prosperous dealer of turpentine and timber.*

*The News & Observer: Recapture of Fugitive
(Raleigh, NC) - The 58-year-old entrepreneur in lumber and turpentine appeared to hold no bitterness towards those who snatched him from the business leadership of Alabama to return to North Carolina and begin serving the 19 years left on his sentence for killing Policeman Oakes in Raeford.

*The Dothan Eagle:
Sylacauga Paper Pleads for an Unfortunate Citizen -
J. B. Davis, the turpentine manufacturer, is not the escaped NC convict in the eyes of the people here, who have learned to love and respect him. It is Davis who our people know, and it is Davis they are interested in. What his past was, no one here cared.

As soon as Lura's mother heard from her, her depression became deeper and more profound. She had always been prone to depression, but this time she was not only depressed, but also physically sick with headaches and stomach problems. Maggie took care of her mother till Lura got back to Raeford on the train, then both girls shared this duty.

Lura had mixed emotions about her Papa being recaptured. She had seen him so happy and productive in Sylacauga. What would this new twist of events do to her and to her family? She was still mad at him for the killing, but she also had affection for him for turning his life around. She held onto the idea Agnes had given her on the train when Agnes materialized and said that her Papa would be free from prison soon. This made Lura feel a little bit better.

In the weeks after his recapture, Lura and her mother received wonderful and loving letters from Gail Jenkins and

Camilla Reid in Sylacauga. In the letters the ladies expressed their affection for Lura's Papa. They said that they understood why Jackson and Aila did what they did, but the people of Sylacauga supported them unconditionally. They promised to begin a campaign to get Jackson pardoned.

Lura thought to herself that if anyone could get her Papa pardoned, then certainly it would be the accomplished Camilla Reid. Receiving letters from the Sylacauga ladies put a smile on Lura's face.

CHAPTER 10
Jackson's Pardon
1930

Jackson had all the time in the world to sit and think in prison. He appreciated that his friends and colleagues in Sylacauga, Alabama, were diligently working for his pardon. Conversely, he knew that the family of the murdered Chief Oakes were working against his pardon. Understandably, the first attempt for his pardon in the summer of 1929 failed.

The second attempt for a pardon was led by Lura's friend, Sylacauga's public librarian, Camilla Reid. She traveled to the prison to visit with Jackson. They had a heart-to-heart talk that lasted over three hours. Jackson knew that Camilla was trying to help him, so he was totally open and honest and told her anything she wanted to know.

At one point during the visit, Camilla said to Jackson, "The whole time you were in Sylacauga you were law abiding, kind to everyone, displayed a calm demeanor, and had no displays of anger. I never saw you drink alcohol or heard anyone say you drank alcohol. From what I've been told, your personality was vastly different when you lived in Quewhiffle prior to the murder, from when you lived in Sylacauga. Why was that the case?"

Jackson took a while to answer, then smiled and said, "I descend from Scottish Highlanders, so naturally I always liked to take a drink. I am sure my drinking was part and parcel of my troublesome uncontrolled behavior. I now see clearly that when

I was drunk, I quickly went from anger to uncontrolled anger. I am ashamed to say this, but I know I was uncaring, violent, and abusive. The slightest provocation like a look or a laugh could set off my anger. I am sure this was unsettling for Aila and my children. I was also often harsh with my children. I really do believe the saying 'Spare the rod, spoil the child.' As I look back on it now, I know Aila and my children were afraid of me. I recall times when I was so drunk, angry, and violent that the children hid from me. I was a bully and I deeply regret it. My family was terrified of me at times."

Camilla could see Jackson's eyes filling with tears of remorse and hear his voice changing to a whisper so he could still talk even though he wept. Jackson continued his story while halting from time to time as emotion overcame him.

"I felt powerful when I was drinking, angry, and violent. When I killed Police Chief Oakes, I felt like the most powerful man in the world. It was only after I spent time in prison and had time to think through all this that I realized how crazy my thinking was. The fact is that the power I felt when I committed murder resulted in me losing my power and my freedom to control my own life. I now realize how stupid I was. Once I got to Sylacauga and got to know Allen Jenkins, I WANTED to change. Actually, I learned those life principles as a boy attending the Sandy Grove Presbyterian Church in Quewhiffle. Getting to know Allen made me remember how I had been raised. I saw how I wanted to live my life, and I have lived that way ever since."

By this time, Camilla had tears running down her cheeks, too. Her heart went out to her old friend. "Jackson, I really think we can get you pardoned, and then you can live your life the way you want to."

Camilla returned to Sylacauga and worked hard to gain support from the community for Jackson. Camilla and a group of her friends and library users in Sylacauga persuaded Alabama newspapers to run a series of articles on the benevolence and kindness of J. B. Davis during the years he lived in Sylacauga.

Here are the headlines from just a few of the Alabama newspapers:

The Anniston Star (Anniston, Alabama) June 25, 1929.
"Alabama Slayer and Fugitive has Become a Model Citizen, Hundreds Testify."

The Huntsville Daily Times (Huntsville, Alabama) Feb. 6, 1930.
"Was Respected in Alabama."

The Dothan Eagle (Dothan, Alabama) Nov. 26, 1928.
"Sylacauga Paper Pleads for an Unfortunate Citizen"

Camilla was setting up a plan with the publication of these newspaper articles. She contacted Jackson and suggested that his family offer a $10,000 gift to the Oakes family on the condition that they not protest a second pardon attempt. Since Aila was against giving this, Jackson's father, Stuart John Kennedy, paid. Jackson's lawyer met with the Oakes family, and they agreed in writing not to protest the pardon in exchange for this "gift."

Next, Camilla reached out to governmental leaders in Alabama and North Carolina, all of whom knew Jackson or the Kennedy family. With the evidence reported in the newspapers of Jackson's changed lifestyle, Camilla persuaded these leaders to petition for Jackson's pardon in early 1930. Some of the people who petitioned for Jackson were Alabama Governor David Bibb Graves, every Alabama State official, and North Carolina county and municipal officers from over a dozen counties.

During the time when the two petitions for pardon were being considered, Lura dreamed how it would be to have her Papa back home. She thought a big party would be just the thing to welcome him home. She planned the details of the welcome home party, deciding it would take place at their spacious Raeford home. The gala would include a pig roast, with a huge cake, a bluegrass band, bagpipe players, and leaders and friends making kind comments about her Papa. A large crowd of friends from Sylacauga would come, including librarian Camilla Reid, who would get special applause for continuing the campaign to get her Papa pardoned, Allen and Gail Jenkins, the minister of the Sylacauga Presbyterian Church, and many others. Lura knew that all her Kennedy relatives would attend.

When it appeared that Jackson would really be pardoned, Lura sat down with her mother to discuss her ideas for the party. She was shocked at her mother's wrath for just suggesting a welcome home party. Aila absolutely forbade the party to be held at her house, even though it was Jackson's house, too. Aila and Lura had a big argument about the proposed party, and then Aila decided to tell Lura the real reason she dreaded having Jackson home permanently, and why she did not want to host a party for him. Aila asked Lura to come to her room and the two ladies sat down.

Aila took a big breath and began. "I want to tell you why I do not want a welcome home party held here. To tell you this, I must go back in time. Your Papa came from a long line of Scots who were known for hot tempers, aggression, and drunkenness.

When I first met him, he was the handsomest man I ever saw in my life. Our parents encouraged us to get married, and I was smitten with him, so I was happy to become his wife. He courted me for three months with flowers, candy and singing Scottish ballads to me. He told me I was as pretty and sweet as a peach, that I was sweeter than sugar, and he wanted to eat me up. He was charming and acted the role of an easygoing and happy person. He was nineteen and I was fifteen when we got married. I had not even started my monthlies then. I was much too immature to marry, and my parents should have insisted that we postpone the marriage until I was older."

Aila paused before continuing. "Our wedding was at the Sandy Grove Presbyterian Church in Quewhiffle, and it started out as the happiest day of my life. After the wedding, Jackson's parents threw a big party at their home."

"Your Papa was perfectly sober during the marriage ceremony, but afterwards he began to drink. He drank just a little at first and it was starting to worry me. I was also worried about what would happen after we went to bed. I did not understand the mechanics of what should happen. When we finally did go to bed, your Papa forced himself on me. My immature body was not ready for this experience, and it hurt tremendously. I kept telling him to stop, but he ignored the protests."

Lura exclaimed, "Mama that is horrible. I never knew! I am so sorry for you."

Aila continued with her story, "The next morning after our wedding night he halfway apologized for his aggressive behavior in bed, but I did not forgive him for a long time. All through our marriage when he was drunk, he would rape me, and this would bring back the horror of my wedding night. This hurt my spirit. I must admit as the years went by, I did enjoy going to bed with him when he was not drinking. He was entirely different then. But these horrible memories have stayed with me all my life."

Aila reflected for a moment.

She continued, "In much of my life, feelings of happiness and pleasure have been foreign to me, and I was afraid to even let myself have pleasure. I tried to be happy and enjoy myself when we were in Sylacauga, and it was too hard. If you asked me what emotion I have the most, it is anger. I am sure my anger rubbed off on all of you children and caused our household to become quarrelsome. Our family isn't the happy family I had hoped for. After you children got out of babyhood, y'all did not pay me much attention.

"Jackson's violence to me, and then all that happened with your Papa's murder of Oakes, his escape from prison, and his recapture; it has all been too much! I want to have extraordinarily little to do with Jackson Kennedy for the rest of my life. I definitely will not give him a coming home celebration at my house."

Finally, on February 13, 1930, Jackson was pardoned by North Carolina Governor Oliver Max Gardner, and promptly released.

In the end, the big celebration did take place, but it was not at Aila's house. The celebration took place directly across the street at the home of Stuart Kennedy, Jackson's father. Everyone attended, just like Lura had planned, and the party went on until way after midnight. Aila walked across the street and attended the party, but just for forty-five minutes.

When Lura's Papa did come home, the tension was obvious between her parents. Her mother had run her household for such a long time by herself that it was difficult to have him tell her mother how to do things, or even suggest how to do things. Aila continued to be mean to Jackson most of the time, and she never shared his bed again. To escape Aila's horrible treatment of him, on most days, Jackson would walk across the street to his father's house and eat all his meals and spend the entire day there. He only came home when it was time to go to bed, and he slept in a separate room from Aila.

Jackson was discouraged with his new life back in Raeford. It was not nearly as exciting and happy as his life in Sylacauga. He was particularly sad at Aila's poor treatment of him. To make himself feel better, he paid $3,650 for a new 1930 Packard sedan. He wanted a diversion. He loved to drive his new fancy car around town and remember the days he drove his old Packard in Sylacauga where he was loved and respected.

It surprised most everyone in Lura's immediate and extended family that her mother decided she liked not having any visitors in her house. After sixteen years of having no guests in her home, Aila decided to continue this practice even though the original reason for the rule was no longer valid. The children that still lived in the homeplace in 1930 included Lura, Louis, and Cecil. They had to abide by Aila's continuing rule of no visitors in the home. Conversely, Jackson said he was NOT going to follow the rule. He made it a point to bring friends home, or welcome friends when they stopped by the house, thus causing an ongoing argument for Aila and Jackson until the day he died.

As soon as Jackson was pardoned, he revoked Angus' Power of Attorney. This made him feel better.

Lura was tired of living under her mother's roof, but with the Great Depression in full swing, she could not secure a job in Raeford, or anywhere else. She applied for jobs, but without success. She even applied for a clerical position with the New

Deal's new Relocation Administration in Washington, D.C., but she did not get that job either.

Since many citizens of Raeford and surrounding areas made their living in the turpentine business, the Depression hit this portion of the state with a vengeance.

Turpentine prices were declining, and some owners had to sell their businesses for pennies on the dollar. By 1939, one bright spot for those in the turpentine business was the establishment of the American Turpentine Farmers Association which stabilized the market. The new association encouraged turpentine farmers to sell turpentine in small bottles to homeowners for the first time. This practice opened a new niche for selling turpentine, and the turpentine business thrived. Jackson's father still had his turpentine business, and he quickly began selling turpentine in small bottles to local stores.

All this turmoil in her house made Lura want to leave home more than ever. She spent time reading and visiting with Laurence and Wanda. One bright spot in Lura's life was the birth of Laurence's and Wanda's baby girl, Olivia. Lura liked to hold baby Olivia and stroke her golden curls, just like Lura had done to Laurence's beautiful blond hair when he was a baby. It made Lura recall the happy times she spent with Laurence when he was little.

As the years rolled by, Lura felt in her heart she would always be a spinster. Her parents were poor money managers, so they were quickly spending their once abundant fortune. By 1940, their precious Raeford house needed repairs, but there was little money to fix it up.

CHAPTER 11
Laurence Disappears
1944

"Has anyone heard from Laurence? It's strange that he's not here yet," said Lura on that Easter Sunday in 1944.

"I hate for us to begin eating before they get here, but if we don't, the food will get cold. Give me a minute and I will call Laurence on the phone," said Lura's older sister Maggie. In a couple of minutes, Maggie returned to the dining room with a deeply concerned look on her face. "Wanda sounded strange. She said Laurence left two nights ago, and she has not seen him since."

"Sometimes Laurence goes on a hunting trip and spends a few nights away from home. I think he's fine. I'm ready to eat," said Lura's Papa.

"Yes, but he always lets someone know his plans ahead of time," said Lura frowning.

Her heart started beating so fast that she suspected everyone heard it. She began thinking,

What to do now, what to do now? Laurence would never leave home without telling me he was going to be away. He particularly wouldn't do this at Easter.

"We might as well eat. I suspect he will show up later today for leftovers," said Maggie.

All Lura's siblings and her parents filled their plates and ate Easter dinner, they looked happy and content. Only Lura was not enjoying the food. Soon everyone was reaching for slices of the two peach pies. Jackson took a slice of pie, and said, "This is the best pie I ever tasted."

"I'm glad you said that about the peach pie because it took all the sugar rations for everyone at this table to make those two pies," said Maggie.

As the afternoon continued, the shadows lengthened, twilight came, and Lura got progressively more worried. By this time, her siblings also began to worry. Several phone calls were made to Wanda's house during the afternoon, but she always said the same thing, "No sign of Laurence yet."

On Monday morning, Lura called Wanda and again, she was told there was no sign of Laurence yet. Lura fretted and could not keep her attention focused on anything else except for Laurence. She called Wanda multiple times that day and got the same response each time.

On Tuesday morning at 7 a.m. Lura called Wanda.

"Wanda, have you called the police yet?" asked Lura.

Obviously frustrated with all Lura's calls, Wanda said in a slightly sassy voice, "No, I have not called the police. Laurence is a big boy, and he is probably having a fun time on a hunting trip."

Lura was now at the end of her rope. She slammed down the phone, and then immediately picked it back up and called the police. She told the authorities about Laurence's disappearance. Then she called Earl and got him to drive her in the Packard at breakneck speed to Laurence's house. The two police officers, and Lura and Earl arrived at the same time. When they all entered the house, Wanda looked strange, angry, but worried. Laurence and Wanda's 10-year-old daughter, Olivia, reached out to embrace Lura, her favorite aunt. Lura could tell that Olivia had been crying, and she looked terribly frightened. Lura tried to comfort the child, but it was difficult to reassure her niece when Lura herself was desperately worried.

The police carefully questioned Wanda and did a search of the house, the outbuildings, and the yard. They found Laurence's wallet and hunting guns, and they noted that Laurence's truck was still in the far corner of the yard.

"It is highly unlikely that Laurence went hunting without his guns," said one of the police officers.

Wanda handed the police officer a piece paper.

The officer read the words aloud:

"Order To Report for Induction"

Greetings, Laurence Kennedy from the President of the United States. Having submitted yourself to a local board composed of your neighbors for the purpose of determining your availability for military service, you are notified you have been selected for training and service. Report to the Fayetteville North Carolina Induction office at 7:15 a. m. on the 25th day of April 1944.

This new evidence made the police theorize that perhaps Laurence did not want to fight in the war and face the possibility of dying in battle. So maybe he left home to avoid that fate. The Police Chief filled out a missing person's report on Laurence, told Wanda to let him know as soon as Laurence returned home, and left.

When the Police Chief and his deputy were in the car leaving Wanda's house, the deputy said, "I have heard rumors that Laurence was running around with Betty Lou who works at Leo's Diner. Maybe his disappearance has something to do with that.

Could there be more to this than Laurence being a draft dodger? Could Laurence' wife have murdered him?"

With an expression of exasperation on his face, the Chief shook his head, and said, "Hush your mouth boy! Wanda is a God-fearing woman, a Sunday School teacher, and a wonderful mother to her daughter, Olivia. How could you even suggest something like that? Do you realize that if Wanda was convicted of murder, she would either go to the electric chair, or spend the rest of her life in prison? Then Olivia would be an orphan. Would that be a better outcome for everyone?"

What the Police Chief did not tell his deputy was that Wanda was his wife's best friend, and he knew that if he suggested that Wanda murdered Laurence that he would be sleeping on the sofa for years to come. To save himself from discord in his marriage, the Police Chief decided to ignore the rumors of Laurence having an affair.

After the police officers drove away, Wanda and Lura sat in the living room in silence. With her hands in her lap and her eyes looking toward the floor, Lura finally spoke.

"Wanda, Laurence would never leave home and not tell you and me his plans. Do you realize how close Laurence and I are? Laurence and I either see each other or talk on the telephone every day. I think you know something about where Laurence is and are not telling us."

Wanda assured Lura she was telling her everything she knew, but Lura knew things that Wanda did not know. Laurence had told Lura that his marriage had become horrible, and he was contemplating divorcing Wanda. Knowing this made Lura suspect Wanda of hiding something, but Lura had no proof. She left Wanda's house totally frustrated and worried to death about dear Laurence.

That night when Lura was all alone in her bedroom, Agnes materialized. She appeared as a blue light, then within a couple of minutes the blue light transformed into the form of a tall woman wearing a long flowing white dress. Agnes, with tears flowing freely and the saddest expression on her face, silently stayed with Lura for a while.

During this visit, Lura begged Agnes for answers, saying, "Dear and loyal friend Agnes, PLEASE tell me what happened to my Laurence? Is he OK? Is he dead?"

Agnes did not reply. She vanished after a few minutes. To Lura this meant Agnes would not confirm Laurence's death because it would cause Lura too much heartache. However, Agnes was telling her in her own way that Laurence was dead.

Lura continued to call Wanda daily for the next three weeks and to get progressively more certain that something sinister had happened. Lura was glad when Wanda told her that the FBI came to investigate Laurence's disappearance. The hopefulness that the FBI might find out what really happened turned into disillusionment when Wanda said the FBI agreed with the Police that Laurence left home to avoid the draft.

Lura loved Laurence better than anyone else on earth, and she could not bear to think of him as gone. She felt she would go crazy if she stayed in Raeford much longer. In Raeford, she would always feel the loss of Laurence acutely.

CHAPTER 12

A Makeover

1945

Despite her love for Laurence's daughter, Olivia, Lura was determined to leave Raeford. Lura's goal was to secure a job far away from Raeford. She could not live in Raeford any longer where everything reminded her of Laurence. Oh, how she missed him, and she felt sure her most important friend and ally was dead, or otherwise he would have contacted her.

Lura wrote letters to every North Carolina furniture store more than seventy-five miles from Raeford, seeking an interior decorator position. After numerous letters back and forth, Lura received a letter from R. E. Quinn's Furniture Company in Wilson, North Carolina, asking her to come for an interview. The letter made her hopeful for the first time since that Easter dinner when she heard about Laurence's disappearance.

As Lura walked down the street in Wilson on her way to her interview, she relished the mild sunny mid-May weather. She noticed dress shops, restaurants, and pretty store fronts. This made her feel happy. Perhaps she could begin a new life here and try to put Laurence's disappearance behind her. Wilson was triple the size of Raeford, and this suited Lura perfectly. She had always thought that Raeford was too small for her.

When Lura first walked into the furniture store for her interview, she immediately felt this was the place for her. A friendly looking middle-aged woman walked up to her.

"You must be Lura Kennedy. We have been expecting you. I am Patsy Smith, and I am a salesclerk here. Mr. Quinn wants me to give you a tour of the store before your interview."

Patsy took Lura to all four floors and told her which furniture manufacturers they used. Patsy and Lura talked about casual things like weather, Lura's trip to Wilson for this interview, and Patsy's family. She wanted to reassure Lura that Quinn's was a wonderful place to work and directed the conversation accordingly.

"Mr. Quinn is a teddy bear. He treats all his employees with kindness, respect, fairness, and generosity. At Christmas he always gives the employees a turkey and a nice bonus. I think you will love working for him."

Then Patsy led Lura to Mr. Quinn's office on the first floor at the back of the store. The walls of the small office were covered in family pictures, and Lura liked that the air in the office smelled of sweet pipe smoke-just the type that her grandpapa used to smoke.

During Lura's interview with Mr. Quinn, she overcame her shyness and boldly said, "Mr. Quinn, I really want this job. The town and the store are exactly what I envisioned for my perfect situation. I assure you, if you hire me, I will be a hard worker, and you will be happy you hired me."

Mr. Quinn asked Lura questions about her education, experience, and her social skills. He was satisfied with all her answers. "Miss Kennedy, I am impressed with you and want to hire you."

Lura tried to restrain her excitement when she heard this. "Mr. Quinn, thank you so much. I will not let you down."

As she signed her job contract, Patsy and several other workers ran into Mr. Quinn's office, yelling.

"The war in Europe is over!"

Lura and everyone cheered, and Mr. Quinn hugged everyone in his office, including his new hire Lura. She felt things were looking up for her.

The next day, Lura looked for a place to live, selecting a picturesque neighborhood on Tarboro Street. There were immaculate small white houses with green lawns bordered with white picket fences. Many of the houses had colorful flowers near the entrance. Sidewalks were on either side of the street, with tall live oak trees beside them. The trees made a canopy of shade over the street.

Lura was pleased to find a suitable and affordable place to live alone, where she did not have to talk to anyone, or cater to anyone. Here she believed she could begin dealing with her grief about Laurence. Lura's apartment provided her blessed quiet in which she could come to terms with her life.

Mr. Quinn must have suspected that Lura did not have furniture, because he called Lura a couple of days after the interview and offered his help in obtaining furniture. He suggested that Lura look at the slightly damaged furniture kept in the back room of the store to see if she wanted to purchase anything. Mr. Quinn offered Lura a great deal. He said Lura could pick out what she wanted, and he could deduct money out of her paycheck until the bill was all paid. Lura selected almost everything she needed from Quinn's. She also visited second-hand furniture stores to purchase the smaller things needed for her apartment. Being an interior decorator, one of Lura's favorite things was decorating her own apartment.

After purchasing the furniture and having it delivered to her apartment, Lura began the task which pleased her the most, arranging the furniture and the decorations. One of the first things Lura unpacked was a handsome picture of Laurence. She held the

116

picture to her heart and said to Laurence, "I think you would be proud of me for my new job and apartment."

Then she gently placed the photograph in the center of her mantle. Next, she unpacked a cross-stitch sampler which her grandmother Kennedy made for her on her fifth birthday. The sampler was a visual representation of Lura's favorite nursery rhyme, 'Hey Diddle Diddle.' It included the happy looking brown cow jumping over the tiny sliver of a yellow moon, the little laughing dog with long ears, the fiddling cat, and the happy faces on the dish and the spoon who were holding hands and running away together. Lura sat down with the sampler in her lap and thought about the time her grandmother taught her to say this nursery rhyme which she had come to love. It had been Lura and her grandmother's special bond, and it became Lura and Agnes' special bond, too. Lura felt her apartment would not be complete without this sampler on the wall.

Once Lura finished decorating and furnishing her apartment, she liked walking through the rooms feeling thankful that she had a job and a pretty new place to live which was far away from Raeford. The apartment walls were light yellow, and the curtains, rugs, and sofa were lime green and yellow. Lura did not prepare the apartment to entertain guests; it was a space just for Lura alone. The only exception would be her one special niece, Laurence's daughter, Olivia.

Lura wrote to Olivia and asked her to come to Wilson for the weekend. She arranged for Earl to drive Olivia to and from Wilson. To Lura's amazement, Wanda allowed Olivia to take the trip. They had a tea party, went to the park, went on long walks, and Lura had time to introduce Olivia to her new life in Wilson. But both nights of the weekend visit, Olivia awoke in the middle of the night screaming and crying. When Lura tried to comfort Olivia and ask

117

her what was wrong, Olivia said, "My poor papa, my poor papa." This made Lura suspect Wanda of foul play more than ever.

Over the first few months at Quinn's, Lura became acquainted with her co-workers. Her goal was not to befriend them, because she did not want to reveal her shady family history to her co-workers. However, she did want to be nice and communicate with them about everyday topics such as the weather, Wilson history, and other nonpersonal topics. Sometimes her co-workers tried to pry, but she had become proficient in redirecting a conversation away from a topic she wanted to avoid. Lura not revealing her family history was contrary to how most people in Wilson functioned. The general practice in this small southern town was that 'everyone in Wilson knew everything about everyone else.' Certainly, her co-worker, Patsy, knew everything about Wilson people, and she particularly liked to share her knowledge with Lura. This suited Lura who appreciated knowing more about some of the people of Wilson, particularly those who were her customers. As an interior decorator, the more Lura knew about her customers' lives, the better she could plan what furnishings and fabrics would fit with the customer's lifestyle.

CHAPTER 13

Lura's Courtship with Tom

1946-1948

One chilly day in January 1946, about six months after Lura started working at Quinn's, a distinguished older man came into the store. He walked up to Lura and asked for her help in selecting a lamp for his mother. It was the general custom at Quinn's that if a customer asked for just one item, the salesclerks would help this customer. Lura decided not to observe the practice on this occasion because there was something about this man that appealed to her. Maybe her interest was increased by his impressive height, or by his handsomeness, by his aristocratic manners, or maybe it was because he still had remnants of red hair on his primarily bald, head. (She was always attracted to people with red hair.)

As Lura chatted to the man about lamps, they also discussed the history of furniture styles.

Lura had a strange thought, *This man seems educated, articulate, and he is interested in things that I enjoy too. I am attracted to him and he seems attracted to me. Wow, it has been a long time!*

She thoroughly enjoyed the time she spent with this customer. He purchased a colorful glass Art Deco lamp. As he was paying for the lamp, he introduced himself.

"I am Tom Davis, and I am from Wilson originally, but now live in Tarboro which is just twenty-five miles from here."

"I'm pleased to meet you. My name is Lura Kennedy."

119

As Tom Davis exited the store, Lura stood still and watched him till he was out of sight. As soon as Tom left the store, Patsy who loved to gossip, came over to talk to Lura about her new customer. "I knew you were interested in Tom Davis since you handled the lamp purchase yourself. Have you ever met him before?"

"No, this was the first time I ever saw him," said Lura smiling.

"Well, let me tell you what I know about Tom Davis," said Patsy. "He's in his mid-fifties. He married Rita Gay Williams when he was a young man. Rita's granddaddy was Alpheus Branch who started Branch Banking and Trust Company. After Rita married Tom, she developed manic depression and she was often debilitated. Rita and Tom had a child named Matilda, and then they divorced when Matilda was two-years-old."

Lura retreated to her office thinking she really did not mind that Tom was divorced, but she was not happy to learn that he had a daughter. Still, she was interested in Tom.

After Lura got home from work, she kept thinking about meeting Tom and about all she learned about him from Patsy. She stood in front of Laurence's picture looking at her dear brother. Smiling and feeling happy she said, "Laurence, what do you think of Tom? I think you would like him. He seems like a gentle soul."

Suddenly, Lura's body was covered in goose bumps. She thought, *Papa used the alias J.B. Davis when he lived in Sylacauga. If I married Tom, my last name would be Davis. Is this a sign?"*

Tom came back to Quinn's the next day and visited with Mr. Quinn. Tom and Mr. Quinn walked into Lura's office. "I have a customer with me whom you recently met," said Mr. Quinn.

"Yes. Nice to see you again, Mr. Davis," said Lura with a surprise in her voice.

"Lura, I want you to know that Tom Davis is a fine man indeed, and I have known him and his family all my life," said Mr. Quinn.

Tom looked a little embarrassed and shy, as he cast his eyelids down. He had no idea that Mr. Quinn was going to say something like that.

"It was such a pleasant experience yesterday when you helped me buy the lamp. I would like to get to know you better. Would you be willing for us to eat lunch together tomorrow at Vanessa's Corner Diner?" asked Tom.

Lura smiled at Tom and replied. "I would like that, Tom. Noon is the best time because that's when I normally go to lunch."

Lura wanted to know more about Tom and his life history, so she pondered all Patsy had told her. After work, Lura walked down the street to see Branch Banking and Trust Company which was begun by Tom's first wife's grandfather. She liked the beautiful neoclassical bank building. There was a plaque on the door of the bank that read, Built in 1903. Lura thought it was ironic that the bank was built the same year she was born. Next, she went to the public library to read about the history of Wilson and the Davis and Branch families. She did not ask the librarian for help since she did not want anyone to know her motives. She found a large number of files on the Branch family and learned they were the richest people in the town. She found information on Tom's family, and they seemed to have been only slightly wealthy over the years.

The next day, Tom arrived at Quinn's at 11:55 and Tom and Lura walked to the diner. Lura noticed that Vanessa's Diner was really a hole-in-the-wall, but she had heard people say the cheeseburgers were out of this world. Both Tom and Lura were nervous. On the way to Vanessa's, they talked about the weather. Once inside, they were seated and given menus, and they looked at the menus in silence.

121

"They have great meatloaf. I am going to order meatloaf, mashed potatoes, and butter beans, and a piece of pecan pie for dessert," said Tom.

"I have been hearing about their great cheeseburgers, so that is what I want," said Lura shyly. After they ordered, Tom became a bit talkative. He asked Lura how she liked Wilson and where she was from. That broke the ice, and they became more talkative.

Lura told Tom the noncontroversial bits about her life.

Lura smiled shyly and said, "My family lives in Raeford, North Carolina, and I attended Brenau College in Gainesville, Georgia."

There was a long awkward silence.

Trying to get her to open up more, Tom said, "When did you go to college and what was college experience like?"

Lura liked talking about her college years. She offered, "When I attended Brenau in 1926, students were not allowed to leave campus without a chaperone. My former roommate, Louise, was expelled from Brenau for riding in a car and going to a restaurant with a man. We had to get up at 4:30 am, clean our room for daily inspection, and go to Chapel before 9:30 am."

They laughed over the standards of behavior imposed in 1926.

Tom told Lura he was born in Wilson, and he attended Atlantic Christian College. He told Lura he loved to read and study diverse cultures.

Tom spoke hesitantly as he told Lura about his marriage, divorce, and daughter. She had the impression that he wanted to go ahead and tell her about the divorce in case she would not want to date him afterwards. She assured him that his history was fine with her, including his divorce. Tom gave Lura a big smile when she assured him that she had no problems with his past.

Next, Tom told Lura about his pride and joy, his daughter.

"Matilda is the most important person in my life. She is tall, slender, has long wavy black hair and hazel eyes. She is charming, has a wonderful smile, and all the boys want to date her. The one dark spot in Matilda's life is her mother's mental illness. It is difficult for Matilda when her mother's manic depression rears its ugly head. Sometimes Rita is well enough to keep Matilda and take care of her, other times Matilda must go and stay with various relatives when her mother must be hospitalized. It is all so sad."

As Tom talked about Matilda, Lura's chest tightened, and she resisted the urge to cross her arms, frown profusely, and quit smiling. Lura had to use her determination not to react as if she felt negative about Tom's description of Matilda. As he spoke, thoughts came into Lura's mind.

I wish he had no children. I bet she is not as pretty as he thinks she is. If only he had no children, he could focus more attention on me.

Next the conversation turned to Tom explaining his job as a cotton broker. He said he had to travel in the southeast states to follow the cotton market, and usually a trip would last from a few days to three weeks. He said he liked staying in the same hotels and enjoyed talking to the same employees each time he visited.

Tom admitted he had been lonesome since his divorce in 1933, and that he had asked few women on dates since then. He looked deeply into Lura's eyes.

"Lura, there is something about you that speaks to my spirit. I am not sure what it is, but I would like for us to get to know each other much better."

Tom explained he was leaving Wilson the day after tomorrow and traveling to Augusta. He said he was not sure when he would return to Wilson, but when he returned, he wanted to see Lura again. They also promised to write letters to get to know each other better.

As Tom walked Lura back to Quinn's, he took out his pipe and began smoking.

"I like the smell of a pipe. That's Prince Albert tobacco," said Lura.

"You're spot on, Lura!" said Tom. "I'll be in touch."

Lura felt a little sad that he was going to be away from Wilson for a while.

Over the next several months, Tom and Lura wrote letters to each other almost every day. It always gave her pleasure as she addressed her letters to him. From their frequent communication, she always knew where to address her letters, either at his home in Tarboro, or at a specific hotel in a certain city.

They began to know each other much better through letters. Lura delighted in all she had learned from his letters. She learned he loved all animals, particularly billy goats and chickens. She learned he had a mild heart attack last year, and he had bursitis in his left arm and shoulder. He liked to sing along with songs on the radio. She learned he could have a temper.

One thing that Lura learned troubled her a bit because it was so different from her own life experience. The troubling factor was that he said he valued family, and some of his favorite memories were sitting on his Mama's front porch at her big house on Nash Street at twilight with his brothers, sisters, nieces, and nephews. The Davis family would drink lemonade while having their feet propped up on the porch railings and talk to neighbors as they walked by. Lura had never done this with her family. In fact, her family always hid from their neighbors by staying indoors.

Tom was helping to heal Lura's deep hurt from the disappearance of Laurence. This was a pleasant surprise for her because she never expected anything to lessen that pain.

Over the Labor Day weekend Tom came to Wilson and stayed with his mother but spent most of his time with Lura. They had a wonderful four days, and both sensed that their courtship was moving along rapidly. Tom at 56, and Lura at 43 were older companions, so they did not want to waste time. Tom's letters became slightly more romantic after Labor Day.

Tom's mother died in March 1947, and Tom was depressed for a long time afterwards. He always admired his mother's faith, her poetry, and her cooking. He loved his Mama, and her death left a hole in his heart which took a long time to heal. To feel closer to Tom and to sympathize, Lura told him about Laurence's sad story. She told him that she and Laurence had a tremendous bond and that they talked every single day until he went missing in 1944. Lura told Tom that she suspected Laurence was dead, and that his disappearance is what propelled her to move to Wilson.

Lura's Papa died one year after Tom's mother. Tom was sympathetic to her and tried to be with her and help her as much as possible with her father's death. Tom drove Lura to Raeford for the funeral. They arrived at Lura's home in Raeford, went inside, and Tom was surprised to hear dead silence. Tom was accustomed to hordes of people coming to pay their respects and bringing food to the bereaved family. This was not the case at Lura's home. Tom and Lura walked around the downstairs of the house looking for family members. Finally, they went into the kitchen at the back of the house, and two ladies were sitting alone at the kitchen table.

"Mama and Maggie, this is my friend Tom," said Lura.

Maggie, with red eyes from crying, stood up and held out her hand for Tom to shake it.

125

"I am pleased to meet you, Tom. Lura wrote to us about you," Maggie said.

"I am happy to finally meet you, but would rather it be under happier circumstances," Tom replied.

Then turning to Lura's mother, Aila, Tom said, "Mrs. Kennedy, let me extend to you my deepest sympathy on the death of your husband."

Aila replied in a quiet voice that lacked any enthusiasm.

"Pleased to meet you, too. I tell you; we have all had a time. I thought I would feel better after Jackson died, but all I feel is emptiness and anger. There has been too much water over the dam."

Tom thought these comments from Aila were mighty strange.

He drove Maggie, Aila, and Lura to the Presbyterian church for the funeral. The church was full of people. Tom, Maggie, Aila and Lura joined the rest of Jackson Kennedy's immediate family on the front two pews of the church. The minister talked about Jackson's life and how he had turned his life over to Jesus when he lived in Sylacauga, Alabama. As Lura was leaving the church, she noticed a large delegation from Sylacauga there to support the memory of her Papa, and this made her smile. Lura was also comforted to have Tom beside her. After the burial portion of the funeral, visitors came up to Lura to speak. Lura introduced Tom to Camilla Reid, and Gail and Allen Jenkins from Sylacauga.

"You are three of the people I most wanted to meet. Lura has told me wonderful stories about the three of you. I wanted to personally say thank you to y'all for helping Lura's father through multiple challenging times," said Tom.

"One way to describe Jackson's character is 'the best portion of a good man's life is his little nameless unremembered acts of kindness and love,'" said Camilla fondly.

126

"Camilla, I think that line is from *Tintern Abbey* by Wordsworth," said Tom.

"I can see that I have a kindred spirit in you, Tom," said Camilla.

Lura felt proud of Tom's literary knowledge, and she smiled at Camilla. They all talked a while longer before moving on to speak with others waiting to pay condolences.

Just then another man walked up and took Lura's hand and said, "I was a young boy when your father came to Sylacauga. Your papa gave me a bicycle, which my poor family could never have afforded. This act of generosity changed my outlook on life. It prompted me to work hard to become successful, and then to help others like your papa did. I have lived my life that way due to your papa."

Two more men who looked like brothers walked up to Lura, and like the previous man, took Lura's hand and said, "I heard what that man said about how good your Daddy was. Let me tell you something amazing about him. When he first escaped from prison many years ago, he came to our house with our cousin and one other convict. Our Daddy gave the three of them warm clothes, some food, and a tiny bit of money to help them out. Three years after this, your Daddy started sending Christmas gifts to our family every single year till he died. He even sent a gift this year. The first gift he sent was silverware for twelve people. We really needed that. In other years he sent clothes, toys, dishes, and books. Your Daddy never forgot our kindness to him. He was a great man, and I came here today to tell you that."

Lura replied gratefully, "Thank you so much. I remember my Papa telling me how he got help from a farmer and his family when he first escaped from prison. You are kind to make it a point to be here today and to tell me that story. Thank you from the bottom of my heart!"

Just then Lura's old college roommate, Louise, came up to Lura and expressed her condolences. She looked a bit older than the last time Lura had seen her back in the 1920s, but still quite fashionable. Lura was impressed that she traveled all the way from Richmond to attend the funeral. Lura introduced Louise to Tom, and they had a lively conversation.

Lura and Tom walked over to the place where her mother, brothers, and sisters were standing. Lura introduced Tom to the rest of her family.

Faithful Earl was also there to pay honor to her Papa. Earl walked up to Lura and said, "Miss Lura, I am so sorry your Papa has passed. It is the end of an era for sure."

"Thank you, Earl. This is my friend, Tom Davis."

Tom reached out his hand to shake Earl's hand and was happy to finally meet Earl whom he had heard about multiple times. "Earl, it is indeed a pleasure to finally meet you. Lura has told me how much you and your family helped her family over the years."

"Now you take loving care of Miss Lura, Mr. Davis!" said Earl.

"I promise," said Tom.

After they said their goodbyes, Lura and Tom got in the car and returned to Wilson. On the way home, they discussed all that had transpired at the funeral and on their brief trip to Raeford.

"Tom, do you remember that man who told us his Daddy helped my Papa when he escaped from prison? I remember hearing about that from Papa multiple times. Papa said the man who helped them had ten children who had to share three spoons to eat their soup. This man just told me that my Papa sent them a silver service for twelve people, and then a Christmas gift every year. It impresses me that he would do this for someone for all those years. That says a lot for my Papa."

"Lura, it indeed says a lot about what a fine man your Papa became" said Tom.

"Before he went to prison, he was arrogant, proud, vengeful, and angry. In Sylacauga, he learned compassion, kindness, and generosity. It was too bad Mama was never kind to Papa after his transformation. If she could have forgiven him, they could have both found at least limited happiness. I hope with all my heart that he has finally found peace," said Lura.

In the days, weeks, and months after the two funerals, Tom and Lura continued their romance which meant the world to both. Because Tom's work required him to travel, and because his home was in Tarboro and Lura's home was in Wilson, they still could not see each other as often as they would like. Their only solace most of the time was the wonderful letters that helped to keep their romance alive.

One of Lura's favorite letters was dated September 19, 1949, and it read:

My Darling Little Lura,

As I sit here in my hotel room, I long for the time we can be together again. Being with you brings me such happiness and contentment. I want to hold you in my arms and read Byron's poetry to you, and drink wine with you. Sometimes I just want to consume you.
With Love, Tom

After receiving such a loving letter as the one dated September 19, 1949, Lura expected to receive a similarly loving letter every day after that. She hurried home from work to find that she had not received a letter from Tom. For a full week Lura did not receive a letter and she was beginning to doubt the relationship. It nearly drove her crazy. But when the next letter arrived, it was well worth the wait. This was her all-time favorite letter from Tom:

My Precious Lura, Sept. 26, 1949

I can just imagine you in your cozy apartment snugly clad, reclining and listening to Ella Fitzgerald on the high fi. You are probably reading a book about interior decorating and having hot chocolate. I WANT TO BE DOING ALL THOSE THINGS WITH YOU TOO!

I have been waiting to tell you this in person, but I can wait no longer. Oh, how I love you Lura! My heart is bursting with love for you. Do you feel the same way? I can only hope and pray. I want to be with you for the rest of our lives. We found each other late in life, and I fully intend to make the most of our remaining days. I want to luxuriate in our love.

I will keep on loving Lura and trusting Lura until the end of time. With every passing day you mean more and more to me. I realize I am getting so dependent on our love.

I promise dear Lura, now I will end with,
I love you, love you, love you!
Yours, Tom

Lura adored this letter, and she kept it with her all the time. She reread it at work, on her walk home from work, on lonely nights, and at breakfast. She almost read it constantly. After a week, the paper was tearing where she had folded it too many times. This letter made Lura over the moon happy.

Matilda Davis at 13-years-old
Family photos reprinted with permission of heir of photographer

CHAPTER 14

Matilda

1948-1949

One evening after supper, Lura and Tom were sitting on the sofa at Lura's apartment holding each other. They had been hugging and kissing and both felt hot, and they didn't want to stop. At this exact moment, someone knocked loudly on Lura's door. Tom and Lura just stared at each other because they didn't want to be interrupted.

"Let's just not make any noise, and ignore the knock, and the person will leave," urged Lura in a gentle whisper. Tom smiled broadly at this suggestion and when he was about to say that was a perfect idea, he heard a loud voice screaming.

"Papa, please open the door. I need you now," cried Matilda.

Matilda's voice sounded frantic and without even thinking about it, Tom jumped up off the sofa, unintentionally making Lura fall on the floor. He quickly opened Lura's front door, and there was Matilda standing in the rain crying her heart out. Tom put his arms around his daughter and tried to console her.

"Honey, what on earth is the matter? Come on in and tell me about it," said Tom as he led Matilda to the sofa.

"Hello, Matilda," said Lura in a cold tone.

Tom sat on the sofa. To his surprise, Matilda sat on his lap and put her head on his shoulder. Matilda continued to shed tears as she told Tom what had happened. Lura sat at the other end of the sofa with her arms tightly crossed over her chest.

"Mama has been so desperately depressed that she has not gotten out of bed for a week. I went to school, then came home. At first, I thought how nice; Mama is bending over the stove to take something out that she cooked for us for dinner. But then I noticed she was not standing over the stove, but rather she was kneeling in front of the stove with her head in the oven! Mama was trying to kill herself. I ran over to Mama and pulled her out of the oven, but she was unconscious." Matilda buried her face in Tom's chest and sobbed her heart out.

Tom knew that his ex-wife Rita's manic depression had been spiraling downward, but he had been hopeful that she might recover or at least improve. Now Tom knew that he must get Matilda out of that environment for good.

"How would you like to move to Tarboro to finish your senior year of high school? I could rent a room for you next to my room at the boarding house," said Tom.

Matilda stopped crying and said, "I would hate to leave my friends in Wilson, but I cannot stand my life the way it is now. Yes, I want to move to Tarboro."

This turned out to be a great move for her. Lura understood the reason that Tom was helping Matilda and that this was the only thing Tom could do. She also knew that she should have been more sympathetic to Matilda, but it was hard for Lura because Matilda got to see Tom much more frequently than she did. Lura could not figure out where her jealousy originated. One of her barely conscious fears was that Matilda would take Tom away from her. In some ways, Lura thought of Matilda like Wanda who made Laurence disappear.

Matilda thoroughly enjoyed all the attention she received at her new high school in Tarboro, particularly from the boys. She was the 'new girl in school,' and everyone wanted to meet her. There was a rumor in Tarboro that Tom Davis was wealthy, and this drew more people to Matilda. She had more dates and offers of dates than she ever did in Wilson. Matilda graduated from high school and took a job at the Tarboro Health Department.

It was at this time that Matilda first met David Aasen who had just returned from World War II in Europe. David was funny, affectionate, athletic, and handsome with black hair and blue eyes. David had made it his goal to marry Matilda. Matilda felt they were quite compatible. They both loved to party and dance to rock and roll. Their favorite dances were the jitterbug, the bop, and the fox trot. They loved to go to Rocky Mount to the Club Rio on Friday and Saturday nights with their friends, and dance to music such as *Pennsylvania 6-5000, In the Mood, Maybe It's Because, Far Away Places,* and *Some Enchanted Evening.* To Matilda, David was rock solid-and she could be sure he would always take care of her, unlike her own parents.

In October 1949, they eloped, but decided to wait a while till they told anyone they got married. When they returned to Tarboro after the elopement, Matilda went back to her father's boarding house, and David went back to his parents' home in Tarboro. They had planned to leave the living arrangements this way until they could afford to rent an apartment and buy furniture. But their plans to keep it a secret were blown away when David's mother found the marriage license. She called Tom, and Tom was furious at Matilda. Tom packed up all of his daughter's clothes and her personal belongings and drove Matilda and her things over to David's parents.

"You need to be with your husband now that you are married, Matilda," said Tom angrily, as they sat in the bench seat of Tom's car.

Matilda pleaded, "I don't even know David's parents. They may not want me to stay in their house with David. Papa, PLEASE do not do this to me. Take me back to my room in the boarding house and in the next few days David and I can work out a place to stay. If you follow through with this, you will humiliate me to death." Matilda started to cry but Tom was fed up with what she had done.

"Matilda, you have made your bed and now you must sleep in it," yelled Tom as he proceeded to take Matilda's clothes up to the porch of her new in-law's house. He pulled Matilda out of the car, then locked the door. He got back in his car and drove off, watching his only child stand in the street looking lost. Then to his relief, he saw a young man walk out of the house and put his arm around his daughter.

Tom went back to his room and called Lura on the telephone. He told her how disappointed he was with Matilda. Lura openly agreed with Tom, but secretly she was glad this had happened. Lura knew it would give her more time alone with Tom. Now that Matilda was married, Tom and Lura dated more regularly, and no longer included Matilda in their dates.

Matilda and David 1949
Family photos reprinted with permission of heir of photographer

CHAPTER 15
Proposal and Marriage
1951-1955

Tom and Lura were happy together and euphorically in love with each other. As the years of their courtship went by, Lura shared more of her horrible childhood memories with Tom. Tom also told Lura of his periods of depression. Tom and Lura shared their heartaches and their successes.

This period of Lura's life was a happy time. Her job at Quinn's was going well, and Lura and Tom's courtship was wonderful. Lura just kept wondering when Tom would ask her to marry him, and Tom was also wondering what Lura would say if he asked her to marry him.

In the summer of 1951, Tom asked Lura to go on a day trip to Raleigh with him. Tom was a little bit preoccupied on the drive from Wilson to Raleigh and he did not talk to Lura too much, but he did hold Lura's hand. Luckily, the temperature was mild rather than hot, and the sky was a vibrant blue without a cloud in sight. They fed the pigeons at the State Capitol grounds, and then they made a short walk to the nearby Mecca Restaurant for lunch. Lura had never been to this popular Greek restaurant before, but Tom knew it well. Tom also knew the owner, Nick Pantelidis, who was originally from Chios, Greece. Nick was outgoing, friendly, and extremely personable. He knew all his regular customers by name. Tom had called Nick before he left Wilson to ask Nick for a favor.

Tom and Lura entered the restaurant and were seated at the best table. Tom ordered two T-bone steaks and a large salad. When Tom and Lura were waiting for their food, Tom reached into his jacket and took out a small box. He took both of Lura's hands in his hands.

"Lura, I love you so much, will you marry me?"

Both Lura and Tom had waited for this day for so long and both wanted a happy married life together. Lura began to cry tears of happiness.

"Yes, darling Tom, yes."

They hugged and kissed, and just then Nick and his entourage came over to wish them happiness. In accordance with Tom's plans, Nick, his wife, his cooks, and his servers circled Tom and Lura's table and did a traditional Greek dance holding hands and singing.

Once the dancing was over and the steaks and salad arrived, they began discussing the logistics of how they wanted to get married. When Tom went to the cash register to pay for the lunch, Nick suddenly appeared. "No. This lunch is my wedding gift to you. Congratulations!"

"I feel like I am floating about one foot above the street because at this moment life is as sweet as it can be," said Lura as they left the restaurant. Both Tom and Lura were elated, and both could not stop smiling and looking at each other.

On the ride back to Wilson, they held hands and talked about their future together. They both agreed they did not want a large wedding. Lura spoke frankly and said she did not want her Raeford relatives to attend, because if they did, she would be reminded of Laurence's disappearance, and the bad memories of her own youth. He seemed a little surprised about this. Then he suggested that they elope and not tell anyone they had gotten married until after the fact. Lura immediately said this is exactly what she wanted. With that decided, they began discussing where to live. They decided to move into Lura's apartment after the elopement since she needed to be within walking distance of the furniture store, and Tom's job did not require him to live in any particular town. They selected Monday, August 11, 1951, as their wedding day.

Once Lura returned to work, she asked for a few days of vacation beginning on August 11, but she did not tell anyone why. She purchased a beige suit for the actual wedding ceremony, and a peach satin nightgown and robe for the wedding night. Neither Tom nor Lura could wait for the big day.

Finally, Monday, August 11 came! Tom arrived at Lura's apartment at 8 a.m. as planned. He came inside and gave Lura a big hug and a kiss.

"Lura, the next time you enter this apartment, you will be a married lady," said Tom.

Tom held Lura's hand as they walked from the apartment to the car. Thankfully, he already had the marriage license.

Lura always loved to anticipate an event she knew would be happy. During the three-hour ride to Chesterfield, South Carolina, she was elated every minute because she knew she would become a wife in a few hours. Tom and Lura talked about the happy memories they already had, and their plans for their married life.

They took a break from the drive about 9:30 a.m. and stopped at an ice cream parlor. Tom had a banana split and Lura had a chocolate milkshake.

"Would you like to have a bite of my banana split? If you would, just dig in. Even though this ice cream concoction is one of my favorites of all time, I am generous, and I will share with you dear Lura."

Lura mimicked his playful and slightly sassy tone and said, "Since this is my wedding day, I think I will have a bite of your banana with cream on it. What do you think of that?"

Tom blushed and felt he was seeing a side of Lura he had not seen before, and he liked it.

Finally, they arrived at the Justice of the Peace in Chesterfield about 12:30. Lura was nervous, but Tom was confident and took care of everything. The Justice of the Peace's office was sparsely furnished with shabby old beat-up file cabinets, scratched wooden desks, and a faded linoleum floor. The air smelled of stale cigarette smoke. Neither the smell nor the dinginess of the office did anything to diminish Lura and Tom's excitement and happiness.

The two required witnesses entered the office, and the Justice of the Peace began the marriage ceremony which was over in less than five minutes.

The newly married couple arrived at the Charlotte Mayfair Manor Hotel for their honeymoon stay. The hotel's dining room was known for elegance, service, and the most delicious food in North Carolina. For their midafternoon wedding lunch, they had crab cakes, oysters, and shrimp, along with asparagus, rice, delicious buttered rolls, and carrot cake for dessert. After the leisurely and filling wedding lunch, they talked and held hands for a long time in the restaurant. Then they went to their hotel room. Tom had bought a bottle of French champagne from the restaurant, popped open the cork, and they toasted to their nuptials. Lura took a long bath and then put on her peach satin nightgown and matching peach satin robe. She scented her arms, thighs, and neck with Tom's favorite perfume, Shalimar. Then Tom took a hot bath.

"I'd love some more champagne, Lura," said Tom. Lura complied, and they toasted again. After finishing that bottle, they sat on the sofa and held each other. They kissed, hugged, and said how infinitely happy they felt. Both were nervous about the next part of their wedding day. They got into bed and Tom put his arms around Lura and Lura put her arms around Tom.

"Tonight, I just want to hold you in my arms, Lura. I want to take this slowly," said a slightly inebriated Tom. "I'm just so tired right now and want to make sure things are perfect." He told Lura that the rest would happen in the nights to follow as they grew more accustomed to one another.

Lura had mixed feelings about Tom saying they should wait to consummate their marriage. For her entire life she had been curious to know what sex felt like. It was frustrating that Tom was making her wait a little longer. Conversely, she remembered her mother told her sex hurt and was horrible. They did indeed consummate their marriage in the next few days. Once this happened, Lura decided that her mother was wrong about sex.

After the elopement, Tom and Lura thoroughly enjoyed telling people that they were now husband and wife. Tom decided that the first person he would tell would be Matilda. He drove to Tarboro and arrived at Matilda and David's tiny house on Porter Drive and knocked on the door. Matilda opened the door and looked surprised to see her Papa so early in the morning.

"Papa is everything okay?" asked Matilda.

"I have some exciting news for you," said Tom with a huge grin.

"Lura and I got married five days ago and I am so happy. I drove over here early this morning so that you would be the first person I told. What do you think about that?"

Matilda put her arms around Tom and gave him a long hug. "Papa, I am thrilled for you. Come on in and tell me all about it. I will make coffee for us," said Matilda.

Matilda and Tom sat down at the red chrome metal kitchen table, and Tom told her all about his proposal in Raleigh with the Greek dancing, the ceremony at the Justice of the Peace, and where they stayed for their honeymoon. Matilda was not one little bit surprised. She was only surprised they had not gotten married sooner.

"Papa, I used to worry about you being all alone. I know you have been through a terrible time with Mama, and I wanted you to be happy and have a wife. I am totally at peace now that you are married to Lura. I also have some important news to tell you dear Papa," said Matilda.

"I bet you are pregnant, is that right?" Tom asked in hopeful anticipation.

"You are right. My baby will be born in March. I want you and Lura to see the baby often and we want you to be the baby's godfather. David and I are so happy, and I can hardly wait," said a beaming Matilda.

Father and daughter talked, drank coffee, and chatted for two hours about the good changes in each of their lives. Tom smoked his pipe and Matilda smoked her cigarettes, and it was a great visit.

When Lura told her family in Raeford about the elopement, the reactions were varied. Lura called her mother on the telephone to tell her. "Mama, I have some news for you." She paused then continued slowly. "You remember that nice man, Tom, who came with me to Papa's funeral? Well, we eloped a week ago," said Lura.

"Why in the hell did you get married that way? If you ever did marry, I wanted it to be in the church with our whole family there. I am so disappointed in you, Lura," said her mother angrily.

Lura ended the call with her angry mother, then called her older sister, Josephine, and gave her the news.

"Lura, I am thrilled for you. I recall him fondly and he is handsome and smart, and he seems to be so much in love with you. I am just delighted. I want to send you a wedding gift, what do you need?" asked Josephine.

Then Lura made the call she dreaded most of all. She called her spinster sister, Maggie, and told her the news.

"Lura, it is just NOT FAIR. Both you and Josephine got married, and I had to stay here and take care of our parents. I had a proposal from Dr. Wilkins, but I had to turn him down due to my duty to mama and papa. I am so angry with you," said Maggie with hot rage as she slammed down the phone.

Even though Lura's mother wanted Lura to have a church wedding, she paid for wedding announcements to be printed so that Lura could mail them to friends and relatives.

Their friends remembered them with wedding gifts such as silver flatware, China, towels, decorative items, tablecloths, and napkins from many of the Kennedys. Earl Brown sent a floral teapot, and Lura treasured it.

A couple of weeks after the elopement, Tom and Lura rode across town to visit Tom's brother and sister-in-law, Stuart and Fanny. Both were happy about Tom and Lura's marriage. Lura grew to be fond of Fanny who was sweet and loving to everyone, particularly Lura. Lura thought Stuart was a bit strange, though. She had seen and heard from other people in Wilson about Stuart's unusual habits. One odd habit was that he would rigidly march down the sidewalk like a soldier, then make an exaggerated military turn to the right when the sidewalk turned to the right. When he got to the street, he would about face, and repeat the same spectacle two or three times. He would entertain himself (and sometimes those watching him) for thirty minutes or longer. Stuart had another habit that either frightened people or made them angry. He first demonstrated this behavior on Halloween day in 1938 when he was serving jury duty at the courthouse. This story was told to Lura by her co-worker at Quinn's, Patsy, who served on the same jury. Patsy witnessed this behavior herself.

"Stuart and I and other people who were serving on the jury took a break on the courthouse steps because it was a beautiful Indian Summer Day."

Patsy paused then continued, "Stuart stood up and put his hand over his brow to shield the sun from his eyes, and he stood staring at one spot in the sky. He stood like that for a long time and others sitting on the steps started looking up at the sky in the area Stuart was looking. They were curious and wanted to see what Stuart was seeing. Then one juror said to Stuart, 'What do you see up there, friend?'"

"I am not totally sure, look over there," said Stuart pointing to the bit of sky just above the corner of the Cherry Hotel.

"I do see something in the sky, but I cannot make it out," said the fellow juror.

Another juror stood up and said, "Where, where is it?"

"There, and I think it looks like a spaceship," said Stuart pointing.

"I know what it is. Martians invaded earth last night and more are getting ready to land again today. We had all better get back in the courthouse for protection," laughed an older female juror.

Most of the jurors started to laugh. Many of them on the steps had listened to the radio last night and heard Orson Welles' program, "War of the Worlds." This was a realistic dramatization of Martians invading Earth. Many people believed the radio program was real and they were scared to death. People all over America went running for their lives because they believed Martians landed on Earth. Others realized it was a work of fiction.

143

This is what inspired Stuart to begin his new trick. He enjoyed it so much that he did this off and on as long as he lived.

"Don't worry about Stuart's strange behavior, Lura. He thinks he's a comedian," said Tom.

Not long after Tom moved into Lura's apartment, they quickly realized it was too small. After a month, they moved to a house on Tilghman Road in Wilson, and here they were able to spread out their belongings. Tom needed room for the antique furniture he inherited from his mother, his favorite being two barrister bookcases. He also inherited several first edition books, a vast collection of religious books, the complete set of the works of Mark Twain, the complete works of Alexandre Dumas, and the 15-volume set of Stoddard's Lectures from 1897.

After a few months of marriage, Tom and Lura got a sweet and loving blond cocker spaniel puppy and named her Sally. Sally followed them around the house and liked to cuddle up with them after dinner. For Lura it was great to have Sally as a loving companion when Tom was away traveling for his work. Both Lura and Tom kidded each other about which of them Sally loved more.

In February 1954, Aila Kennedy, Lura's mother, died at the age of seventy-nine. She had been a difficult person since her husband murdered the police chief. As an old woman, she was described as cantankerous. Because she would not let people in her home, nor go to the homes of people in Raeford, her funeral was not well attended. Aila's children were sad that their mother died, but relieved they no longer had to put up with her anger and negativity.

Maggie was fifty-eight-years-old when her mother died, and for the first time in her life, she did not have to take care of others. Maggie had always dreamed of getting married when she no longer had to be responsible for her parents, but now her health was poor, and her looks made the possibility of attracting a husband unlikely. After her mother died, Maggie just stayed home and continued to complain. At one point, Maggie realized that she had become much like her mother. She was now a bitter old woman who was unhappy with her life.

At the time of Lura's mother's death, Lura and Tom had only been married for three years. This was a happy time for the newlyweds.

They relished all their time together, but particularly enjoyed their annual vacation. The first summer after marriage they went to Wrightsville Beach, on the southeastern coast of North Carolina. The cooler ocean breezes were like paradise to them. They enjoyed walking on the beach, gathering shells, eating delicious seafood dinners, and relaxing together.

On another summer vacation they went to Lake Lure, a man-made lake which flooded an old town when it was created. Lake Lure also had a much cooler climate than Wilson because it is in the foothills of the North Carolina mountains.

When Tom and Lura had been married for four years, Lura became interested in bringing in more business to Quinn's Furniture Store. Just like she did when she did a methodic search for interior decorator jobs, she made a list of all the potential clients in Wilson who needed their place of business redecorated.

The first potential client she contacted was the owner of Wilson's tallest hotel, the Cherry Hotel. She was overjoyed that he agreed to see her on Friday, March 23 at 11:30 in the morning. The six story Cherry Hotel was the tallest and the most elegant hotel in Wilson.

Lura was walking toward the Cherry Hotel at 11 a.m. on the specified morning. She had planned to arrive a few minutes before her appointment, as she always wanted to be on time or early.

She was within thirty feet of the hotel when out of the corner of her eye, she saw something falling from a window on the top floor of the hotel. She saw what looked like a huge bundle of clothes falling out the window. She watched the bundle as it fell, and to her horror as it got closer, she saw arms and legs in the bundle. She heard a loud thud as the bundle hit the sidewalk just ten feet from where she was standing. For the second time in her life, she was paralyzed with fear. Other people nearby screamed or ran to the body. As Lura stood there unable to move or speak, her mind began to play strange tricks on her.

Rather than focusing on the blood and gore on the sidewalk, Lura stared at the herringbone pattern on the victim's jacket. It was clearly visible because the victim landed on his face and chest. Lura's mind went to a strange thought. This man's jacket looked just like the one she and Tom gave Stuart for Christmas last year. When she realized the man was her brother-in-law, Stuart Davis, Lura fainted.

Understandably, Tom was distraught at the suicide of his dear brother. Both he and Lura did all they could to help Stuart's widow, Fanny. Tom seemed more irritable after this, and he found fault with Lura more often, too.

Tom liked a clean kitchen and orderly house, and Lura's standards for an orderly house did not always match Tom's standards. Lura was hurt when Tom would make demeaning comments about her housekeeping. He told Lura when he found breadcrumbs on the kitchen counter or on the floor. He also told her when the living room was messy, or if he noticed any other messy area of their house. To Tom, he was just communicating, as if he said, "the newspaper did not arrive today." But to Lura, he was criticizing her specifically, and she was tired of his criticism.

146

Sometimes when Tom complained, Lura would say to herself, *You can just go back to work in Atlanta or Dallas and leave me and Sally here alone. That is better than you pestering me about these inconsequential things.*

But Lura was non-confrontational and she did not say these words to Tom. She would always say meekly that she was sorry. The reason she did not show her anger and disappointment was that she had witnessed anger between her own parents too many times and she vowed *not* to act like either of them.

Like all marriages, Tom and Lura had good times and tough times. They planned for a vacation in 1957, but fate had another plan.

CHAPTER 16

Lura's Cancer

1956-1958

Lura had been feeling a bit nauseous with mild stomach pains, so she took a few days off from work to rest and recover. While Tom was on a business trip to Atlanta, she decided to spend this day rereading all the letters and postcards which he had sent her over the years. First, she arranged the correspondence in chronological order and began reading the first letters Tom sent to her in 1946. As she read phrases like *I will love you till the end of time, and I think of you constantly Lura*, tears of happy remembrance stung the back of her eyes. She delighted in reliving the exciting time of their courtship. By the time Lura reread Tom's most recent correspondence, she couldn't help but notice the difference in tone between the first letters and the most recent postcards which were hastily written and short to the point. *Arrived here safely. Will be back Saturday afternoon. T.*

Lura sighed as she felt that the butterflies of new love had been replaced by the casual companionship of a five-year marriage. Lura thought about her relationship with Tom. He still traveled about half the days of the year, and Lura knew Tom was sick and tired of traveling and being away from home so much. Conversely, Lura liked him away some of the time. She liked privacy, making her own choices, and being the only occupant in the house-other than Sally.

Lura quit rereading the letters and reminiscing because her stomach began to hurt more. She put a hot water bottle on her abdomen, took a sleeping pill, and fell into an uneasy sleep with dreams of Laurence disappearing, and her father leaving home.

By three in the morning, her stomach pains felt like someone was repeatedly stabbing her abdomen with a knife. Lura felt she was dying. As she lay there, her actions were erratic, and she was almost unconscious. Her reactions to the pain went from crying like a baby with her mouth open, to screaming, and then to moaning. Somewhere in her mind, she realized she should call for an ambulance, but her brain was too foggy, and she failed to act.

Tom arrived home mid-morning, and he could hear Lura's screams as he attempted to unlock the front door. He could barely put the key in the lock because his hands shook violently. His mind was trying to imagine what was happening to Lura. Was someone inside trying to kill her? Once inside, he yelled frantically,

"Lura, where are you, what is wrong?"

He followed the sound of her screams to the bedroom and was horrified to see her rolling back and forth in the bed and holding her belly which was swollen like she was seven months pregnant.

"Honey, what is happening?" he asked gently.

He picked up the phone, called the ambulance, and knelt beside her bed, trying to make Lura understand that he was there at her side. He did not think she noticed his presence.

The ambulance arrived and took Lura and Tom to the Woodard-Herring Hospital in Wilson. Even though the hospital was only a few blocks from their house, Tom felt like the ambulance ride lasted an hour. Once inside the hospital, the doctors quickly examined Lura and gave her an injection to make the pain almost disappear. The doctor said Lura had an intestinal blockage and would need surgery. The doctor wanted Mrs. Davis to have the best possible surgeon, so he immediately contacted Dr. Michael Pishko at the Pinehurst Hospital.

Arrangements were made to take her there immediately by ambulance. Tom quickly got a taxi to their house, and then drove his car back to the hospital. With the sirens screaming in front of him, he followed Lura's ambulance. Lura was transported to the Pinehurst Surgical Hospital, in Pinehurst, North Carolina. Tom did his best to keep up with the speeding ambulance, but it was difficult driving due to his nerves and shaking hands.

To calm himself he talked to Lura and said, "Hold on darling. You are going to be fine; we will take great care of you, and you will be as good as new. I love you! I love you!"

Talking to Lura made him begin to cry, and his tears flowed freely, making it dangerous to drive. Tom remembered that often when he was distraught or sad about something, he would talk to God. Silently Tom said, *God, please don't let her die. Be with her and hold her close to you in your arms. Please comfort her and give her a peaceful spirit.*

He talked and prayed to God most of the time during the drive.

As soon as the ambulance arrived at the Pinehurst Surgical Hospital, Dr. Pishko met the ambulance and gave directions for Lura to be prepared for surgery. From lengthy phone calls between Dr. Pishko and the Wilson physicians, he had been thoroughly briefed on Lura's condition. He had Tom sign forms giving him permission to do the operation, and to even do a colostomy if necessary.

Once Dr. Pishko opened Lura's abdomen and visualized the bowel, he knew from years of experience that Lura most likely had colon cancer. During the operation, he performed a colostomy which rerouted the intestines, so elimination would take place through an opening in her abdomen. After several hours of surgery, he sent samples of Lura's tissues to the pathologist.

During the surgery, Tom had been pacing up and down the hall outside of the operating room. Finally, Dr. Pishko walked out of the surgical suite, and saw Tom who was waiting just outside the door.

"Your wife has colon cancer, and this caused her colon to be totally blocked, which leads to swelling of the abdomen, and severe pain. I did a colostomy on your wife. She is as well as expected for now. I will talk with you again later today regarding her condition. Do you have questions?" Dr. Pishko asked.

Tom shook his head to indicate no. He was too tearful to utter a word. Dr. Pishko patted Tom's shoulder to give comfort.

Dr. Pishko kept Tom informed regularly. The next day he met with Tom again to reassure him. He put his hand on Tom's shoulder and said, "I believe your wife will be fine. You try to get some rest and I will talk to you again soon."

Tom was numb. He was comforted that Lura was still alive, but he was worried to death with the diagnosis. When Tom entered Lura's room, she was almost unconscious from the powerful pain medications she was taking. Tom knelt beside the bed, held Lura's hand, and prayed aloud, "Dear God, give us your healing presence and be with us, please take away all Lura's pain and give us peace. In Christ's name, Amen."

After Tom met with Dr. Pishko alone, the two men went into Lura's hospital room and Dr. Pishko told Lura the same news, that she would be fine. He told her that many people lead long and productive lives with a colostomy. After the doctor left the room, Tom and Lura talked for a long time.

"Tom, hold me. I am so cold," said Lura shivering.

They held each other for a long time and then shed tears openly.

After a couple of weeks, Lura felt stronger. She was still in the hospital with attentive nursing care. At that point, Dr. Pishko came to Lura's room and had a discussion with Tom and Lura about the various aspects of Lura's recovery.

"Mrs. Davis, you are now cancer free. We will keep you here in the hospital for a couple of months, then you can go home. One possible negative outcome of this operation is you might develop peritonitis. If your abdomen begins to hurt badly once you get home, you must get to a doctor immediately. Other than that remote possibility, things should progress nicely. Some husbands help their wives by handling the colostomy bag for them. So, Mrs. Davis, if you have a hard time with it, then perhaps Mr. Davis can handle the bag for you. If you choose to do this then Mr. Davis could feel more involved in your care," said Dr. Pishko.

At this suggestion, Tom and Lura blushed noticeably.

"I will leave you two alone to discuss things and check in with you later," said Dr. Pishko as he exited the room and closed the door.

Tom looked embarrassed. Both Lura and Tom loathed discussing the care of the colostomy bag. After a few moments of awkward silence, Tom was wracking his brain to say something.

"Dr. Pishko is a great doctor, and I am confident he has given you the best care possible."

"Tom, I would rather manage the bag myself. I know I can learn to do it and I have two more months here for the nurses to teach me what to do," Lura replied.

"That's fine, Lura. Whatever you want to do, that is what we will do," Tom replied in relief as he looked out the window.

"Tom, I need to close my eyes and be quiet for a while," Lura said wearily.

"That's fine," said Tom. He was grateful for some time with his own thoughts.

Lura's mind was going ninety miles an hour. Despite being cancer free, she was depressed and angry. Managing the colostomy bag was difficult and it could sometimes leak, which would cause her much embarrassment. Even when the bag was perfectly in place, Lura was worried that it would leak in the next couple of hours, so she was perpetually in a worried state.

The next week Lura's older sister, Maggie came to visit Lura in the hospital and brought a huge vase of yellow roses. Maggie opened the door to Lura's room and walked in quietly.

"Maggie, those flowers are beautiful. How kind of you to bring them to me," said Lura.

"Are you feeling any better today, Lura?" asked Maggie.

"Not much better," sighed Lura. "Not much better."

To Lura's horror, she felt something wet and warm on her abdomen and smelled the unmistakable odor of feces. Lura looked at Maggie and could tell that her sister noticed the smell too.

"Could you go and get my nurse for me? I need a few minutes with her," said Lura.

"In the meantime, Maggie, why don't you get some lunch in the cafeteria and then come back to see me."

At the request, Maggie quickly left the room to look for the nurse. Lura's eyes filled with tears, and she wondered how she could go on like this. It was just too much to deal with. After a few moments, Lura's nurse entered the room.

"Mrs. Davis, don't you worry one minute about this. It happens sometimes when a patient is trying to get used to managing the bag." The nurse expertly fixed everything while reassuring Lura that she would become proficient handling the bag. Lura just needed practice.

In July, Tom drove Lura back to their house in Wilson. Sally was beside herself with joy to see her, and Lura felt the same way. Lura let Sally lick her face as she relished the wet feel of Sally's soft tongue, and the smell of doggie breath which Lura rather liked.

Tom was happy to have Lura home. By this time, Lura did not need help with her care, as she had become proficient in taking care of herself. Tom was relieved. Two weeks later he went back to traveling, and Lura resumed working at the furniture store.

Tom never told anyone, but he had a visceral revulsion to Lura's colostomy. He unconsciously began to do little things that told Lura of his revulsion. Prior to the surgery, Tom would enter their bedroom without knocking, or he would enter the bathroom when Lura was in the tub. After the surgery, he would always knock before entering. Tom and Lura used to spoon in bed with Tom wrapping his arms around Lura and letting his hands rest on her abdomen. Now they still spooned in bed, but Tom was careful not to touch Lura's tummy. Lura knew what Tom was doing and why. She still loved him, but she was saddened that the physical side of their relationship had changed.

154

Tom tried to act cheerful by saying that he was lucky that she was alive and lucky she had beaten cancer. He told her that he was proud of her for her strength and courage in undergoing the surgery. He made it a point to compliment Lura often.

Sadly, when Lura was completely healed, Tom once again started criticizing her for her inadequacies in housekeeping. This made her unhappy, particularly now that she had lived through cancer. Lura pondered Tom's motives. She thought maybe he was worried that she might become an invalid in the future, and he dreaded this. She certainly did not want to become a burden to him.

For whatever reason, he criticized her. Tom's behavior often made Lura uncomfortable when they were together. It made her self-conscious in her own home. Even when Tom acted completely normal, Lura was worried that he now viewed her negatively. She was surprised to find that she was occasionally happier when he was away traveling on business, because then, she and Sally could enjoy the house without having to think about Tom and what Tom was perceiving.

CHAPTER 17

Christmas Comfort

1957

Christmas Eve 1957 found Tom at the YMCA in Dallas sitting on the bed in his room. He decided to look for a friendly bar and have a few drinks. He walked along the empty streets and entered the first bar he saw. His eyes slowly adjusted to the dim light. When he could see once again, he saw one customer at the bar, a young man in sloppy clothes, and the bartender, a heavy Italian looking older man, who like Tom, looked lonely. He sat down in an empty seat in front of the bartender.

"What will you have?" asked the bartender as he placed a small white napkin in front of Tom.

"Whiskey, please," said Tom.

"Where are you from?"

"Wilson, North Carolina. How about you?" asked Tom. The bartender smiled broadly, moved closer to Tom, and put his elbow on the bar.

"I have been to Wilson and spent a lot of time there. I used to be in a musical quartet, and we performed at Mamona Hall in Wilson several times every year."

"Heavens to Betsy, it's amazing that you have been to Wilson! My name is Tom Davis, and I am pleased to meet you."

Tom extended his hand to shake the bartender's hand, and the bartender reciprocated and shook Tom's hand warmly.

"I am Stefano Liotta, and I am from Sicily, originally."

Tom spent the next four hours talking with Stefano, drinking whiskeys, and enjoying the companionship. Tom learned that Stefano moved from Sicily to New York City, and eventually to Dallas. He was married, then divorced. Then Stefano told Tom he wanted to know about Tom's life and all the details of what brought Tom to Dallas, and to this bar on Christmas Eve. Tom could tell that Stefano really wanted to have a lively conversation on Christmas Eve, to feel human companionship and not be alone. Sadly, Tom felt the same way. Tom, who was naturally a private man, rationalized that he would never see Stefano again, so why not tell him about his life? It was always easier to tell complete strangers personal things, so he felt at ease.

"My story is long and convoluted, but if you want to hear it, I will tell you my saga," said Tom. He paused then continued. "Stefano, why would a sixty-seven-year-old married man be over 1,000 miles from his wife on Christmas Eve? It is because even though I long to be with my family, my small income as a cotton broker does not provide us enough income to meet our expenses. This is a sad fact, and one that I have tried to change, to no avail. I try to keep up appearances for my wife. I try to be cheerful to my wife in letters, postcards, and Christmas cards. I tell her to enjoy her Christmas, and I tell her that I am enjoying window shopping and going to Neiman Marcus, but I am not enjoying my time here in Dallas, at least not until I entered this bar tonight. The fact of the matter is that I am depressed, and I know there is little I can do to remedy this." Tom paused and sighed and looked down at his lap.

"Tom, tell me more about why you are depressed and more about your life," said Stefano.

"Well, my depression comes from several factors. I have been married two times in my life. My first marriage was to the beautiful Rita Gay Williams. Rita had long black hair, dramatic olive skin,

157

and light grey eyes. When we got married, she was thirty-three and I was thirty-eight." He laughed. "Rita told me she only married me to get me to stop asking her to marry me. That should've been a sign of things to come, right?"

Tom paused, shook his head, and took a swig of his whiskey.

"At the beginning of our marriage, I was deeply in love with Rita. During the first four months of marriage, I discovered Rita's likes and dislikes and her peculiar ways. She did not like me to hug her or make love to her. This was devastating and surprising to me. I overheard Rita telling a friend that she did not like sex because it was thoroughly disgusting and messy."

"That's a shame," said Stefano.

"Rita often seemed like two entirely different people. We got married in June and for the first four months, there were arguments and hard feelings between us. Then Rita totally astounded me in October 1928. She turned into the sweetest and most loving wife that any man would want to have.

She did not know how to cook because before we married, she lived with her father who employed a great cook and other servants. Rita now wanted to learn to cook, so she had her friends help her prepare meals for us. They would come over in the afternoon and instruct her in every step for making a superb meal. When the meal was ready, the friends would leave, and Rita would quickly take off the dress she wore for cooking, slip on one of her many fringed flapper outfits, put on make-up, and greet me at the door with a big kiss.

We would have lively conversation as we ate the delicious dinner. Then Rita said she wanted to either go dancing or have hot sex in the bedroom. Some nights we did go dancing, but I liked the latter choice better, so we did more of that.

"Can I get you a refill? You look like you need one," said the bartender.

Stefano gave Tom another refill.

"As time went on, Rita's moods switched vastly every few months. I kept a record of her mood swings in my address book. I absolutely did not understand Rita's behavior."

"I had a friend who experienced this same thing. I think they have a name for this. I think it's manic depression, or something like that," said Stefano.

"You might be onto something my friend." Tom continued his story. "In the summer of 1930, we found out that Rita was pregnant. Both of us were happy about the baby. Rita was in a good place mentally during her pregnancy. She had our baby on January 31, 1931, and we named our beautiful baby girl Matilda Branch Davis. After Rita had the baby, she behaved normally for a while-tenderly taking care of Matilda. I loved our baby immediately and felt a bond with her that I knew would last forever. When Rita became a mother, I loved her more than I ever loved her before, and I was hopeful that her prolonged periods of depression were over. But my hope was unfounded. Rita's depression, exhaustion, and unhappiness revealed itself when Matilda turned two months old. I was worried about Rita and the baby."

"This sounds awful, Tom. What happened then?" asked Stefano.

"Then the ugly side of Rita's personality came out in full force. She said over and over that she never wanted to have sex again, that it hurt to have sex, and it hurt to have a baby. Then she told me the devastating news that she did not want to live with me any longer and that she wanted a divorce. I tried to persuade her that we should stay together. It was no use. Finally, I had to move to Arkansas for three months to get the divorce. Arkansas' divorce laws are more lenient than those in North Carolina." Tom downed his whiskey, and Stefano replaced it with a fresh one.

"After the divorce, I changed jobs and became a cotton broker. With this new job, I traveled about half of the time. I moved back into my old room at my mother's house in Wilson. I visited Matilda each time I came to Wilson, and throughout her growing up years, I was able to be a loving father and a friend to her. When Rita became sick, our relatives took Matilda in and took care of her." Tom paused, wiped a tear away from his eye and took another swig of his whiskey.

"Rita absolutely broke my heart, and it was many years before I ever even looked at another woman. One consequence of my divorce from Rita was that now I experience periods of deep depression. My periods of depression usually last about two weeks."

"I'm so sorry to hear all of this. I hear many stories like yours inside these walls," said Stefano.

"Rita and I divorced in 1931, and she died in September of 1957, just three months ago."

"You said you got married again?" asked Stefano.

"Yes, Lura is my second wife. We met in 1946, and as soon as I met her, I knew I wanted to get to know her better. Lura and I took our courtship slowly and got to know each other well before we discussed marriage. Our courtship was happy, and our marriage was good. In the beginning of our marriage, we had sex occasionally. Now we like to hug each other in the evening and I like to hold her in bed," admitted Tom.

"In January this year, Lura began complaining of stomach pains. Finally, she went to see the doctor and found she had colon cancer. She had to get a colostomy just to survive."

"I'm so sorry to hear this," Stefano said.

"Stefano, this year has been horrible. So, here I sit on Christmas Eve in Texas, and I feel like a failure as a breadwinner and as a husband. My small paychecks barely cover our expenses, and now with Lura's medical bills our finances will be even worse. All I can do is the best I can do and this Christmas I sacrificed being at home in exchange for staying in Texas and working before and after Christmas to make more money."

Stefano had a look of compassion on his face, and he spoke. "Tom, I can tell you have faced some devastating situations in your life, and here you are on Christmas Eve feeling sad. One thing that helps me when I feel overwhelmed and melancholy is to think of a time in my life when I was genuinely happy and try to relive every moment of that time over and over. Would you tell me about a time in your life when you were happy, and all was right in the world?"

Tom was quiet as he pondered Stefano's question.

Then he smiled broadly and said, "Matilda's baby girl was born in March 1952, and she named her 'Gay' as tribute to her grandfather, Edgar Gay. I remember Gay's baptism in October when she was eight months old at Calvary Episcopal Church in Tarboro, and I was her godfather and one of her sponsors. I remember it was a brilliant warm Indian summer day with a totally blue sky and I recall the beautiful hues of purple, blue and yellow that fell on the floor and on the baptismal font, cast by the stained-glass windows. I looked at my granddaughter and felt all the love in the world for her, and when the priest said, 'I mark Gay as Christ's own forever,' my heart soared, and I was totally at peace and overjoyed. Just remembering that wonderful day makes me feel joy again."

"Stefano, you are a wise man, and you have helped me more than you know. First you helped me by reaching out to me on Christmas Eve when I felt all alone, then you helped me by encouraging me to recall and relive a wonderful day in my life. Now it is your turn to tell me your life story."

Stefano told Tom about growing up in Sicily and how his cousins were in the Mafia, and this frightened him. He had two uncles, one of whom fathered twenty-two children, and the other was killed by the Mafia. Stefano loved to visit the ancient ruins of temples. He also spent time in Greece, particularly on the island of Chios, where he helped the village baker with the communal oven that cooked foods for the entire village. Stefano spent at least thirty minutes telling Tom about his Sicilian ex-wife, Francesca. He described her lovemaking, her temper, her cooking skills, and her crazy family.

Tom asked Stefano questions as he told his story. He wanted more details about the Greek temples and the communal oven. Stefano delighted in telling his story, as it made him feel closer to his family in Sicily.

Midnight was closing time for the bar. Stefano and Tom warmly shook hands and said their good-byes.

Tom walked back to the YMCA to his room, laid down on the bed, and looked out the big window. He saw a huge lighted cross on the Republic National Bank Building nearby. The cross stood about two hundred feet tall and 120 feet wide and was made of lighted windows in the offices of the bank. Tom felt this cross was like an embrace from God reminding him that Christmas is about Christ and His love for His children. The cross and spending time with Stefano helped Tom feel much better on this most unusual Christmas Eve.

In Tom's prayers that night he said, "Thank you God for the gift of your son which came to us all those years ago on Christmas night. Earlier today, I felt sorry for myself and all alone, but you directed my path straight to Stefano. You knew that I needed companionship and a connection to another human being. Now with the bright light of the massive brilliant cross shining in my window, and with your love lighting my path, I feel joyful once again. Amen."

Tom holding baby Matilda
Family photos reprinted with permission of heir of photographer

CHAPTER 18

More Tragedy

1958 -1959

"Agnes, MY CANCER HAS RETURNED! Can you come here? I need you," Lura whispered.

Lura began to smile slowly as she saw a familiar blue light beside her bed that slowly transformed into a young woman wearing a long flowing white dress.

"Lura, my friend, you are going to be fine and live to be over ninety-three-years-old. Do not worry about this cancer. This is the last time you will ever have surgery," said Agnes.

With those words, Lura felt her body relax for the first time in an exceptionally long time.

"Agnes, I hope you are happy now. You look exactly like you looked when we were roommates at Brenau. You have not aged a bit," said Lura to her ghostly friend.

Agnes returned a bright smile.

Lura then thought of something that had been on her mind for a long time. She was afraid of the answer, but she asked Agnes anyway.

"Agnes, is my brother Laurence dead?"

"He is dead, but he is at peace. You see Lura, where Laurence and I dwell, all is loving, peaceful, and forgiving. No one experiences pain or sadness. Laurence and I spend a lot of time here together basking in the perpetual sunlight and praising God."

"Lura, do you remember how much we loved to laugh when we were young girls in Quewhiffle, and when we were young women at Brenau? I will tell you something funny about where I dwell now. We are surrounded by perpetual light. Well, I must admit sometimes this luminosity becomes bothersome and we long for twilight or candlelight. It is impossible to find any shade here. Can you imagine angels using their wings to shield their faces from this constant brightness? Even though I am now a spirit and not a human, I see the humor in that. I thought that story might bring you mirth."

Lura grinned as Agnes vanished and the hospital room became pitch black. She thought, *Agnes would appreciate the darkness in this room now.*

Lura already knew in her heart that Laurence was dead, so hearing this from Agnes did not upset her. She was at least relieved that her dear Laurence had found peace at last, and that Agnes and Laurence were together in heaven.

Lura's cancer symptoms had begun in late September 1958 with severe abdominal pain. She returned to Dr. Pishko in Pinehurst. This visit from Agnes occurred the third night after Lura's surgery to remove more of her colon. As with her previous surgery, she stayed in the hospital for two months, and then returned to home to Wilson.

In the months after her second cancer surgery, Lura's physical health improved, but her mental health began deteriorating. Due to her depression, Lura took a leave of absence from her job. To Lura it felt like she was spiraling down into a bottomless pit of melancholy. Some days she felt so hopeless and forlorn that she could not face getting out of bed. She feared becoming a burden to Tom and she feared he would abandon her. She lived in agony with a black despondency that permeated every fiber of her being. She was desperately seeking a solution to her agonizing never-ending black depression. Lura's mental state gnawed at her sanity during both her waking hours and her troubled sleep.

In the wee hours of the morning on Saturday May 30, 1959, she had two horrible dreams back-to-back. First she dreamed she was standing in Brenau's auditorium watching Agnes' lifeless body hang from the balcony. Next she dreamed she was standing beside the Chief of Police in Raeford when her father murdered him, and her father also shot her in the chest. After these terrifying dreams, she realized there was no escape from the horrible life she was living.

Lura made a decision about her future that would stop all the madness. Ever so quietly and silently, she arose from the warm bed she shared with Tom. She put on her robe, and silently closed the door to the bedroom behind her. She went into the living room, and picked up her beloved Sally and rubbed her. Not wanting Sally to witness what was to come, she placed her in the laundry room.

Lura sat down at Tom's rolltop desk in the living room, and removed Tom's thirty-two caliber Smith & Wesson revolver from the drawer. Shaking with fear, she pointed the gun at her left temple. When she was just about to pull the trigger, Tom ran into the living room.

"No Lura, No!" yelled Tom, his voice frantic. He ran to Lura and grabbed the gun. They struggled, causing Lura's colostomy bag to burst open. Then Lura heard the deafening noise of the gun shot, the echo of the shot, then complete silence. She was waiting to feel the pain of being shot. Then she realized that she was not shot, and that Tom was no longer struggling to take the gun away.

"My God, it's Tom, not me," she whispered.

Tom's limp body fell to the floor. Lura could not breathe. She felt paralyzed with fear and could not move. She saw blood gushing from Tom's head, soaking the white rug. Suddenly Lura's eyesight failed, and she could not see anything at all.

Lura began screaming, "Tom, Tom, Oh My God."

Even though Lura could not see, she stooped down, reached for Tom's body, and laid down beside him to feel if he was still breathing. Tom was still. There was no breath. Lura started screaming again. She felt Tom's blood covering her hands, arms, and face. The blood on her hands felt slightly sticky. She did not care. She just wanted to be as close to Tom as possible.

Hearing the screaming and the gunshot, Lura's next door neighbor ran over and investigated the living room through the large picture window. The neighbor began shaking as she saw Lura and Tom laying on the floor covered in blood. She ran home and called the police.

Lura cradled Tom's head in her arms and rocked him gently. That was the first time she noticed the smell of her own feces since her colostomy bag had gotten dislodged. For the first time, she did not care one bit about this. She heard sirens getting louder, then brakes squealing, then car doors slamming, then banging on her front door, then the voice of a man.

"This is the police. Open the door or we will break the lock."

Lura did not reply, she just kept rocking Tom's dead body. The policemen broke the lock, ran into the room, and witnessed a woman covered in blood holding a lifeless looking man with a bloody and wounded head. The gun was lying in this pool of blood.

This was the strangest time in Lura's life, and she did not know what to do. She still could not see anything. She heard the policemen talking but could not comprehend what they were saying. Lura heard flash bulbs popping so she figured someone was taking pictures. For Lura, time seemed to stand still, and all her attention was focused on cradling Tom.

167

Lura could feel the arms of two of the police officers lifting her off the floor.

"Let's get you up, honey," said a female police officer.

Then they laid Lura down on the sofa. The lady police officer put wet towels in Lura's hands so she could wipe away some of the blood.

"I cannot see anything, I am blind," said Lura.

The lady police officer used the wet towels to wipe Lura's face, arms, and hands, and afterwards she held Lura's hand. She was gentle, and Lura was grateful.

After about thirty minutes, the coroner, Robert Goudy, arrived and introduced himself to everyone. Lura's mind was clearer by now and she remembered that Robert Goudy had been a frequent customer at Quinn's Furniture Store. The coroner examined Tom's body and pronounced him dead.

"Mrs. Davis, I am so sorry," said the coroner.

Lura began to cry. The coroner then said in a gentle voice, "Tell me what happened."

Lura had considered what she should say to this question. She felt there was no point in telling them that it all started with her trying to commit suicide.

Lura began her version of what happened, "Tom had been despondent for the last two months. We have both grieved because I had colon cancer and have had two surgeries for cancer. This morning Tom got out of bed before me, which was unusual. I heard strange noises in the living room, so I got up quickly and came into the living room, and I saw that Tom had a gun in his hand and tears running down his cheeks. He had such sad eyes. I was fearful he was going to kill himself, so I ran over to him and tried to take the gun away from him. We were both holding the gun when it went off, then he fell to the floor." Lura sobbed as she finished her story.

"I laid down beside him to see if he was still breathing, there was no breath. I held him and comforted him. Then my eyesight vanished."

"Mrs. Davis is there someone, maybe a family member, we could call to come and be with you now?" asked the coroner.

"My sister-in-law, Fanny Davis," said Lura.

"I will get one of the police officers to go pick her up and bring her here then," said the coroner.

As soon as the police officer arrived at Fanny's house, Fanny was at the door ready to go. She already knew that Tom was dead, as gossip travels fast in a small Southern town. Fanny said she would go to Lura. After a short ride in the police care, Fanny opened the front door, and what she saw made her chest constrict. She saw Tom's bloody body on the floor surrounded by photographers taking pictures, and Lura on the sofa covered in blood.

"Now that you are here to take care of your sister-in-law, let's move her to her bedroom to give you two ladies more privacy," said the female police officer.

The female police officer and one other officer gently lifted Lura off the sofa, carried her to the bedroom, and laid her down on the unmade bed. Lura moaned softly. Fanny got a bucket of warm water from the kitchen, towels from the bathroom, and came into the bedroom, closing the door behind her.

"Lura, it is Fanny come to help you dear."

"Fanny bless you! If I ever needed you, I need you now," said Lura in a strained voice.

Fanny walked over to the bed and held Lura's hand and stroked her arm. Both ladies shed tears and were silent for a long time.

"Lura, is it okay if I use these soft towels and warm water to clean you up a little?" asked Fanny.

169

Lura nodded her head, so Fanny gently and slowly wet the towels in the warm water and wiped Lura's face, arms, and hands. It was not possible for Fanny to get all the blood from around Lura's fingernails. She could see and smell Lura's burst colostomy bag, but she did nothing to clean that up. Fanny concentrated on wiping Lura's face, arms, and hands that were stained with blood. Fanny cared more about being a comfort to Lura rather than getting her cleaned up.

"Lura, do you want to talk about it?" asked Fanny.

"I cannot talk about it yet," said Lura emphatically. "You talk to me. You have been through this before with your dear Stuart. To take my mind off what happened here, tell me the circumstances when Stuart died. I need to think of something other than Tom."

Fanny thought it was strange that Lura wanted to hear about Stuart's suicide at a time like this, but she took a deep breath and began her story.

"Some people in Wilson thought Stuart was odd, but I thought he liked to have fun and play jokes. I knew him much better than the townspeople, of course. I do not know what motivated him to go to the Cherry Hotel on March 23, 1956, and take his own life. For thirty-five years he had been a successful tobacconist, with a lovely home and a good marriage. That fateful day started like any other day. I cooked a Southern breakfast of bacon, sausage, eggs, homemade biscuits, and coffee. We talked about our garden and a birthday party we were supposed to attend for a neighbor that night. He kissed me goodbye and walked out the door on his way to work.

"At 10:45 on the morning of March 23, 1956, he checked into room 629 in the Cherry Hotel. He took off his green Fedora hat and placed it on the chair. He placed his glasses on the dresser. He removed the screen from the window and propped it up against the door of the closet.

"Lura, I can only guess what he must have been thinking at that point. Was he thinking he had a poor marriage, or that he did not earn enough money, or that life was boring? If only I could have been with him in that room and pulled him back inside. But I was not there to stop my dear Stuart.

"He sat on the windowsill and then jumped. Of course, you witnessed him jump, and I would imagine that was one of the most horrible experiences of your life. He left no note explaining what he did. The newspaper had an article about his suicide. It said he jumped just ten minutes after he checked into the room. No one heard any commotion before, during, or after the fall." Fanny paused and looked at Lura, then continued."

"The fall crushed dear Stuart's chest and both of his wrists were torn apart. Lura, I felt numb and stunned for days after that. The only thing that helped me to survive was my faith in God. That happened two years and ten months ago and I still hurt from it. I still miss him. But time is the great healer, and time helped me to feel better. So dear Lura, you will get better with time, too."

Fanny said to herself, *I hope this is not too much for Lura at this point. I think she just wants to think of anything other than Tom.*

After a couple of minutes of silence, Lura spoke and her voice sounded a little stronger. "You took my mind off my situation for a little while and it helped me. Would you help me go to the bathroom and get in the tub and soak for a while?"

CHAPTER 19
The Funeral
1959

Tom's funeral service was brief. At Episcopal funerals, generally little is said in the eulogy about the personality of the deceased. However, this priest mentioned Tom's profound knowledge of art, music, and literature-particularly the classics. Lura felt emotional too, but she did not shed tears at the funeral.

At the graveyard, people expressed condolences to her. Earl and Lura spoke briefly, but then Matilda and David walked up to Lura. She had dreaded seeing them. Lura noticed the grief on Matilda's face, her tear-stained eyes, and the look of utter tiredness that goes with despondency over losing a close family member unexpectedly.

"My poor Papa. I cannot believe he is gone. I did not get to say goodbye or express my love to him," cried Matilda. David had to help Matilda stand, as she was about to fall to the ground in her grief. Once Matilda seemed a little stronger, David said to Lura, "Lura, I do not think that Tom committed suicide. Tom was always so meticulous in his financial records, and he took immense pride in his genealogical materials as did his father before him and his father before him. A man with this temperament would not do this. He would not leave Matilda with no explanation. You told us you went blind when you saw him lying on the floor. Could it have been an intruder who killed him?"

Lura just stared at David with a puzzled look on her face.

After this, other people came up to Lura and expressed their condolences. Lura looked exhausted. As she started walking toward the car to leave the cemetery, Matilda walked up to Lura again.

"I hope David did not upset you with what he said earlier. My husband can be direct and seem harsh at times. I apologize if he upset you more than you were already upset by the circumstances. You do not have a husband or children. I do not have a mother or a father. You could be a part of my family now that my Papa is gone. Please think this over Lura."

"I will give that some thought, Matilda. Thank you." Lura said formally.

Immediately after the funeral, Earl drove Lura to her house in Wilson to get Sally, and then on to Raeford.

On the ride to Raeford, Lura began thinking about all that had happened. She felt some guilt that it was really her own actions that caused Tom to die. She had been trying to commit suicide. When Tom attempted to stop her from killing herself, they both struggled with the gun, and the gun went off. She was sorry he died, but a portion of her was glad that Tom would no longer be able to criticize her for little inconsequential things. Lura was worried about what David told her at the funeral. He said he did not believe that Tom killed himself. Who did David really believe killed Tom? And if David suspected Lura of killing Tom, maybe the police would decide she was guilty of murder, too.

Lura no longer wanted to kill herself. Too much had happened since her suicide attempt. After all, Agnes had told her (on good authority) that she would live to be over ninety-three-years-old, and she would not be ninety-three for another thirty-eight years. There must be something she was supposed to do for the next thirty-eight years.

CHAPTER 20
First Month After the Funeral
1959

"Lura, you are here, and I am so glad. I am going to take good care of you and pamper you. Josephine is also coming to stay with us," Maggie said welcoming Lura home to Raeford.

Lura was pleased at Maggie's welcome, but Lura knew Maggie's kindness now was due to Tom's tragic and unexpected death. She expected Maggie to revert to her confrontational personality within a week, and she dreaded it.

Over lunch, Maggie told Lura the news of the town. There wasn't much news, except that the neighbor's cat had fifteen kittens, and the roof at their house was leaking profusely when it rained.

After lunch Lura picked up her dear little dog, Sally, and went to her old bedroom to settle into her surroundings and rest. As she sat in her familiar bedroom with Sally in her lap, Lura wondered if the house itself would give her any solace, or just bring back horrible memories of Laurence's disappearance, bitter arguments between her parents, and discord with her siblings. She was worried about her own supply of money. Now she had to pay for Tom's funeral, and she knew that because Tom did not leave a will, a third of his assets would go to Matilda and two thirds would go to her. She decided she would write a letter asking Matilda to relinquish her third of Tom's estate.

When Matilda received the letter from Lura asking her to turn over her inheritance from her father's estate to Lura,

Matilda was furious. Matilda felt Lura was greedy and that she did not deserve Matilda's portion of the estate. Also, Matilda knew the Kennedys were rich, so why should she give her share to Lura?

Lura was indignant that Matilda did not agree to give Lura the money immediately. Matilda's hesitancy made Lura angry at her and made Lura hate Matilda even more than when Tom was alive.

Matilda told Lura she needed time to think over Lura's request. But before Matilda had time to discuss it with her husband, Matilda got a second letter from Lura, making the same request.

She tried to justify why Matilda should give her rightful inheritance to Lura. She said that everything in the bank account had been earned by both Tom and Lura since their marriage, and that Lura had willingly gone without a maid and done her own housework to save money. Lura also pointed out that she had medical bills to pay and that she had no guarantee that she would not have a recurrence of cancer.

The third letter from Lura to Matilda was more insistent and just restated all the reasons Matilda should give Lura Matilda's share of the inheritance. This third letter made Matilda decide to turn her inheritance over to Lura, because Matilda believed Lura would ask Matilda for her inheritance over a hundred times if that's what it took to get Matilda to agree.

Lura had horrible dreams every night for a month. Four of the worst dreams were about Laurence disappearing when he was a baby, Tom's death, seeing Stuart Davis' body falling from the top of the Cherry Hotel, and Agnes committing suicide.

While in Raeford, Lura received a letter from the Chief of Police in Wilson. Just holding this official letter in her hand made Lura begin to cry. She let the letter sit on her desk for two hours before she opened it. Unable to wait any longer, she ripped open the letter. The police chief said as soon as she returned to Wilson, she was to call him on the telephone, and then come to the police station the next day to answer questions. All during the rest of her visit, she often thought of having to go to the police station, and how she dreaded it!

The next week, Lura's four brothers came for a visit and were exceedingly kind and attentive. Louis, the pharmacist, brought Lura medicine to calm her nerves and help her sleep.

After Lura had been in Raeford for two weeks, there was a knock at the door. Lura was astounded to see Wanda at the door. As soon as Lura saw her, she thought to herself, *this is surely Laurence's murderer. If only I had proof.* She entered with a sad looking red geranium plant in her arms. Both Wanda and Lura looked extremely uncomfortable to be in each other's presence. This was the first time Lura had seen Wanda since Lura moved to Wilson, and Lura was shocked at how much Wanda had aged. She now had gray hair and large dark circles under her eyes. Neither Wanda nor Lura wanted to see each other, but Wanda had come to express condolences for the sake of propriety. She placed the geranium on the table.

"Lura, I know you always liked geraniums, so I brought this. How are you?" she said with little to no emotion.

"I guess you could say I am doing okay under the circumstances," said Lura in a slightly sassy voice.

Then there was dead silence in the room. Lura's sister Maggie in an uncharacteristic manner tried to calm the atmosphere by chiming in.

"Did you hear that the musical, *Gypsy,* opened on Broadway last month? Lura and I like musicals a lot. Don't you?" said Maggie.

Again, dead silence in the room. No one uttered a word. Maggie tried again with another topic that was more familiar to both ladies.

"Wanda, did you see last night's television show-the *Wonderful World of Disney*? Lura and I watched it and just loved it. We have been looking at a lot of television since Lura came. Some of my favorite shows are *Leave it to Beaver* and *Father Knows Best*," said Maggie.

"I like all of those shows, too," said Wanda.

All this time, Lura wanted to somehow give Wanda a message that she knew that Laurence was dead. Lura felt she had it on good authority that he was dead because Agnes said he was dead. Agnes had not told her that Wanda caused his death, but Lura believed this with all her heart. Just then Lura had an idea.

"You know, Tom and I used to enjoy going to the movies better than watching television. I just love some of these thrillers. Have you seen them?" asked Lura.

"I'm not much into thrillers, Lura," said Wanda.

"Too bad. You should check out these three movies, *Anatomy of a Murder* with Jimmie Stewart, *A Bucket of Blood,* and *The Headless Ghost*. You can learn a lot about how to commit a murder from these movies."

Wanda's face turned red, she squirmed in her chair, and she began to tremble slightly. This made Lura smile and say in her mind's eye,

Wanda, I think you DID kill Laurence and now I am making you feel nervous about it.

Wanda stood up abruptly and said she had to run. She walked out the front door slamming the door behind her.

"Good riddance," said Lura.

Just then the front door opened again and Lura thought, *Please God, don't let it be Wanda.*

It was not Wanda, but Josephine, Lura's older sister, carrying a huge box in her hands.

"Hi Lura. I am here to take care of you and try to make you feel better. I took off time from my teaching job in Virginia just to help you. Look what I brought for us three sisters to eat," said Josephine.

She unpacked the box revealing tasty homemade sweets, apple butter, molasses, crackers, an assortment of cheeses, and homemade sweet pickles. The last item she removed from the box was an African Violet plant for Lura.

"If tasty food can make you feel less sad, then let's eat," said Lura.

The three sisters made a feast of Josephine's gifts.

That night after Maggie went to bed, Josephine came to Lura's room to talk. They talked about good times in Quewhiffle as children, Laurence's disappearance, being widows, and Maggie.

Then Josephine mentioned a topic she had been wanting to discuss for a long time.

"Lura, I know it is too early for us to retire now and we both still have jobs, but when we do retire, I want us to come here to this house and live together. Lura, we could be so happy," she said.

"I am fifty-six now, so I still have several years to work. You are older so you can retire earlier. Josephine, you are forgetting one huge obstacle to us living happily in this house and that obstacle is our sister, Maggie. You know how moody and judgmental she is. She is only being nice to me now because of

Tom's recent death. Josephine, why do you think she is so mean and so much like Mama in personality?"

"Maggie is jealous of people who are happy or who are married. Both you and I were married and so she is particularly jealous of us." Josephine paused then continued. "Mama told Maggie that she and Papa expected her to remain unmarried and stay here at the house and take care of them. Maggie did just that. I must admit that was benevolent of her. Maggie does not have a retirement income since she never had a job. She is bitter about her choice to stay at home and take care of our parents."

CHAPTER 21
Wilson and Raeford
1959-1978

After spending the first month of her widowhood in Raeford, Lura returned to Wilson. The first night back, Albert A. Privette, the Wilson Chief of Police, knocked on her front door. He was a short older man with a thick neck, and he smelled of cigarette smoke. His mannerisms were polite but businesslike.

"How are you Mrs. Davis? I sent you a letter, and I thought you were going to call me," he said.

"I have been too heartbroken to talk on the phone, but we can talk now," she said.

She offered him a seat on the sofa, and she took the easy chair facing him. They sat in silence for a moment.

"Let's get to the matter at hand," said the police chief awkwardly.

"Who owned the gun that killed your husband?"

"My husband owned the gun," she replied timidly.

"Is there mental instability in your husband's family?" he asked.

"Well, his brother Stuart committed suicide by jumping from the top of the Cherry Hotel a few years ago," Lura replied, relieved to be talking about something other than how Tom died.

"Was your marriage a happy one, and did your husband have any reason to kill himself?"

"We were only married eight years, but it was a happy marriage, even if we had challenges. The fact that I had two surgeries for cancer was depressing for both of us. Still, that is no reason to commit suicide," replied Lura quietly.

"You did have gun powder on your hands, but that is expected since your hands were also on the gun. We know that you were both holding the gun when the gun went off. You were attempting to stop your husband from pulling the trigger."

There was a pause in the conversation, and finally he cleared his throat.

"Unless you have anything else you can tell me, you have answered all my questions."

"I don't, sir," said Lura.

"That will be all for today. Thank you, Mrs. Davis."

Lura showed the Police Chief out the door hoping that would close the case.

She did not sleep one wink that night. She kept reliving the scene when Tom died. She got out of bed and walked around the house, but everything reminded her of the excruciating chain of events when Tom died. During the long sleepless night, she decided she could no longer live in this house. She needed a fresh start.

Early the next morning she checked the newspaper for apartments for rent. She saw an advertisement for an apartment on Vance Street in the Anderson Apartment complex. She grabbed her pocketbook and walked over to the apartment. The landlord gave her a tour of the spacious apartment with large windows and abundant sunshine inside. Lura rented it on the spot.

Lura hired Earl and his brother to move her furniture from her old house to her new apartment, and they arrived two days later. Lura had a happy visit with the two men and caught up on Raeford gossip. Afterwards, Lura gave them a guided tour of Wilson in the Packard.

When Lura settled into her new apartment, she decided she liked it much better than the house where she and Tom had lived. This apartment contained no bad memories.

Lura telephoned Mr. Quinn, her employer, and told him she was ready to come back to work. She resumed her old job the next day, and her boss was happy to have her back. He told her to select some new furniture and accessories from the store at an 80% discount and to make her home as comfortable as possible. Lura was grateful, as she wanted to get rid of Tom's desk in the living room, and other pieces of furniture that reminded her of that most horrible day. This transformation of Lura's living situation made her feel better and more like her old self.

Lura and her sister-in-law, Fanny Davis, saw each other frequently. They had a lot in common as both were women who worked outside the home and they were widows of two brothers.

Fanny came over to Lura's apartment at least once a week, and Lura did the same. Lura usually did not seek out friends, but Fanny was special to Lura. She was humble, affectionate, kind, and generous, even though she had little money.

Fanny loved dogs, particularly Sally. She would bring her small brown dog Charlie over to Lura's house to play with Sally. It made Fanny and Lura laugh to watch their canine shenanigans. Charlie was a talented and perceptive little dog, which was particularly helpful to Fanny because she was beginning to lose her eyesight. Her little dog watched Fanny and was always there to help her. If she dropped a towel on the floor, he would pick it up and give it to her. Fanny could also ask Charlie to bring her things like her glasses case, the newspaper, or her umbrella. Charlie would obey instantly. Lura and Fanny often talked about the bond they shared with their dogs. Both admitted they talked to their pets and thought the pets really understood what they said.

Lura was glad to be back in her routine work at Quinn's. She still missed Tom dreadfully, but she managed to be okay with only her little dog Sally.

To her surprise, her older sister, Josephine, began sending Lura letters regularly. Some of the letters again suggested that when Lura and Josephine retired, they should move into the old homeplace in Raeford.

Josephine's most recent letter read:

"Lura, you have been a good sister to me. When we were younger, we were not close, but now as older adult women, we are close, and I want us to grow closer as we get older. I really do love you. How I wish we were together now. I've thought of you constantly. You know I have always tried to live right and do the honorable thing."

Lura contemplated Josephine's suggestions.

Lura also received a letter from Tom's daughter Matilda suggesting that Lura spend the upcoming holiday with Matilda's family. Lura smiled and put the letter in a safe place and thought, that's not going to happen. She had no intention of spending Easter or any other holiday with Matilda's family, and she had no plan to reply to Matilda's letter.

Lura received a second invitation for the Easter holiday, this time from her oldest sister Maggie. She asked Lura and Josephine to come to Raeford for Easter in 1960. Lura accepted this invitation because she felt an obligation to visit.

A week later, Lura arrived at the Raeford train station, and dependable Earl met her. They were glad to see each other and talked easily. As he drove Lura in her Papa's huge old Packard sedan, Lura thought, I cannot recall a time that Earl was not in my life.

"Miss Lura, I know that you knew Miss Agnes and I were close friends years ago. You were standing beside me at Agnes' funeral when her mother reached out to me in kindness and said she appreciated my friendship to Agnes."

Lura replied, "Agnes confided in me about that when we were both in college at Brenau. It's too bad that you two did not end up together, and I am sure it was societal expectations that prevented this from happening. Agnes told me how much she cared for you. Did you realize that she was trying to protect you from any negative consequences from society by not being your girlfriend?"

"I did know that," Earl said sadly.

They were both silent for a while.

As Earl drove the old Packard slowly up the circular driveway, he said, "Miss Lura, this old house needs some tender loving care. It needs paint, yardwork, and a new roof."

"I know it needs repairs. We are just trying to find enough money to pay for the most essential things first," Lura replied.

Earl took Lura's luggage into the house and they were greeted by sisters Maggie and Josephine.

"Miss Lura, do you want me to take your luggage to your room?" asked Earl.

"Yes, please, I am plumb tuckered out," answered Lura.

Lura and her two sisters followed Earl upstairs to Lura's old room. It had not changed at all. The expansive room had a big four poster bed with a canopy, several tables, and a sofa and two side chairs in faded colors of blue and yellow fabric. Maggie plopped down on the sofa. "Those steps will give me a heart attack one day."

Lura sat down at the other end of the sofa and propped her tired feet on the huge ottoman in front of the sofa.

"Lura, would you like me to unpack your suitcase for you?" asked Josephine.

Lura looking exhausted said, "That would be great. I just do not have the energy to move."

The three ladies chatted about local gossip in Raeford. Josephine began unpacking Lura's clothes, putting some on hangers and some in the chest of drawers. She saw a beautiful yellow suit and matching flowered hat.

"This is the prettiest Easter outfit I have ever seen, Lura! Where on earth did you get it?" asked Josephine.

"Tom's sister-in-law, Fanny Davis, used to work at Barshay's Dress Shop in Wilson. When wonderful clothes in my size went on sale, she would put the items away for me and I would come in and buy the outfits. She selected this for me. It is too bad her poor eyesight has caused her to quit her job."

"My new Easter outfit is lime green, but not nearly as beautiful as yours," said Josephine.

Maggie watched and listened to all the discussion of beautiful Easter clothes, and she felt her blood pressure rise. She walked over to Josephine and yanked Lura's new yellow dress and yellow hat out of Josephine's hands. She put the dress against her own chest, so it looked like she wore it; then she propped the yellow hat on her head at an unattractive angle. She took exaggerated long steps around the huge bedroom with the dress against her chest, and the hat on her head at a crooked angle, as she dramatically shouted in ever-increasing decibels.

"Look at Maggie, look at Maggie, the poor old lady who cannot afford a new Easter outfit like her sisters. Don't you two feel guilty that I was the one who had to stay home and take care of Mama and Papa when you were able to get married, have careers, and earn money? You two can buy any Easter outfits you DAMN well please. Well, you should feel guilty. I am mad as hell about it!"

With that, Maggie threw the hat and dress on the floor, and walked briskly out the bedroom, slamming the door behind her.

Lura and Josephine just stared at each other and shook their heads back and forth in dismay. Josephine looked at her watch. "Exactly thirty-eight minutes after you arrived Maggie had a hissy fit. I like to time her outbursts. She is as mad as a cat with tin cans tied to its tale."

"Why did I come here for rest and relaxation, knowing Maggie would be here? I must be a fool," said Lura.

"As Maggie gets older, she is more and more meanspirited, just like Mama," said Josephine.

This sort of a confrontation accompanied each visit Lura, and Josephine made to Raeford. In addition to Maggie's hateful demeanor, another reason Lura and Josephine did not come to Raeford as often as they could was that the house was in bad shape. Neglect and the elements had taken their toll on the house. Rain, heat, humidity, and ice caused significant deterioration. Maggie had no money to pay for house maintenance. Lura, Josephine, and their brothers made financial contributions periodically for house repairs, but their money paid for less than half of what was really needed for restoration.

Lura stayed in Raeford a few more days. Maggie was pleasant some days and hateful other days. On the Saturday before Easter, Josephine and Lura took Maggie to Lucy's Boutique and bought her a new pink Easter outfit with a matching pink floral hat in various hues of pink. Maggie was ecstatic about her new Easter outfit.

The three old Kennedy sisters looked the epitome of spring at Easter services at the Presbyterian church. Lura in yellow, Josephine in lime green, and Maggie in pink looked like a pretty bouquet of flowers. Each wore shoes and a hat to match the color of her outfit. The ladies also wore white gloves and carried their spring pocketbooks. Some of the townspeople whispered about the secrets the sisters held in that old house.

After this Easter visit, Lura and Josephine continued to come to Raeford, but usually only once a year. The house continued to deteriorate each year. By 1965, the house had no hot water, no heat, no working oven, and a roof that leaked profusely. Lura's one consolation about the house was that her mother who had died in 1954 was not living in this decrepit old house now. Lura and Josephine did not know how Maggie managed to live there alone year-round.

The once rich Kennedys had spent most of the money they received for their land at Quewhiffle, and much of the money Jackson made in Sylacauga. They squandered their fortune on poor investments, new cars, and beautiful clothes, although spending money on beautiful clothes was strange because they did not go anywhere to wear the fancy clothes.

From time to time, Matilda continued to write letters to Lura asking her to come for a visit. Lura never responded. Matilda knew Lura still had Tom's family bible, almost all her own baby pictures, and the extensive Davis family genealogy records. Matilda wrote to Lura and requested these items, but Lura received the letter and as with all the others, she put it aside. She took this letter with her on her next visit to Raeford to see Maggie and Josephine, and read it to them at dinner.

"Lura, maybe you should give Matilda some of the things she is asking for," said Josephine.

Lura's face turned to an ugly shade of red, and a stubborn look appeared on her face.

"I have decided that Matilda does not deserve Tom's belongings. Those belongings should rightfully be mine because I am his widow. Matilda was Tom's daughter, not his wife. Matilda abandoned him when she went off and got married to David without asking for Tom's permission. No! She will not get anything of Tom's as long as I am living. That's the end of it!" said Lura passionately.

When Lura went to bed that night in the Raeford house, she realized that anger was a major attribute of her own personality, as well as the personalities of her sisters and brothers. She believed that the anger came from being emotionally damaged by her mixed-up family.

In Lura's day-to-day life in Wilson, she could hide her resentment of her family because she did not see them often. But every time Lura came to Raeford, Maggie's behavior reminded her of how their family life was shattered. It seemed the siblings remained in touch with each other only out of duty.

In the summer of 1967, Lura's beloved dog began to behave differently, and she quit eating. Lura had begun the practice of letting Sally sleep with her after Tom's death. Sally would snuggle up to Lura's abdomen with her four feet facing the side of the bed. One morning when Lura woke up early, she noticed Sally was not in her usual place, but near the foot of the bed. Lura reached out and put her hand on Sally's back so she could tell if she was breathing. The little dog was cold to the touch and there was no breath and no heartbeat. Lura pulled Sally's cold and lifeless body into her lap and held her for a long time. Lura told Sally how much she meant to her, as she stroked Sally's back and rubbed her head. Sally had been with Lura through thick and thin and Lura was absolutely devoted to Sally. Lura sat there in her bed holding her precious Sally and crying tears that wet Sally's beautiful blond coat. It took several days for Lura to stop constantly thinking about Sally. After Sally's death,

Josephine sent Lura more letters than before, and she also sent small gifts from time to time. Josephine was trying to help Lura feel better.

Sometimes Lura questioned Josephine's plan for the two of them to go back to Raeford and live together in their parents' old house after retirement. Both sisters had some bad memories there at this house; however, Josephine and Lura finally decided to move to the old Raeford homeplace after they retired. Their plan was to travel most of the time and use the homeplace as a place to stay between trips. This method would be much cheaper than renting a place for the two of them to live, and then also paying for hotels when they traveled. One hurdle they knew they must overcome would be to have money to pay for needed repairs on the house. Both sisters also worried about the difficulty of living with Maggie

On September 18, 1973, Lura received an early morning phone call from Josephine. This alarmed Lura because she and Josephine communicated by letter, and almost never by telephone.

"Lura, please sit down," said Josephine.

"I just sat down, what is happening?" asked Lura.

"Maggie died last night. Earl went over to the house at about 8 a.m. to do some work and he found her. Earl said she was still in bed and appeared to have died in her sleep. He said she looked peaceful."

"Oh Josephine, we have waited for this time to be able to move into the house without Maggie. But now that the time has come, I am heartbroken that she died. I am particularly unhappy that I seldom had a good relationship with my sister. I feel like this even though I was the one who tried to keep the peace and she was the one who lashed out at me. I feel wretched about everything," said Lura.

"I agree with you dear Lura. I feel overwhelmed about her, too. We need to begin planning her funeral. Can you meet me at the Raeford house this afternoon?"

Maggie's funeral was much better attended than was her mother's. Maggie did have some friends in Raeford who loved her, and for that Lura was grateful.

After the funeral, Duncan McMillan, the family lawyer met with Lura, Josephine, and their brothers. The lawyer read Maggie's Will. She left the house and most of its contents to Lura and Josephine. Even though Lura and Josephine expected to inherit the house, they were deeply grateful that Maggie willed the house to them. Maggie left several specific items of furniture and personal belongings to her brothers, nieces, and nephews.

In the four days following the funeral, Lura and Josephine got cost estimates for house and appliance repairs or replacements. Over supper one night at the Raeford house, the sisters talked about Maggie.

"Lura, it was unfair that Maggie did not receive money for taking care of our parents in their old age. If our parents had been better money managers, they should have set up a trust for Maggie's living expenses, and for the upkeep on the house. But Mama and Papa never did this, and neither did you nor I, nor our brothers," said Josephine.

"I also believe we should have met as a group to decide how to provide for Maggie and how to take care of the house. Of course, all of us had such little money that it was hard to be that generous," said Lura.

The two sisters calculated a schedule for the repairs, and then planned to move to Raeford a few weeks after the repairs were due to be completed. Lura and Josephine went back to their jobs, gave notice of their upcoming retirement dates to their supervisors, and kept working at their jobs until all was ready for their move to Raeford.

Lura and Josephine retired and moved to Raeford in December 1973. To Lura it seemed strange to live in this old house again. So much had happened in her life. Lura chose the largest upstairs bedroom and the adjacent sitting room as her personal space. She furnished this space with her own furniture and accessories from her Wilson apartment. One thing that struck Lura when she moved from her modest apartment in Wilson back to this house was the abundant space in every room. Lura thought that it was a pity she did not have the money to fix up this old house using all she had learned over the years as an interior decorator.

After Lura and Josephine moved to Raeford, they lived a simple life. Faithful Earl came over to do small handyman jobs for the sisters every week. He also served as their chauffeur by driving them to the grocery store, to the beauty parlor, and to the Presbyterian church in their Papa's old Packard. The sisters always wore hats and gloves to church, even though hats and gloves were no longer fashionable. Sadly, the plans the sisters had made to travel extensively did not come to fruition. They only made a few trips to the beach and to Richmond, and then due to the cost of travel and their own declining energy levels, they stayed at home.

Long before they moved back to Raeford, Lura and Josephine decided that they wanted almost no visitors in their home once they moved to Raeford. They were continuing their mother's strange isolation rules, even though there was no reason for this to occur. Of course, they allowed Earl to come and go as he pleased, and many of his visits included payment for services rendered.

Lura and Josephine got along great the first several years they lived together. They had so much in common; being sisters, being widows, and having experienced heartache from childhood.

191

Lura loved to sit in her favorite cushioned rocking chair on the expansive back porch of the house. In one hand she held a tall glass of wine and in the other hand she held her favorite current novel. She liked to position the rocking chair so that the sun shone on her back and legs. This was heaven to her.

Josephine liked the same thing on the sun porch, but she would choose a beer rather than a tall glass of wine and her book would be about travel in China, which was something she hoped to do before she died.

When Lura first returned to Raeford, several former friends and acquaintances called her on the telephone to welcome her back to Raeford. They invited her to their homes. There were only a few friends that Lura wanted to see, and to those she suggested they meet at a restaurant. Once she got to see these friends, to find out how they looked in their old age, or to learn the facts of their lives, she never contacted them again. Lura and Josephine were satisfied to have Earl be their only visitor.

CHAPTER 22
Lura's Nephew
1979

In early Spring 1979, Lura received a letter from Jeremiah Murry Green of Virginia. Lura had never heard of this person and was curious as to why he was writing to her. She opened the envelope and read that he claimed to be the illegitimate son of Lura's brother, Louis. He asked for a photograph of his father. In the letter he said that he knew his father was dead now, but in 1977, he came to Raeford with the purpose of finding his father. He knew that Lura lived in the Kennedy homeplace, and his plan was to go there to ask how to locate his father. But when he was only two blocks away from the Kennedy homeplace, he became too afraid to proceed. He feared being treated poorly by his father or other relatives, so he left Raeford and went back to his family in Virginia.

Inside the letter, Lura carefully examined a picture of Jeremiah. Lura believed that he was the son of Louis because the two men looked so similar.

Lura held the letter in her hand as she walked to the sunporch to find Josephine who was reading another book on China.

"Did you know that Louis had an illegitimate son named Jeremiah Murry Green? asked Lura.

"That seems as likely as that our three cats are out chasing elephants," snorted Josephine.

Lura handed Josephine the photograph of Jeremiah and his letter. Josephine read the letter and studied the photograph intently for several minutes without saying anything.

Finally, she said, "Lura, those brown eyes of Jeremiah look exactly like Louis' brown eyes. I think he is telling the truth. We should welcome him with open arms."

Lura hesitated, and slowly tears gathered in her old eyes as she said, "Our poor family cannot stand one more scandal. We must ignore this letter. If we communicate with this young man, I think I will explode from too many horrible things happening."

So, Lura folded the letter and put it away.

CHAPTER 23

Laurence's Fate

1979

Lura often thought about her niece, Olivia Kennedy Montgomery, daughter of Lura's favorite brother, Laurence. Usually, Lura did not make long distance calls, but Agnes had visited Lura last night and told her it was important to call Olivia. It had been a long time since Lura and Olivia had spoken.

Lura dialed Olivia's number and after a few rings, a voice answered.

"Hello," said Olivia.

"Olivia, it's Aunt Lura. How are you?" said Lura.

Olivia gasped, "I can't believe this is happening. Aunt Lura, I was just contemplating calling you, but dreading how you would react to my news."

"Whatever it is, just tell me, Olivia."

"Okay. Do you remember me having those horrible headaches and visions of violence as a child? I know you do because when I spent the night at your house, you would comfort me when I woke up from a nightmare. Well, over the years those visions have gotten so much worse.

"It all started when my Papa disappeared when I was ten-years-old. About six months ago I could no longer stand it anymore, and I went to see a psychiatrist. He suspected I had witnessed something violent in my childhood and that I was repressing what I witnessed.

195

"He put me under hypnosis to try to uncover what had happened to me. He did several sessions of hypnosis, and finally asked my permission to videotape the next hypnosis sessions so I could watch them. I gave permission." Olivia paused then continued.

"What I saw when I watched myself under hypnosis frightened me to death. Do you really want to hear this Aunt Lura? It's about your dear Laurence and what happened to him, and it is gory, so I warn you ahead of time."

There was silence then Lura said slowly and quietly, "Of course, do continue Olivia." To take away some of the pain of shocking news about Laurence, Lura dug her nails into her arm until she drew blood.

"During the first hypnosis session, the psychiatrist asked me if I recalled anything unusual during the time my father 'disappeared.' Aunt Lura, here are my very words I said under hypnosis. I know I said these things because I wrote them down word for word. I said,

I remember seeing Papa's bloodstained body lying on the floor. He had no clothes on, except a bloodstained rag was covering his groin. I laid down next to him to see if he was breathing. He was not breathing and his body was ice cold.

Olivia stopped before continuing.

"At a later hypnosis session, the psychiatrist asked me if I had seen any further evidence of what happened to my father in the days after his disappearance."

At this point Olivia began to cry. She needed reassurance from her aunt that she really wanted to know everything. Once again Olivia asked Lura if she wanted her to continue, and once more Lura said yes.

Olivia continued with her story. "I remember seeing bloody pots and pans in the kitchen sink. I remember seeing a huge box in the back of Uncle James's truck. I remember hearing Mother and Uncle James talking and dragging that box across our yard to the outhouse. The psychiatrist asked me 'Why didn't you report all of this to the police?' I replied that if I had told the police what happened, and they did not believe me, then the police would take me to my mother." She paused before continuing.

"Every few months from the time my Papa 'disappeared' until I left home to go to college, Mama would say to me, 'Olivia, do you remember anything about the time your Papa disappeared?' Whenever she asked me this, I would say, 'All I remember is that he left and never came back.' I knew that as long as I lived with my mother, that was the only answer I could give and remain safe. I was afraid if I told the truth that she would harm me, or even kill me like she killed my Papa."

Lura listened intently, with her anger boiling up.

"After the hypnosis session was over, the psychiatrist said to me, 'I think you need to contact the FBI and the Hoke County Sheriff and tell them what you told me. As you requested, I made videotapes of what you said under hypnosis, so you have those tapes as detailed accounts of what happened.'"

"So, what did you do, Olivia?"

"Aunt Lura, I did what my psychiatrist suggested. I traveled to Raeford last month and met with the local police, and afterwards with the FBI in Hoke County. They viewed the videotapes of my hypnosis, and just two days ago they reopened my poor Daddy's missing person's case. They made plans to excavate Mama's property. They asked me not to tell a living soul about this because someone could move Papa's bones to a new location to protect Mama. I went by to visit you and Josephine, but you were not at home and Earl said you two had gone to Wrightsville Beach for a couple of days. I made Earl promise not to tell you or anyone else I was in town."

Lura shocked Olivia by saying, "Olivia, no matter how much I would hate being present when dear Laurence's body is unearthed, I MUST be there when his remains are uncovered. I dread it, but I owe that to my dear brother. Promise me that you will take me with you when his body is exhumed."

"I understand, Aunt Lura, and I promise. I am coming to Raeford again in a few days. I will call you before to let you know when it will happen."

After Lura hung up the phone, she vomited until she could only throw up bile. The bitter taste in her mouth helped to distract her from the reality of what she had just learned. After the vomiting stopped, Lura took her favorite framed picture of Laurence off the mantle and put it against her chest and gently rocked the picture back and forth as she moaned Laurence's name repeatedly. In her wildest imagination, Lura could not have guessed that this was the true fate of her dear Laurence. Her only consolation was that years ago, Agnes promised her that Laurence was with Agnes in heaven, and that both were at peace.

While shedding tears, Lura told Josephine the news that Wanda had killed Laurence. The two old ladies were in shock. They cried in each other's arms.

There was something else that worried Lura about the news of Laurence's death. Lura knew there would be massive publicity once these facts were widely known. News travels fast in small towns.

Olivia did not tell her mother that her father's missing persons case was being reopened, and that her yard was going to be excavated to locate her father's bones.

Wanda learned this life shattering information from a close friend at the police department. Wanda began preparations for the excavation. She finished wrapping the Christmas gifts for her daughter and grandchildren and placed them in the backseat of her car. She took out the ingredients to make chocolate chip cookies and lemonade and put them on the kitchen counter. She stood on a stepstool to reach the best crystal and china to use when serving the refreshments, and she wrote a note.

Three days later, Olivia called her aunt again. "Aunt Lura, do you still want to be with me when my Papa is unearthed?"

"Yes, I do," Lura replied.

"I will pick you up at 7 a.m. tomorrow morning."

"I'll be ready," Lura replied faintly.

When they arrived at the farm, they saw a backhoe, five police cars, and FBI vehicles in the yard. Lura saw a group of men standing around. They were the coroner, the Hoke County Sheriff, two deputy sheriffs, and others she did not know.

Once Olivia and Lura got out of the car, a nice policeman spoke to Olivia, "Can you walk with us to show us where the privy used to be?"

Olivia and Lura walked across the large yard holding hands. Seventy-six-year-old Lura looked frail but determined to be there. Olivia pointed to a piece of land about ten feet square, and slightly sunk into the earth. "It was here," she pointed.

Olivia and Lura stood beside the former site of the privy for a long time, watching the backhoe remove a thin layer of soil, and then the soil was put in a sifter that allowed bits of soil to fall through, but kept everything solid. The forensic scientists and the coroner examined what remained in the sifter after the soil dropped away. After about an hour, one policewoman brought two chairs so Olivia and Lura could sit down.

Soon the excavation crew and others who gathered for this gory task began smelling the alluring aroma of chocolate chip cookies, and the smell came from the direction of Wanda's house.

To Lura's absolute amazement, Lura saw Wanda walk out of her house toward the former privy.

"What in the world is she doing?" Lura whispered incredulously.

Wearing a stylish dress, Wanda served warm chocolate chip cookies on fine china dessert plates and poured lemonade into tall crystal goblets. She played the role of a gracious southern hostess and displayed generosity, politeness, and kindness to everyone present. Everyone except Lura enjoyed the delicious cookies and chilled lemonade. When Wanda extended a glass of lemonade towards Lura, Lura looked at Wanda with intense hate, then turned her head away in disgust.

In Wanda's outward appearance and mannerisms, she seemed calm and peaceful and perfectly at ease. Conversely, on the inside, Wanda was falling apart because she knew life would change forever that day.

When one of the workmen said they should begin recovering bones in about thirty minutes, Wanda placed the pitcher of lemonade and the cookies on an outside table, and then without anyone noticing, went back in the house through the back door.

She proceeded out the front door, walked to her car, opened the door, got inside, and drove to the edge of her farm. She parked her car, sat still for a few minutes before turning the motor off.

Wanda thought, *I am glad James died before any of this came out. I was the one who talked him into killing Laurence, so it was not really his fault what happened to Laurence.*

She saw that the ribbon on one of her Christmas gifts for Olivia was crooked, so she adjusted it. Then she opened her purse and took out a note she had written a few days ago which read,

My brother James and I killed Laurence because he was having an affair and he had threatened to leave me. I am sorry.

Wanda Kennedy

Then Wanda ended her life with a pearl handled .32-caliber pistol. No one heard the gun shot and Wanda was not discovered until the next day.

Back at the excavation site, the police officer that was sifting the soil paused. He said, "Here is the first bone. I can see it has been hacked in several places as if someone used an ax."

He put the bone in a sifter and placed it closer to Olivia and Lura so they could get a better view of the dirt covered bone.

As quick as a frog can grab an insect with his tongue, Lura grabbed Laurence's soil covered bone in her hand and held it tightly. She held the bone to her chest with both hands and rocked her body back and forth.

Lura whispered repeatedly, "Laurence, Laurence."

Even though it was against police protocol for anyone other than police officials or FBI to touch human remains, everyone present allowed Lura her grief and did not rush her. Lura did this for several minutes and the people present bowed their heads and did not utter a word. Their behavior was a token of respect to both Lura and Laurence. The only sounds anyone heard were Lura's voice pitifully saying "Laurence" and the beautiful bird song of two nearby robins.

Finally, Olivia gently touched Lura's shoulder.

"Aunt Lura, we have to give this back to the police so they can continue their investigation for Papa's sake."

Olivia was thankful that the police officer allowed her aunt to handle the evidence and did not snatch it from her.

After Lura gave the bone back to the police officer, the work of the excavation sped up. Soon bone after bone was unearthed and gently put in a special box just for this purpose. The policemen and the coroner said they thought they found all the bones other than the skull. They dug a while longer for the skull, but it was not in this location. The only person who knew the location of the skull was no longer living.

Once the excavation was completed, Olivia and Lura got in the car, and Olivia drove Lura home.

"Aunt Lura, you are a very brave woman, and you were a devoted friend and a loving sister to my Papa all his life."

No matter how much Lura anticipated the publicity, it was more than she ever imagined. Reporters swarmed the town and knocked on Lura's door repeatedly. Of course, Lura kept the curtains drawn and did not answer the door. It was all too much, and it made Lura physically sick.

One morning when the publicity was the most intense, Lura said to Josephine, "Oh My God! How our family has suffered over the years, and how the good name of our family has been ground into the dirt. To me it has been important to be somebody and to have high standards, but how can we possibly overcome all we have had to bear?"

A funeral for Laurence was held a few weeks after his bones were unearthed and released to the Kennedy family for burial. Lura attended as did her entire family. At the end of the funeral, a women walked up to Lura. "My name is Meg McGinnis, and I have some things to tell you about your brother. Here is my phone number and address. Will you call me?"

Lura was surprised and she vaguely recalled that there was a Meg that had been a worker on Laurence and Wanda's farm.

"I will call you when I get home in an hour."

After she arrived home, Lura dialed the number Meg had given her.

"Thanks for calling me Mrs. Davis. Can you come to my house now? I have much to tell you."

Lura hung up the telephone and picked it up again and dialed Earl's number. Luckily, Earl answered the phone.

Lura said, "Earl, I really need your help. Can you come now and drive me out into the country? I have some important business to conduct. I may be there for a few hours."

Earl sensed that Lura's request was tremendously important to her. "I will be there in five minutes," he said.

Earl drove Lura to Meg's house, accompanied her to the front door, and then returned to the car to wait.

Lura's legs trembled, and her heart felt heavy as she knocked on Meg's door. Lura did not know if Meg would try to harm her. Meg slowly opened the door and gestured for Lura to come in and sit down.

"I have information on exactly what happened to your Laurence. I know you loved him. He was always truly kind to me, and even continued to let me live on the farm when I was too sick to work. If you want, I will tell you what I know about your brother and his death, but I must warn you, some of it is gory."

Lura swallowed and said in a whisper, "I want to know everything."

Meg began. "Four days after Wanda reported Laurence missing, I was rocking on the front porch of this very house at twilight, enjoying watching the lightning bugs in the shrubs. It was a pleasant, peaceful evening. I saw my dog, Champ, approach the house with something big hanging from his mouth. Champ often brought me dead birds, or small rodents and he was plenty proud to give his prizes to me. But what he had in his mouth this time did not look like a dead rodent. He walked up on the porch and placed the thing about a yard from my feet. I could see it was the size of a big cantaloupe, and it smelled like rotten meat. I was getting alarmed. There was blond curly hair on it, and the thing was leaking pink liquid onto my porch. I could not identify what type of animal this was."

Meg paused, caught her breath, then continued.

"Usually I praise Champ when he brings me a 'prize.' Because Champ wanted my praise and had not received it yet, he used his nose to push his 'prize' closer to me. His movement caused the object to spin around. Then I could plainly see what it was, and what I saw almost made me have a heart attack. Your dear Laurence's eyes were looking directly at me, and I was shocked beyond belief that Champ had brought me Laurence's severed head."

Meg paused because Mrs. Davis looked like she was going to faint.

She said, "Oh Mrs. Davis, you look white as a sheet. Do you want me to get you something to drink, some nice pink lemonade, or a cold compress? I know this is so hard to hear. I thought it might bring you some closure. You still have the option of not hearing all of this."

"Just some water please. You are right, I am feeling faint, but I want to know everything I can about my Laurence. We were as close as brothers and sisters could be, and the day he went missing was the worst day in my life."

Meg gave Lura a glass of water and she drank it.

"Please, go on with the story," Lura said.

"You can understand that I needed to get as far away from that head as I could. But even though I wanted to run, my body was paralyzed with fear, and I could not move or speak. It was a dreadful feeling-to be deathly afraid, and unable to move. I wanted nothing more than to get away from the horrible spectacle.

"Well, after two minutes, I was able to scream and run out into the yard near the road, and I threw up. Poor Champ was trying to be persistent in bringing me the prize, so he lifted the head again to bring it to me. I screamed at him to drop it. Champ dropped it, then he came out in the yard and sat by me looking puzzled. I stayed far away from the front porch for half an hour just shaking and trying to gain enough courage to go back and do something.

"Since I live alone, I am the one who must handle everything. Eventually I went back in the house and got several brown grocery bags and a pair of gloves. I put on the gloves, then put Laurence's head in the first bag, and then put four more bags around the first bag. Then I walked in the house and put the bags containing Laurence's head in my freezer. I did not sleep one wink that night knowing Laurence's head was in my house."

Lura was horrified by this story. She needed some air. She said, "Meg, let me take a break because what I am learning is about to kill me."

Lura stood up slowly but lost her balance and had to sit immediately back down. She tried again and this time succeeded, but on shaky legs. She rejected Meg's offer to help her to stand up. Finally, Lura stood up and opened the front door and breathed in huge breaths of air. She looked like a person dying of thirst who is drinking her first mouthfuls of water. After about ten minutes, she was ready for Meg to continue her narrative.

Lura said, "Please continue."

"Early the next morning, I went over to Wanda's house and told her that I had something to show her, but she had to come to my house to see it. I told Wanda it was about Laurence. As Wanda followed me back to this house, she looked extremely nervous, and she said little. We went inside the house in silence, and we were standing by the freezer. I opened the freezer and took out the bag, and I then took Laurence's head out of the four bags, unfortunately some of the brown paper clung to his frozen head. Because I wanted Laurence to look as respectable as possible, I tried to remove the strips of brown paper that clung frozen to his head. Wanda recognized Laurence's head immediately.

"Wanda screamed, 'Get that thing out of my sight! Put it back in the freezer.' Then she started hyperventilating, and her eyes were pleading. I did as she said, and she calmed down a bit and was just crying quietly. Wanda wanted to talk so we sat down, and I let her speak. This is what she said to me."

"'Meg, you are already involved with what happened to Laurence, so I want you to know the whole story. Laurence had been running around with another woman and wanted a divorce from me. He told me about this horrible news in such a matter-of-fact manner that it infuriated me. I was so angry. I went to the home of my brother, James, and told him the horrible news. I also solicited James' help in the remedy that I had in mind. Finally, James drove me back to my house, and I went inside. I was no longer crying because I had decided on my course of action for the next day. I gave Laurence one more chance to do the honorable thing and give up the woman. He said no, he would not change his plans to divorce me. So, James and I killed Laurence, dismembered his body, and threw his body in the outhouse.'"

"At the end of Wanda's story, I asked her what she wanted to do with Laurence's head. She said that she would take it home and decide later."

"I said to Wanda, 'You are a good God-fearing woman who teaches Sunday school, a great mother to Olivia, and you have worked hard all your life. If your story got out and you went to jail, that would not help the situation. It would make Olivia an orphan. What is past is past and we cannot change it. Wanda, you have always been kind to me, giving me money when life was so hard, and bringing me food when I was sick. I will not tell your story to another living soul as long as you live. I cross my heart and hope to die.'"

As Lura listened to Meg's story, Lura's eyes were as big as saucers, her skin coloring grew pale, and her skin became clammy. Lura was mesmerized by Meg's story, and she looked straight at

207

Meg's face as the horrible saga unfolded. Lura felt she might miss something essential if she glanced away from the storyteller.

"Wanda and I hugged for a long time, then I put Laurence's head in four fresh bags and handed it to her. I watched Wanda as she walked home carrying the bags containing Laurence's head."

Meg looked at Lura's face and went on. "I know a bit more of the details of all that happened. Wanda told me about these details over the years. Do you want me to tell you what else Wanda told me? I do not feel I am betraying her now that she is dead, too."

"Yes, I want to hear all of it. I owe it to Laurence," said Lura.

Meg reached in her large pocket and removed a notebook. Lura could see there was handwriting on the pages of the notebook.

"What I wrote in this notebook is exactly what Wanda told me about Laurence's murder. It is in her own words. She told me at various times, and each time, I would always write down the exact words she said to me. I wrote this because I wanted to remember all she said, and I wanted a record of this in case I ever needed it."

Meg paused and looked at the cover of the notebook for a moment, then handed the notebook to Lura so she could read it.

Lura began reading:

These are the true words Wanda Kennedy said to Meg McGinnis over the years about the murder of Laurence Kennedy. Recorded by Meg McGinnis.

On Easter weekend, 1944, here is what happened. When I learned Laurence was going to leave me for another women, I talked my brother, James, into helping me kill Laurence. My brother came to my house and brought three bottles of whiskey, hammers, and saws. He hid the tools on the front porch. Whereas James just pretended to drink, Laurence drank until he got stinking drunk.

Once Laurence was unconscious, we put down a tarp on the floor near his chair, pulled him onto the tarp and then dragged him to the front room of the house which we never use. We used tarps to keep the blood from covering the floor.

James raised the largest hammer and forcefully hit Laurence in the temple with a sickening thud. Laurence's ear started to bleed, and his skin tore open. I eagerly took one of the other hammers and hit Laurence several times in different places on his head and each time at the place the hammer hit, there was an indentation on Laurence's head and then a lot of blood. After this, we suspected he was dead.

James checked and Laurence was definitely dead. I told James to undress Laurence, and afterwards I took a butcher's knife and cut off Laurence's privates. James gasped and asked me why I did that because that was not in our plan. I just smiled.

To my exasperation, James began to feel too sick to finish our work tonight. I knew that was a fine kettle of fish because by leaving his body in the house overnight, we might be caught. Olivia was spending the night with a friend, but she was supposed to come home in the morning.

In any case, we decided to leave Laurence's body in this room and come back the next evening and finish our work.

I spent hours cleaning up the blood. I put the pots and cake pans we used for collecting the blood in the sink to soak. I went to bed about three in the morning.

The next morning Olivia arrived home early from spending the night with a friend because she was sick. She came in the kitchen and questioned me about bloody pots and pans. I told her I cut my hand.

I was amazed that I was not sorry. I gave Olivia medicine for her upset stomach mixed with sleeping pills so she would sleep for a long time.

I sat on the front porch most of the next day because I did not want to be alone in the house with Laurence's dead body.

Finally, at about 5 o'clock James came back and brought a big cardboard box with him in this truck. We did our gruesome work, dismembering Laurence, so that the parts were small enough to throw in the outhouse. We put all the parts and the torso in the large cardboard box and dragged it to the outhouse which was at the back corner of the yard. It took all my strength and over three hours to drag that box clear across our big yard.

We had forgotten to bring a flashlight and it was a dark night, so we could not see well. James dumped the portions of Laurence's body in the outhouse hole and with each piece that fell in, we heard a splash. When only Laurence's head was left to throw in, I said that I wanted to do that part myself. I asked James to step out of the outhouse and give me some privacy. I held Laurence's head up so that his face and my face were inches apart. I kissed his bloody dead lips, and threw his head in the outhouse hole, or at least I thought I did. The fact that your dog carried off Laurence's head tells me it must have missed the hole and fallen on the outhouse floor.

Meg watched Lura as she read this. Lura's tears fell on the pages of the notebook. When she finished reading, she sat still as a statue with her eyes closed for a couple of minutes. Then she opened her eyes and handed the notebook to Meg.

"I have to go home now," said Lura as she stood up, walked out the front door of Meg's house unsteadily, and got into her Packard with Earl sleeping in the driver's seat. She woke Earl by saying, "Let's go home now. Earl, I want you to know that you are my loyal friend."

CHAPTER 24

Lura and Josephine

1979-1993

After Laurence's horrible death was revealed, Lura and Josephine's relationship changed. Josephine annoyed Lura with irritating questions and hateful comments such as:

- *Why did you leave the lid off the jelly?*
- *Why did you open that window?*
- *Lura, I do not like to hear you play the piano.*
- *You are a horrible musician.*
- *You are giving me a headache.*
- *Why do you have an irritated look on your face?*

To isolate herself from Josephine's irritating behavior, Lura spent most of her time in her bedroom or her sitting room on the second floor. She also arranged for a separate telephone line to be installed so that she had her own personal phone and phone number, preventing Josephine from picking up another house phone and eavesdropping on Lura's phone calls.

This negativity between the sisters went on for over two years. It saddened both of them.

Lura knew she was getting physically weaker. It was now hard on her to go up and down stairs, and so she took more naps. She was also diagnosed with rheumatoid arthritis in her hands and wrists. This was particularly debilitating for her because it meant that she could no longer manage her colostomy bags proficiently.

Lura's declining health worried her because being clean and smelling good was essential to her. Another difficulty of Lura's diminishing strength was that she could no longer push the heavy vacuum cleaner, or bend down to use the dustpan, or sweep up the dirt from the floor.

By 1986, Lura's legs were too weak to manage going up the stairs anymore. The house had only one bedroom downstairs and it was occupied by Josephine. Lura knew Josephine's bedroom was plenty large for the two of them to share, but she worried that Josephine would be against sharing her room with her. So, Lura decided to try an experiment to see if she could get Josephine to invite her to move into her bedroom.

For the next several days, Lura was extra nice to Josephine. She made a big breakfast for the two of them each morning. She cooked bacon, fried eggs, toast, and grits. Lura did a decent job cooking despite her arthritic hands. As the two sisters sat down for breakfast on the third morning in a row, Josephine started a conversation.

"These scrambled eggs are delicious," she said.

"Thanks. I think so, too. I used a little cream and cheese in them to make them extra tasty."

As the sisters sat there eating, emotion overcame Lura, and her eyes began to tear up. She covered her eyes with her gnarled and knotted hands, and tears trickled down her old, wrinkled cheeks. As she wept, she made pitiful little whimpering noises like a puppy.

To Lura's surprise, Josephine expressed kindness and compassion by hugging her. In a voice that sounded genuinely concerned, Josephine said, "Lura, Honey, what's wrong?"

Lura looked at Josephine through her tears and said, "I'm losing my strength, Josephine; I just cannot manage the stairs any more at all. How on earth can I get to my bedroom? I have become a weak old woman."

"We'll just get Earl to move your bedroom furniture to my room. There is plenty of room for all of your furniture and all of my furniture in that one room," said Josephine.

Josephine said exactly what Lura had hoped and prayed she would say. Lura hugged her sister, and felt the huge emotional rift between them evaporate.

"Lura, I know I have not been easy to live with for a while. The reason for my negative behavior is that I feel so alone in all the world. But now I am going to help you and you are going to help me and we will watch out for each other. I feel like my body is failing me too, and it scares me to death. We must be a rock for each other and build each other up with kindness and compassion."

After that morning, the two sisters helped each other, and were kind to each other for the rest of their lives. As the years passed, the two sisters slowly grew remarkably close and loving to each other once again. Even though each of them was hospitalized from time to time, the two sisters managed to hold things together. Luckily, when one was sick, the other was usually well. Lura's ailments were gastrointestinal in nature, whereas Josephine's were usually respiratory. Even with their health problems, they were content in their self-imposed isolation.

Every few years Lura received a letter from her stepdaughter Matilda inviting her to come for a visit. Lura never replied, she just placed the letter with all the others she had received over the years from Matilda in a shoebox.

CHAPTER 25
A Serendipitous Meeting
1993-1994

Sometimes in life strangers meet by complete happenstance and this sets in motion a completely different and unexpected outcome. This is what happened one bright beautiful Tuesday morning in April 1993. Elsie Everette from Raeford was on vacation in Beaufort, North Carolina and she walked into a flea market to look for prisms. Matilda and David Aasen usually work as salesclerks in this flea market on Thursdays, but because their friend was under the weather, they were working this day for her.

When Elsie came to the cash register to pay for her prisms, David said, "Where are you from?"

David was a great conversationalist and loved to talk to all the customers.

"Raeford, North Carolina," said Elsie.

Both Matilda and David were astonished. By this time, Matilda seldom thought of her stepmother anymore. That chapter in her life had closed forever. Or had it? But maybe there was a tiny crack in that long ignored chapter of Matilda's life that seemed to be opening, just a little.

For the next thirty minutes the three of them had an intense conversation. Elsie told them that Lura and Josephine were her distant relatives, that they were recluses, never letting anyone in their house. Matilda told Elsie that Lura was her stepmother, and she had not seen her or heard from her in over thirty years.

215

Elsie said that no one in Raeford even knew that Lura had a stepdaughter. Over the course of the conversation, Elsie felt great sympathy for Matilda's inability to communicate with Lura and obtain her family Bible and baby pictures. Elsie happily agreed to Matilda's request – for her to let Matilda know if Lura went into a nursing home or died. Matilda felt she might have a chance to get her belongings under these circumstances.

Matilda called her grown daughter, Gay, and told her about this serendipitous meeting with Elsie.

Gay said, "Mama, I think this is all so strange. I wonder if this meeting with Elsie has a hidden meaning."

Then Gay learned she needed to take a trip to Pinehurst for her job early next year. Matilda suggested that Gay go to Raeford after leaving Pinehurst because it was only twenty-four miles away. So, the plan was set for Gay to try to see Lura.

After the January 1994 Pinehurst meeting, Gay drove to Raeford. Gay had a strange feeling in the pit of her stomach as she pondered the outcome of this day. In Gay's heart of hearts, she did not believe that Lura, her step-grandmother would agree to see her today. The last time she saw Lura was when she was seven-years-old at her grandfather Tom's funeral. Now thirty-four years later, she wanted to try to see this mysterious woman again, if she could.

She figured there could be three different endings to this day:

(1) Lura would welcome her with open arms (unlikely),

(2) Lura would let her inside the house and talk to her, but behave coolly, or

(3) Lura would refuse to see her step-granddaughter.

She decided not to be upset with any of the potential outcomes because she did not have emotional energy invested in the relationship with Lura. There was no relationship, only an attempted relationship.

216

Gay arrived in Raeford about 1 o'clock in the afternoon. Lacking Lura's phone number and address, she had to do a bit of detective work to find her. She tried the police station first and talked to an elderly policeman with a kind face. She told him that Lura Davis was her step-grandmother, and she wanted to locate Lura's house and go see her. At that moment, all the policemen stopped what they were doing, perked up their ears, and listened to the conversation with great interest. The elderly policeman gave the others a strange look.

"Honey, we never knew Miss Lura had any stepchildren, much less step-grandchildren. We knew she was married, but we thought that her husband had no children. Regardless of that, you look like a nice lady to me, so I am going to help you. Come this way."

The officer led Gay to the other side of the building, and she noticed that the policemen were whispering to each other and staring at her. The news of Lura's step-granddaughter coming to town spread like wildfire. The nice policeman led Gay to the tax collector whose office was also in the same building as the police station. The tax collector was a stylish looking woman in her 40's with big orange earrings, and a tweed suit to match.

"Betty Jo, honey, I have some big news for you. This is Lura Davis' step-granddaughter, and she needs directions to Lura's house," he said.

"Bo in the next office just told me about you, ma'am. This is such a surprise because Lura never mentioned having any relatives other than the Kennedys," said Betty Jo.

Gay reached out to shake Betty Jo's hand and introduced herself. Betty Jo told Gay she would drive her car to Miss Lura's house, and that Gay could follow her. Betty Jo drove about a mile and then pulled her car into a grand circular driveway, stopping in front of an imposing brick two-story house that was at least one hundred feet from the street. Gay parked behind Betty Jo. Both ladies got out of their cars.

"It looks like no one's home," said Betty Jo. "Why don't you wait in your car, and I'll go knock on the door."

Gay waited impatiently until Betty Jo knocked on the door and returned to the car.

"As you can see, there's no answer. This is probably the day that Earl takes Miss Lura to the beauty parlor," said Betty Jo.

"What do you suggest I do?" asked Gay.

"Why don't you get some lunch at the Wagon Wheel Restaurant and then come back. Miss Lura should be home by then."

Gay took Betty Jo's advice and went to the Wagon Wheel Restaurant. The smell of fried chicken, homemade biscuits, and hush puppies permeated the air and made the place seem homey. A friendly looking waitress came to Gay's table holding a pad and pencil.

"Darling, you can sit wherever you want," she said.

All the tables were occupied, but small town folk being helpful and kind, noticed that this stranger needed a seat. Several customers shifted their seats and moved their food to make an empty table. Gay sat down and thanked them. The waitress came over and placed a glass of sweet tea and a menu labeled 'The Wagon Wheel' on Gay's table. She said that the catfish was great today, so Gay ordered that with sweet potato fries. One of the men who had vacated the table where Gay sat overheard her order.

"Good choice," he said.

"I know you are not from around these parts. I hope you are not having trouble. I saw you walk into the police station," said a woman from the next table.

Gay smiled and thought about how different it must be to live in a small town of 5,000 people, like Raeford.

"I sure hope you get to see Miss Lura and her sister, Miss Josephine. They almost never let anyone in that house," said the man.

Gay thought, *how on earth does this man know what I am here for? Typical small town grapevine must be working at the speed of light today.*

"Miss Lura and Miss Josephine are at my sister's beauty parlor now. I just left there. By the time you eat and drive back to their house, Earl should have them back home," said the friendly woman.

"Who is Earl?" asked Gay.

"Earl Brown is just about the only person Lura and Josephine allow in their house. They have known him all their lives. Earl's father and his grandfather have always worked for Lura's family, and now Earl takes care of Lura and Josephine. Earl is Miss Lura's and Miss Josephine's chauffeur, butler, handyman, delivery man, and grocery shopper. The ladies don't go out much, but when they do, Earl drives them. Earl is the kindest man you will ever meet. I just do not know what the two ladies will do when Earl passes."

Then the woman changed her demeanor from outgoing and friendly to dead serious, and she lowered her voice, and moved closer to Gay and said,

"I do not know what you know about Lura and her family's past, but there are skeletons and secrets in every closet of that old house. People in the town want to know what has really gone on behind those closed and forbidden doors. There are rumors of murders and ghosts. I tell you; I would never go in that house."

Then the lady put her hand on Gay's shoulder and spoke in a motherly way.

"You be careful now. Don't get drawn into that Kennedy quagmire. You will be better off if she doesn't let you in."

These reactions about Lura first from the policemen, and now from this lady alarmed Gay, but she still wanted to see her step-grandmother.

Gay easily found her way back to the old Kennedy house. As she walked toward the front door, she noticed what a stately and fine house this must have been in its heyday. The house was situated on an exceptionally large lot, and contained four massive chimneys, three dormer windows, and torn awnings over the doors and windows. On this second visit to the house, there was a massive black Packard dating from the 1940's parked underneath the portico on the right side of the house.

Gay boldly walked up to the front door and rang the bell, but it did not work. So, she knocked loudly on the door. As she waited, she noticed the cobwebs in all the corners of the door and windows. The house seemed like an incredibly old lady, once beautiful, refined and meticulously groomed, and now in the declining years of her life. What a shame! Gay waited for a long time after she knocked. She waited so long that she would have left if she were not trying to see Lura. She reasoned that if she left now, she might never get to come again. As Gay pondered these thoughts, the door was slowly opened by a nice-looking black man- slim, kind, and with a friendly smile.

"Can I help you, Miss?"

"I hope so. My name is Gay Aasen Corey, and I am the step-granddaughter of Lura Kennedy Davis. I am forty-one-years-old, and I have not seen her since I was eight. I came to visit her today."

Earl smiled a warm and caring smile.

Gay wondered, was he thinking, *I could have known and loved this child if circumstances had been different?* Had Lura told Earl that she had a step-granddaughter? Maybe she had never acknowledged Matilda or Gay to anyone.

Earl held up a finger and said, "You wait here, Honey."

It seemed to Gay that he had more life in his step as he turned to go to tell Lura that her granddaughter was here. It took about ten minutes for Earl to return to the door. With his head held low, he ever so slowly opened the massive front door again. He just stood there, pursed his lips, and shook his head back and forth in an exaggerated way.

"I am 86 today, and it's my birthday. I hate to tell you this, but Miss Lura will not see you."

Even though Gay had prepared for this outcome, and knew it was the most likely one, she felt like she had been slapped in the face. To Gay, it was tragic that this 84-year-old woman was not even allowing her own step-granddaughter in the house. It would just have taken only seconds for Gay to walk inside and for her step-grandmother and her to be reunited. It was not so tragic for Gay who had a husband, a daughter, loving parents, a career, hobbies, interests, and college degrees, but it was tragic for Lura. All those years between Tom's death in 1959 till this attempted visit in 1994, Gay and her mother Matilda had tried to reach out to Lura numerous times, invite her to special occasions, and to share family life with them. Now, here is an 84-year-old woman in a decaying house, not having anyone in to visit, and only going outside twice a week. How could she choose not to see Gay after all these years? Gay wanted to know what makes someone like this, and what circumstances in Lura's life made her choose being alone rather than being with her family? Gay was determined to try to find out what would make a person this way.

Matilda and David
Family photos reprinted with permission of heir of photographer

CHAPTER 26
Lura & Josephine at the Nursing Home
1995

In June 1995, both Lura and Josephine's health deteriorated rapidly. Neither sister could adequately take care of herself, much less each other. Lura now fumbled with her colostomy bags and quickly became bedridden.

Josephine was doing her best to take care of her sister but unfortunately, she stumbled over a pile of books on the floor and couldn't get up. Prior to the fall, she was bringing food and water to their bedroom and the sisters ate their meals there.

Now there was no one to bring Lura and Josephine food and water. The two sisters were in a pickle, and to make the situation worse, both telephones had been cut off for nonpayment.

Both Josephine and Lura were desperately worried, and knew they needed help to survive.

"Josephine, this probably serves us right for not letting anyone come into our house," said Lura.

"I'm not so sure anymore, Lura. Things need to change," said Josephine from the floor.

"We might die here in our bedroom, then our bodies would decompose, causing a horrible smell all the way to our neighbor's yard. Then the police would come, and we could have a joint funeral," said Lura.

This scenario envisioned by Lura was not to happen. The next evening Earl Brown was at the front door calling Lura and Josephine, but they were too weak to respond with more than a whisper. Earl could not hear them speak.

Earl used his key to open the front door. When Josephine and Lura heard this, they looked at each other, and they both said a little silent prayer of thanks.

When Earl walked into Lura's and Josephine's bedroom, the sisters were never so happy to see anyone in their lives.

Earl looked shocked when he saw the ladies.

"Miss Lura, Miss Josephine," he repeated over and over. He shook his head back and forth and tears were falling down his dear black cheeks.

First, Earl went to get two glasses of water. He handed Lura her glass. She could hold the glass, but her throat muscles did not allow her to swallow the liquid.

Earl then tried to help Josephine by holding the glass of water to her lips, but she could not swallow either.

Earl stood there looking at the sisters for a few minutes. His shoulders slumped and his hands were on his hips.

"Miss Lura and Miss Josephine, you need lots more help than I can give you. I am going to go across the street to use the telephone and call for an ambulance."

Lura lost consciousness when Earl left the room to call the ambulance.

Lura stayed in the hospital for a week and was then taken to Autumn Care Nursing Home. Josephine stayed in the hospital one day longer than Lura did. Both sisters were too weak to feed themselves. It took many days of nutritious food and physical therapy for them to get better. Both sisters did improve, but neither of them could walk unassisted, and their hands were not dexterous enough to cook or clean a house. Lura was an utter failure at taking care of her colostomy bag. The sisters had been hopeful that they could return home, but now they saw this would be impossible.

At the nursing home, the sisters had separate bedrooms, but they shared a sitting room with other residents.

Duncan McMillan, the sisters' lawyer and cousin came for a visit. After exchanging pleasantries, Duncan got down to business.

"I think you two are going to be here for a long time. We need to decide how to pay for your care here. I am happy to figure that out for you, but do you want me to tell you all the details of what I have in mind?"

Both Josephine and Lura looked into each other's eyes, and then in unison said an emphatic,

"NO!"

"That's Okay," said Duncan, a little surprised. "Why don't you tell me what you have been up to lately and who has been to see you."

Lura and Josephine had a nice chat with Duncan. They asked about his mother, and about the Presbyterian church where all three of them were members.

"I will respect your wishes and handle everything. You two will be taken care of," said Duncan.

He then said his goodbyes and left.

Lura called the nurse to take her back to her room, as she felt totally exhausted.

Lura sat alone in her room pondering what Duncan had said. She knew their only option would be to sell the house, but she was glad that he didn't mention it.

Lura had an ability that few people have. She could decide to put something out of her mind and act as if it did not happen, or even to act as if it would not happen. She did this when she accidently killed Tom, and she did it now to remove any thought of relinquishing her beloved Raeford homeplace.

CHAPTER 27
The Davis Family Bible
1995

As promised, when Elsie Everette met Matilda Aasen two years previously at the Flea Market, she wrote to Matilda in October 1995 saying that Lura and Josephine had been placed in a nursing home. Elsie also said that Lura's house and all its contents would be sold at public auction in late November. Elsie suggested that Matilda contact her stepmother's attorney.

Matilda asked her daughter Gay to contact the attorney. Gay explained to Duncan McMillan that the house contained her grandfather's family Bible, family papers, pictures, and genealogy materials. Gay asked if she and her mother could come to Raeford and meet with him. She also asked if he would be willing to have someone gather up all the Davis family papers, genealogy materials, and newspaper clippings so Gay could take them home with her. The attorney agreed to meet with Gay and Matilda at Lura's house three days later.

As Matilda and Gay entered the circular driveway of Lura's property, Matilda commented on the faded glory of the once beautiful and stately home. The expansive front porch was covered in tiny paint chips from the paint peeling from the windows and doors. The unkempt yard had clearly not been tended to for a long time. Gay recalled the hurt she felt the previous year when she tried to visit her step-grandmother at this house, to no avail.

Duncan McMillan, a handsome man in his 40's, welcomed Matilda and Gay, and unlocked the beveled glass French doors which were covered by heavy bed sheets to prevent curious people from seeing into the house.

Gay and Matilda eagerly followed Duncan into the long-forbidden house. At first glance, Gay and Matilda noticed the fourteen-foot ceilings, the excellent quality of the hardwood floors, and the feeling of expansiveness of the house. To Matilda's surprise, hanging in the entrance hall was a familiar portrait of one of Matilda's ancestors.

"That is a portrait of my ancestor, James Davis," said Matilda.

Duncan took the portrait off the wall, and said, "This is now yours."

Gay was perplexed that her step-grandmother chose to put a portrait of a Davis ancestor in the focal point of the house, rather than a portrait of a Kennedy ancestor.

"It is indeed ironic that your ancestor's name was James Davis, because when Lura's father, Jackson, escaped and lived incognito in Alabama for fifteen years, he used the alias, James B. Davis," said Duncan.

Matilda thought this was a strange comment but did not ask for an explanation because there was so much to see and explore.

"Now let's take a quick look around the house and gather your things," said Duncan.

Gay and Matilda followed Duncan through the fifteen spacious rooms of the house. In the kitchen, Duncan introduced Matilda and Gay to three middle-aged women. "These women have been working hard for a month to clean the house and prepare it for the auction. I asked them to gather your family pictures, documents, and letters. Those materials are in the six large cardboard boxes at the front door."

Duncan led Matilda and Gay up the wide and majestic staircase. They walked through all the expansive rooms on the second floor, but much too quickly for Matilda to see all she wanted to see.

Then they proceeded to the attic. The attic was full of old treasures. Gay saw a wooden baby crib, a child's highchair, dolls, a large wicker bedroom suite, and much more. Matilda came across two more framed Davis family portraits and Duncan said she could have them. Duncan, Matilda, and Gay quickly walked through the rest of the attic, but nothing else looked familiar to Matilda.

Returning to the dining room, Duncan picked up a large and ancient looking book. "Here is your Davis family Bible."

Matilda took the treasured family heirloom in her hands and then hugged it to her chest.

Just then Matilda spotted something on the table which she had been seeking. She reverently picked up a pocket watch which she had not seen in thirty-six years. She opened the watch and saw her own childhood photograph looking back at her.

"This is my father's pocket watch, and I would love to take this home. He used to play with me by saying 'Matilda, do you want to see a monkey?' and then he would open his watch and show me my own picture."

"I wish I could say you could take that watch home with you now. But if I said that, I would not be looking out for Lura's monetary interests. If you want the watch, you will have to bid on it at the auction," said Duncan in a businesslike manner.

Gay could tell that Duncan's reply embarrassed her mother.

Then Duncan quickly changed the subject and said, "I am going to stay in the dining room to go over some auction business. Matilda, you and Gay can look through the house again and see if you see anything else that belonged to your father."

"Thanks Duncan. We will do just that," said Gay.

Then Matilda and Gay went into the kitchen where the three cleaning ladies were putting glassware into boxes for the auction tomorrow. The oldest cleaning lady with her hair in pink curlers spoke first.

"Mr. McMillan told us that you are the daughter of Miss Lura's dead husband Tom, but no one in Raeford ever knew you existed."

"It seems that Lura never told anyone about me. I do not know why," said Matilda.

The slightly younger cleaning lady with beautiful blue eyes, a pretty figure, and a strong southern accent weighed in.

"The Kennedys were mighty strange people. My sisters were amazed that I agreed to clean this house since this is where that man had his head and feet cut off. I tell you, *no one* in the town was ever allowed in the yard, much less the house. I know secrets about this house. This is the spookiest house in town and there are hundreds of stories about it. Y'all are probably wondering why I even took this job. Well, I wanted to look at all those things in the house which we could never see before. You might say I am plenty curious. This house was the nastiest I ever cleaned."

The other two cleaning ladies nodded in agreement and rolled their eyes.

The cleaning lady with the pretty blue eyes continued speaking. "When we got here, we found twenty-one dead rats, cobwebs throughout the house, dead bugs, and filth. Miss Lura has not been able to look after herself for a long time. Poor Miss

Lura forgot how to take care of her colostomy, so we found nasty rags and colostomy bags everywhere-particularly under her bed. The smell! Lord have mercy! I thought I would throw up the first few days I was here, but I guess a body can get used to most anything."

Just then, Duncan walked into the kitchen and interrupted the fascinating story. The three cleaning ladies instantly stopped talking and went back to their work, as if they knew they had been gossiping out of turn and wasting time. Duncan was holding a framed photograph.

"I saw this in the formal dining room. I asked the cleaning ladies to leave all the things in the room where they found them, so this photograph must have been in a place of prominence for a long time. Matilda, I can tell this is a younger version of you and I'm sure you would like to have it. So, have you seen enough of the house this morning?"

"Yes, and we certainly appreciate the family Bible, the three portraits, and the boxes of Davis papers," said Gay.

Duncan and the three cleaning ladies put the portraits and the six boxes in Matilda's car.

When Gay and Matilda drove away, they discussed the astounding stories they heard and had experienced at Lura's house.

"What those cleaning ladies told us was incredible," remarked Gay.

"Yes indeed!" agreed Matilda.

To both Matilda and Gay, this experience was the culmination of years of trying to get Matilda's family Bible and family papers from her stepmother. But the visit was also the beginning of trying to understand why Lura rejected all their attempts at friendship and inclusiveness. Both Matilda and Gay marveled at the comments by the cleaning ladies and were amazed to learn that the people in Raeford also agreed that Lura and her family were strange. They commented upon the sadness and tragedy which Lura's family endured.

"It is hard for me to even wrap my arms around all we have heard and seen on this trip. Gay, what words would you use to describe this trip today?" asked Matilda.

"These words come to mind: haunting, eventful, historic, confusing, contradictory, sad, and tragic." They both agreed that this visit was the most memorable and eventful that they had experienced in a long time.

CHAPTER 28
The Boxes Reveal Secrets
1995

As soon as Gay returned home from her step-grandmother Lura's house, she started going through the six large, corrugated boxes that Lura's lawyer had given them. She decided not to read all the materials thoroughly the first time she went through the boxes. She simply took a quick glance at each item. Some of the items included letters, Confederate money, Matilda's baby pictures, and hundreds of newspaper clippings.

Gay's interest and curiosity about the contents of the boxes was so intense that she could not tear herself away from the boxes, other than to telephone her mother three times to tell of new discoveries. She continued examining papers until the wee hours of the morning when her husband called from the bedroom and said he felt like an abandoned husband.

The next day, Gay left her job at about noon, drove home, and launched into her treasure hunt again. The most poignant thing Gay found was an ordinary shoe box with the word IMPORTANT written in large letters on the lid. Inside the box were all the things Matilda's family had sent to Lura over the years, Gay's wedding announcement, pictures of Gay as a child, Valentine's cards, Christmas cards, a letter from Gay, and fifteen letters to Lura from Matilda.

Gay tried to reason why Lura would write the word important on the box if she did not value her stepdaughter and her family enough to let them visit, or even communicate. Gay wondered if Lura felt her life was better for not allowing Matilda and her family to have a close relationship with her. To say the least, Gay was shocked that Lura kept all those mementos. Gay felt the expected outcome should have been for Lura to throw the items away as soon as they were received. The fact that she held onto them certainly had a hidden meaning.

There were multiple newspaper clippings about Lura's father Jackson Kennedy killing the chief of police in 1912, going to prison, escaping, and living in Alabama under an assumed name. There was an incredibly sad letter from Jeremiah Green to Lura written in 1977 saying that he was the illegitimate child of Lura's brother, Louis.

By examining the boxes, Gay learned much more about her own family, but she was totally overwhelmed by the violence, dysfunction, and mental instability in her step- grandmother's family.

CHAPTER 29
The Viewing Day
1995

Twelve days after Matilda and Gay went to Lura's house to obtain their family Bible, they were back to view the contents of the house and attend the big auction the following day. The auction company advertised this day as the "Viewing Day," which meant this was the day when anyone could come in the home and look through all that was there in preparation for the auction. This was the day that the Raeford people had waited for, because while the Kennedys lived there, almost no one was ever allowed to enter the house, or even the grounds.

Matilda and Gay arrived early. They wanted as much time as possible to view the house and its contents. As they walked leisurely through the stately but deteriorated house, they felt happy that no one was rushing them, or watching them, and that no one even knew who they were. This anonymity gave them the freedom to observe the comments and behavior of others as they walked through the house. Gay had the strange thought that today's totally unrestricted access to the house and its contents was a payback for the time two years ago when her step-grandmother would not let her in the house.

The first room they visited was the elaborate music room containing a grand piano and two harps and two harp stools. Several people were walking in and out of the room. Gay walked over to a small bookcase and began picking up books on the history of the Scottish Highlands. A hot discussion/argument was in progress between a lady with teased blue-black hair who was sitting on the piano bench, and a thin older lady sitting on one of the harp benches.

"I fixed Miss Lura and Miss Josephine's hair for the last thirty years. They came to my beauty parlor every Wednesday morning at 11 a.m.," said the lady with the blue-black hair.

"They were always immaculately dressed, but they almost never talked to anyone. If I asked them about the weather or mentioned an event in the news, they might reply with a few words, but they never talked about their family or specific people. Once I asked Miss Lura about Miss Wanda's horrible treatment of her husband Laurence, and Miss Lura just ignored my comment and opened a magazine. She acted as if she never heard my comment."

The thin older lady jumped up off the harp bench and spoke angrily, "What the devil do you mean by saying Wanda treated her husband horribly? Wanda was my best friend, and her husband deserved everything he got. Wanda even told me what she was going to do before she did it. Don't you EVER say anything bad about Wanda. Wanda brought her daughter up right, took her to Sunday School, and taught her right from wrong. Wanda was generous to everyone in Raeford. She loved making cakes for Raeford people when there were weddings, funerals, or baptisms. She was my loyal friend."

One of the rooms Gay found most interesting was the library. In this room were what must have been a thousand or more books. The focal point of the room were the two beautiful antique barrister bookcases with glass doors. These bookcases were empty because all the books had been put in liquor boxes on the floor. At least one third of the books had the name 'Davis' stamped or written on the inside of the book covers, and some of the books were published as far back as the 1700s.

"How in the world did your Papa have so many books when he lived for a long time in a boarding house?" asked Gay of her mother.

Matilda replied, "He only gained possession of the books when his mother died. Papa loved these books and particularly treasured the ones from James Davis."

Gay said, "I am going to rearrange these books so I can buy all the books that belonged to our Davis family, plus a few others that are interesting to me."

Gay sat down on the floor and rearranged the books so that she knew which boxes of books she should bid on. In the end, she had twelve liquor boxes containing only the books she planned to buy. She wrote down the color and the wording on the boxes, so she could easily identify the boxes for the bidding.

The saddest room in the house was Josephine and Lura's bedroom. This room contained the shabbiest furniture in the whole home. The broken drawers of the dresser and the leaning sleigh beds were worn out from years of use.

Matilda and Gay went to the second floor and into one of the bedrooms. Lura's hairdresser and her thin friend were continuing their controversial conversation in that room. "I cannot believe I am really in Lura Kennedy's house. For years, I have been hearing stories about this place. And of course, all these years no one was allowed in the yard, much less the house. I wonder where in the house that murder was committed?" said the hairdresser.

Gay and Matilda were particularly interested in the second floor that contained the huge cedar closet. As they walked into this bedroom, once again the hairdresser and her friend were talking loudly and proudly about private aspects of the Kennedy family. Just then the hairdresser said, "Aila Kennedy was a *bitch,* a pure *bitch.*

237

She was hateful as all get out to her husband Jackson. And I guess it was because he humiliated her all those years. She was a bitch to almost all her children, too. Lura was the only one her mother liked even a little bit. She even cut her son Angus out of her will entirely. That was just not fair, because he was the son that visited her and did the most for her."

"These Kennedys ain't as high and mighty as they thought they were. This family has always been hotheaded-particularly Jackson Kennedy. Just look what he did," said the friend.

Then Lura's hairdresser and her friend left the room. Gay felt like the hairdresser and her friend were trying to figure out who Matilda was, or trying to shock Matilda, or trying to provoke a reaction from Gay or Matilda. It was all perplexing, but fascinating. Gay said, "Being here feels like being in the *Twilight Zone.*"

Matilda and Gay entered the large closet which was permeated by the fragrant cool aroma from the cedar panels on the walls and ceiling of the closet. They enjoyed examining the gowns; ball gowns, prom gowns, and wedding gowns. The dresses dated from different time periods in the last one hundred years. Gay liked the short flapper dresses with an abundance of fringe. Interestingly there were seven identical flapper dresses in assorted colors. Just then an incredibly old woman and a slightly younger woman entered the closet. The older woman picked up the red flapper dress and looked at it for a long time. "I remember Lura telling me that she wore this to her first dance at Brenau College. She was happy then. I am glad she found some happiness in her life," said the older woman.

The ladies who were discussing Lura's red flapper outfit left the room. Gay and Matilda continued to look at the dresses and noticed most of them were in various stages of dry rot, some so

238

fragile that just to touch the fabric made it disintegrate. The clothes were falling apart, just like the house, and just like Lura.

Matilda and Gay looked around the house a while longer; they even looked at the buildings in the back of the house, containing old furniture and scattered papers. Many papers mentioned business dealings of J.B. Davis and Sylacauga, Alabama. There was an old file cabinet whose drawers were opened to expose papers that had yellowed with age. In plain sight they saw letters signed by Allen Jenkins, cancelled checks, and deeds to property in Alabama. There were also thick ledgers on the old desk.

To Gay and Matilda, much of the enjoyment of this day came from the hundreds of people who came through the house and made comments about the family. What they said was sensational and some of what they said was slightly incorrect. Gay was able to understand most of what they said because by this time, she had read every scrap of paper in the six boxes which Lura's lawyer, Duncan McMillan, had given her.

Gay and Matilda did not know it, but Earl also visited during the open house. Whereas Gay and Matilda saw the house and its belongings as an adventure and an opportunity to right a big wrong done to them, Earl thought of this day as the end of a family. To him, it was a sad and tragic day. Earl walked slowly through all the rooms, reliving poignant memories, both good and bad. Mostly he remembered the kindness that Lura and some of the other Kennedys showed him throughout his life. When Earl walked into Lura and Josephine's bedroom, he sat down in a broken-down chair and tears rolled down his old cheeks.

CHAPTER 30

The Auction

1995

The long-awaited big day of the Kennedy auction caused quite a stir in Raeford. The newspaper headline read, "Mystery House Opens Its Doors." The people of Raeford relished learning about long held secrets in the Kennedy family.

Sadly, the weather was overcast and cold which was not an ideal day for an outdoor auction. As Matilda and Gay arrived in the vicinity of the home, there were cars parked everywhere. Over one hundred people filled the auction seats. The auctioneer was a heavy, slightly balding man in a big warm coat. He told jokes and made-up funny stories as he encouraged people to bid on the items.

Soon after the auction started, the auctioneer put up a group of pocket watches for sale. Matilda bid on her father Tom's pocket watch, and after several bids, she bought it for $400. Matilda also purchased five other old pocket watches. Gay and Matilda were successful and were able to buy all the items they wanted. Gay bought a wooden chest of drawers, a wooden bed that belonged to Lura's father Jackson, two antique barrister bookcases which belonged to Tom's grandfather, and every one of the books she had previously chosen for purchase. Matilda bought some china and other smaller items. Gay and Matilda stayed until the very end of the auction.

After the auction ended, Gay and Matilda walked through the empty house one last time. They felt sad for Lura and her family, for the tragedy of their lives, and for all they lost with the auction

Afterwards, Gay asked an auction employee how she might rent a truck to transport her new purchases home. A man standing beside Gay spoke to her. "I am Buddy Blue, Lura's nephew, and I understand you are Tom Davis' granddaughter. Elsie Everette told me that y'all would be here, and I have been looking for you two. I can help you with getting a truck and loading it for you in the morning." Buddy Blue looked to be about sixty-five-years-old, slightly chubby, with thinning hair and a nice smile. He spoke in the raspy and hoarse voice of a heavy smoker.

Gay replied, "Elsie told us about you, too. We will surely accept your kind offer of the truck. Thanks so much. If you follow me to the other side of the yard, I will introduce you to my Mama, Matilda."

They walked across the front yard to meet Matilda.

"From Elsie Everette, I understand that you and I are both amateur genealogists, Miss Gay. That is terrific. Elsie said you want to know more about the Kennedy family," said Buddy Blue.

Reaching Matilda, Gay introduced her mother to Buddy. Buddy and Matilda hit it off right away, being about the same age, and both interested in family history. After the three of them talked for about fifteen minutes, Buddy smiled and made an offer.

"If y'all are free, you two can come to my house tonight for dinner. I'm cooking soup in the crock pot, and it will be hot and delicious on this coldest day of the year."

Gay and Matilda looked at each other and nodded their heads at the same time.

"We'll come by about 6:30 p.m. if that's alright Buddy," said Gay.

Little did Gay know at that point that she and Buddy would become friends and he would help her to understand Lura and the Kennedys better.

CHAPTER 31

A Visit to Lura

1995

Gay had been pondering a visit to see Lura and Josephine all day long. She finally suggested it to her mother. Matilda was undecided if she wanted to see her stepmother, as Lura had shunned her all her life. Matilda thought it might seem strange just to walk into Lura's room in the nursing home after all those years. In the end, Gay convinced her to go, if they kept the conversation light, friendly, and did not talk about the auction, or anything controversial.

Autumn Care Nursing Home was a short ride from Lura's house. Both Gay and Matilda were nervous as they entered the nursing home and got directions to Lura's room. Standing in front of the door to Lura's room, Matilda closed her eyes, took a big breath, and knocked softly on the door.

She heard a soft voice say, "Come in."

Matilda and Gay walked in and saw a tiny old lady lying on the bed with traces of red in her mostly gray hair.

"Matilda Davis Aasen and her daughter Gay are here to see you Lura," said Matilda.

Lura looked at her two guests as calmly and as casually as if they visited her daily.

"Hello, I am glad to see you. How are you?" said Lura.

Matilda was extremely uncomfortable, and she shook slightly, but her outward appearance was upbeat and cheerful. Matilda had always been a brilliant conversationalist who could talk to anyone about anything, so she knew she could live through a brief conversation with Lura, even if she was play acting.

"Everyone is fine at home. The weather surely has turned cold, Lura."

Lura, Matilda, and Gay talked for about ten minutes about insignificant, unemotional things. Gay asked about Earl and about Lura's 103-year-old aunt who also lived at this nursing home. When Matilda and Gay were beginning to say their goodbyes to Lura, she interrupted and said, "Please go see Josephine, I know she would want to see you. Her room is the next room down the hall from mine."

"Yes, we will stop by to see Josephine," said Matilda.

Matilda and Gay said goodbye to Lura, and they closed the door to Lura's room. Matilda and Gay paused a moment and looked at each other with an expression of great relief and hugged. Matilda and Gay were as close as any mother and daughter could possibly be, and they often knew what the other person was thinking.

Next, they walked to Josephine's room. As they entered the room, Matilda spoke. "Josephine, Matilda Davis Aasen and her daughter are here to see you."

Josephine replied with a happy sounding voice and a smile, "Hello Matilda, hello Gay."

At that moment, Gay was thinking, *Josephine must have remembered that Mama's daughter was named Gay. It is amazing that she remembers my name after all those years. Had I been an occasional topic of conversation for Lura and Josephine? Why did Josephine remember my name? Maybe it was when I attempted to visit them last year and Lura turned me away.*

Josephine seemed more mentally alert than Lura. She volunteered comments during the conversation and seemed to be thoroughly enjoying the visit and talking to Matilda and Gay. The three ladies had a nice warm conversation. Matilda felt more comfortable talking to Josephine because she had always treated her kindly.

When Matilda and Gay were back in the car on the way to Buddy Blue's house, Matilda spoke softly. "The visit was not what I expected. It was not an ugly visit, and it gave me some peace. I am glad we came. I still do not understand why Lura lived her life the way she did, but coming to see her made my heart go out to her and I felt some affection and caring."

Gay replied, "When Josephine remembered my name, I must admit my heart skipped a beat. I would have loved to have had those two ladies in my life growing up, to have spent time with them here in Raeford and in our home too. I would have loved to have known Earl. I think Earl had a lot of love to give everyone. Mama, I am tremendously glad we came here today, and I suspect that even though both Lura and Josephine acted very casual about our visit today, that in reality they were profoundly moved and extremely happy that we came to see them. In retrospect, the visit to Lura and Josephine means almost as much to me as the return of our family's belongings."

CHAPTER 32
Buddy Blue
1995

Gay and Matilda arrived at Buddy Blue's house. He lived in a small bungalow with books in every nook and cranny, and papers scattered about which bore the evidence of an avid genealogist's home.

"Welcome! I am dying to ask you about your visit to Lura and Josephine," said Buddy.

"I tell you what Buddy. I was astonished that both Lura and Josephine acted as if we saw them every day. They acted like it was the most normal thing in the world for Gay and me to come for a visit when I have not seen them for thirty-five years. The visit was peaceful, brief, and fine. They were friendly, particularly Josephine. We only spoke of casual things and made no mention of the auction. The visit brought me some peace."

While Buddy, Gay, and Matilda were eating the aromatic vegetable soup and cornbread, Buddy started talking about the Kennedys.

"I can tell you two ladies are perplexed about the Kennedys and why they lived as they lived. I am going to tell you more about my family so you can understand them better. Much of what I will tell you came from my grandmother's memories. My grandmother was Lura's father's sister. For over sixty years, my grandmother lived directly across Main Street from Lura and her family in Raeford. The two families never visited each other.

They never even went into each other's yards. The only exception to this is that Lura's father, Jackson Kennedy, took his meals at my grandmother's house after he was pardoned and released from prison because his wife, Aila, was hostile and mean to him. He died in 1948 and Aila died in 1954.

Buddy took a sip of soup and continued.

"As a kid, I played with my friends in my grandmother's front yard, and in the street in front of the house if our games required more room. That street separated my grandmother's front yard from Lura's front yard. I know this sounds strange, but I was taught to never step foot in Lura's yard, and I never did. I knew better, and everyone in Raeford knew better, too."

"Buddy, do you mean if your grandmother had a big Christmas party that spilled over onto the front porch, and into the front yard, that Lura and Josephine never walked across the street to enter into the festivities?" asked Gay.

"That's exactly right, as strange as it sounds. We did see Lura and Josephine peeking out from behind the living room curtains sometimes, trying to watch the party," said Buddy.

"That is the saddest thing I ever heard, Buddy," said Matilda.

"Why did they isolate themselves like that, Buddy?" asked a puzzled Gay.

"Because after Lura's father escaped from prison and set up a second identity in Alabama, he would come to Raeford two or three times a year. It was imperative that when he showed up at his house in Raeford that no visitors were there. If there had been visitors, the visitors could have turned him into the authorities.

"To protect Jackson from being discovered and sent back to prison, Jackson and Aila came up with a plan. That plan was that outside of immediate family and Earl's family, no one else was allowed in Aila's house. Then Aila and her children extended their self-imposed isolation by not visiting in the homes of anyone they knew, too. The most amazing thing was even after Jackson was pardoned, and there was no reason in the world to isolate themselves from others, Aila still refused to let visitors come to the house.

"Aila was a bitch of a woman. She is the one who insisted on keeping this rule. Not allowing visitors to come to the house when Lura and her siblings were young, screwed up Lura big time.

"Lura had tragedies in her life. Her father committed murder, her beloved brother Laurence was murdered and dismembered, her husband Tom committed suicide, and Lura's best childhood friend, Agnes, committed suicide. It was too much, and it harmed Lura for life."

"Then why do you think Lura refused to communicate with me all those years?" asked Matilda.

"Lura had horrible role models for parents. Her mother was a bitch-always stirring up trouble, not giving affection to her children. You may be interested in why Aila was a bitch. She had a hard life too. She and Jackson married when she was fifteen and she was much too young and immature to marry. I heard through the grapevine that when Jackson got drunk, he would violate Aila.

"Then after Jackson killed the police officer and went to prison, Jackson left Aila with nine children to raise alone. That was too much for her to handle. Aila seemed uninterested in her children, and she did not give them the affection which they desperately needed. She did not express love to them and so they did not know how to express love."

Buddy shook his head and then continued. "Aila was like a caterpillar who never became a butterfly. Both Lura's grandmother and my grandmother often talked about Aila's inability to be a mother in the natural way. She had arrested emotional development and never developed her social skills further than a 15-year-old girl. This happened because of Jackson's repeated sexual violence against her. Aila also did not experience the love of being a mother as most women do. She seemed detached from her children. She seemed like she was watching her life unfold from outside herself. When the children were young, she was tired and weary, and she approached motherhood as if it were mechanical. Her personality was irrevocably harmed by Jackson's violence toward her as well as others."

"Buddy, you're starting to sound like a psychologist, and I'm glad. Lura's life and her reasons for living her life as she did weigh heavy on my heart. Please tell us more," said Gay.

"Well, Aila harmed her younger children by not explaining where their father went after he killed the police officer and was taken to prison. She thought she was doing a good thing by protecting her children from this horrible knowledge. But what happened was that it made all the younger children worry that anyone could disappear at any time. For Lura, this fear was particularly harmful because she worried about Laurence disappearing. Lura and Laurence were as close as siblings could be. Also, for Lura and all the children, their father was absent most of their growing up years. Lura, like her mother, also lacked people skills."

Buddy breathed heavily and then continued. "Laurence and Lura were the only siblings that had a close relationship. No one else in the family said, 'I love you' to each other – ever."

"Who told you that, Buddy?" asked Gay.

"Lura's brother, Angus, told me that. And as the experts say, a lack of physical and verbal affection can harm a child for life. One good thing in Lura's family was that Earl Brown, and Earl's father before him, were loyal servants and friends to the Kennedys all their lives. Earl really cares for Lura and Josephine and he continues to visit them in the nursing home as his health allows."

"I met Earl last year when I went to Lura's house for a visit. He looked terribly sad when he had to tell me that Lura would not see me. I could tell by his demeanor that he was kind, sensitive, and caring," smiled Gay.

Buddy shook his head and pressed on.

"To me, one of the saddest times for the Kennedy family was the time that Wanda and Laurence's daughter, Olivia, thought her Daddy had abandoned her. Someone told her that a man picked up her Daddy in a small airplane. Poor Olivia got excited every time she saw an airplane flying overhead because she believed her Daddy might be coming home. She always looked for airplanes."

"That's so odd," said Gay.

"The ironic thing is that deep inside, Olivia knew her Daddy was killed and chopped up by her mother. Olivia saw some evidence of the murder but could not recall all that had happened. She knew enough to be afraid that her mother was going to harm her if she told anyone what really happened. One result of all the violence which Olivia witnessed was that she told the best ghost stories when all the cousins gathered in the attic or under the house at my grandmother's home. Her tales of murder, blood, and gore scared me and my cousins to death."

"Surely some people in Raeford knew that Wanda killed Laurence," said Gay.

"Sure, they knew. My Daddy knew, and the Chief of Police knew, but because his wife was Wanda's best friend, he did not report it. Lura's parents knew, and Aila was mad as hell that Wanda did this to her son, but she reasoned that reporting it and getting Wanda sent to the electric chair would not be good for Olivia."

Gay and Matilda found the fact that people in Raeford knew that Wanda killed Laurence and did not report it to be astounding. Perhaps it was clan loyalty, or Wanda teaching Sunday School, or people feeling they could decide Wanda's fate themselves.

"Buddy, did the people of Raeford know that Lura's father often left Sylacauga and came home in secret to Raeford to visit his family?" asked Gay.

"Many surely did know this. When he got to Raeford, he would often stay in one of the many outbuildings behind the main house. He kept documents about his turpentine mills in Sylacauga in those outbuildings. My grandmother always knew when he came home, and so did my father. One thing that protected Jackson was that Raeford people and people in this part of the country loved and respected his father, Stuart John Kennedy, and out of loyalty to him, they never turned Jackson in."

The wonderful visit with Buddy went well into the night. Most of the things Buddy recounted were familiar to Gay from her careful reading of the documents and newspaper clippings in the boxes. But some of what she thought she knew was confusing and hard to piece together. She was glad that Buddy made the events much clearer, and that he did it willingly. Mother and daughter were deeply grateful that Buddy reached out to them and offered his home, his food, his confidences, and his friendship.

CHAPTER 33
Agnes Visits Lura
1997

Lura had been feeling poorly for days. The aides in the nursing home assured her that everything was going to be fine. She knew differently because it was hard for her to talk or to drink water. She felt the end was near.

One night in her nursing home bed she thought about her dear friend Agnes. Lura and Agnes's ability to communicate had changed over the years.

Now Lura could speak to Agnes in the softest whisper, or even just think what she would say, and Agnes could still hear every word or every thought coming from Lura.

Lura summoned her friend, and Agnes materialized in a haze of blue smoke within a couple of minutes.

Lura spoke to Agnes in her thoughts.

"Agnes, thanks for coming for a visit tonight. I feel my time on earth is coming to an end and I wanted to talk to you, tell you my thoughts, and to clarify my motives and feelings. Some of this I may have told you before, but I get confused now. Please bear with me."

"I'm listening, my dear Lura," whispered Agnes.

"I got along great the first several years after I returned home to Raeford after I retired. In the early days, several former friends and acquaintances called me on the telephone to suggest we get together. I chose not to see almost any of them.

"Then, about ten years after I returned to Raeford, my health began to fail. I took more naps. I had developed rheumatoid arthritis in my hands and wrists a few years earlier. My poor hands were aching all the time. The arthritis in my hands meant I could no longer manage my colostomy as proficiently as before. Also, it was more difficult for me to clean our house, and the house was getting dirtier with every passing day."

Lura was silent for a moment collecting her thoughts.

"Do continue, Lura. I'm listening," said Agnes.

"My legs were too weak to manage going up and down stairs anymore, therefore, I got Earl to move my furniture downstairs into Josephine's bedroom and we shared the room. Time passed and I was in and out of the hospital over the next several years. My ailments were gastrointestinal in nature but thank God my cancer never came back.

"In early 1994, there was one visitor that I asked Earl to turn away, and now I am questioning if I did the right thing. The person was Gay, my stepdaughter Matilda's daughter. In my heart's core, I really wanted to meet Gay and get to know her. Over the years, I had glimpses of Gay's life. She was born in Tarboro a few months after Tom and I married. After Tom died, Matilda mailed me pictures of Gay as a child and adolescent from time to time. Matilda also mailed me an invitation to Gay's high school graduation, and Gay's wedding. Gay sent me two handwritten letters when she was an adolescent. She seemed truly kind in her letters. Also, Gay would often visit my good friend, my sister-in-law, Fanny Davis, in Wilson. Gay always asked Fanny about me and asked Fanny to say hello to me on her behalf. Fanny is a good judge of character; therefore, I think I would have liked Gay if I had allowed myself to get to know her. Fanny told me that Gay was smart and loved reading, particularly the classics, and was fascinated with genealogy. Maybe she had a lot of Tom in her, and I could have witnessed that if I had let her in my house.

"I have also questioned my choice of not getting to know or spend time with Matilda. Years after Tom's death I began to ponder my choice. If I had chosen this path, then I would have gone down a vastly different road indeed. Did I make the right decision? What has been the outcome of choosing the lonely road? I had the satisfaction that I avoided Tom's descendants because I was jealous of Matilda. It helped me to avoid facing my guilt about Tom's death by not being around Matilda and her family. When Gay came to my house and tried to visit, I pulled the curtains aside just enough to look at her. She looked like Matilda. Both have jet black hair. Gay also has a professional demeanor, and sadly she appeared somewhat vulnerable. In any case I chose NOT to see her that day. Did I make the right decision? Probably not."

"One poem that reminds me of my choices in life is, *The Road Not Taken* by Robert Frost. Do you know that poem, Agnes? If you do, recite it for me please."

As directed, Agnes recited the words of Robert Frost:

Two roads diverged in a yellow wood,
And sorry I could not travel both
And be one traveler, long I stood
And looked down one as far as I could
To where it bent in the undergrowth.

I shall be telling this with a sigh
Somewhere ages and ages hence:
Two roads diverged in a yellow wood, and I—
I took the one less traveled by,
And that has made all the difference.

254

"That was beautiful Agnes. Thank you, dear friend! I have more to say to you."

Lura continued while she still had the strength to direct her thoughts.

"Our poor Earl died just a few months ago. He used to visit Josephine and me here at the nursing home. We feel lost without Earl.

"Recently I have been reminded of the choices I have made in my life. Maybe I am extra sad today. At this point in my old age, all I want is not to hurt, not to worry, and to be at peace. Matilda and Gay came here to visit a couple of years ago. That visit did not disturb my peace.

"Dear Agnes, thanks so much for being with me and letting me tell you all of this. Soon I will be where you and Laurence are, and we will be together forever. That makes me so happy."

Agnes stepped to the head of Lura's bed and removed an old framed cross-stich sampler from the wall. It was handmade by Lura's grandmother years ago. Agnes put the sampler in Lura's hands, and then Agnes looked at Lura and nodded her head in the manner she did when they were young. Agnes, looking young just like she did the day she ended her life at Brenau, and Lura looking terribly old and small, held hands and began reciting:

Hey Diddle Diddle....

They only got as far as "the cat and the fiddle," and Lura stopped breathing, and Agnes vanished.

ACKNOWLEDGMENTS

I thank Jerry, my wonderful and indulgent husband and best friend since we were 13-years-old, for proofreading, making suggestions, and putting up with many days and nights of spending time alone when I wrote my novel.

I thank my wonderful daughter, Catherine Bright, for helping me with formatting, suggestions, my book website, and marketing.

I thank Frank and Rhonda Amoroso, my publishers, and friends, who helped me transform from writing scientific literature to writing a completely new genre of literature. They kept me encouraged, offered suggestions, and sometimes gave me examples of how I could improve a passage.

I thank David Kennedy, my great friend and a fellow history and genealogy lover, for his careful and detailed analysis of the manuscript and his tremendously valuable suggestions. You will never know how much you helped me, David.

I thank Joyce Bush, my lifelong friend from England, who read the manuscript multiple times and made excellent suggestions for the psychological motivations of the characters in the book. Joyce was such a supporter that I can never thank her enough.

I thank Susan Hance, freelance writer, who carefully read the manuscript and made helpful suggestions regarding my novel's layout and characterizations.

I thank my neighbor and friend, retired English teacher Kim Roberts, for her meticulous reading of the manuscript, and her many suggestions.

Many family members also read the manuscript and offered helpful suggestions- Cousin Edna Gaston Lovelace, Cousin Mershon White, Cousin Alice Boseman, and Cousin Nerita Flake.

I thank my friends Carla and Gary Cantrell and Fran and Bill Woodruff for helping me to enhance the southern dialect of my novel during several of our yearly trips to Edisto, South Carolina. I particularly thank Carla for several useful edits after carefully reading the manuscript.

I thank my friends Joan Blanton, Jo Bowes, Kathryn Cando, Jana Utley, Alice Preville, and Jeanne Kennedy for reading the manuscript and making suggestions.

I thank Maren Jensen for helping me with the typing of the manuscript.

I thank Dr. Bill McMillan for reading the chapter on Lura's cancer and colostomy and keeping my 1950s medical language accurate to the time period.

I thank Dr. Linda F. Carners-McNaughton, Archeologist and Curator of the Cultural Resource Project at Fort Bragg, North Carolina.

I thank Benjamin Barton, Collection Development Librarian, Trustee Library, Brenau University, Gainesville, Georgia.

I thank Lynn McKaim, Brenau Alumnus, whom I met by chance. She had been helpful in making opportunities for me at Brenau University.

I thank Agnes, Brenau University's ghost.

AUTHOR'S NOTE

I have been writing this novel for almost three decades. The inspiration for the novel came to me from attending the auction of Lura's home and family possessions in November 1995. At the auction, I overheard gory stories and saw odd reactions of the townspeople, and I knew I wanted to know more. I used my librarian's research skills to seek out newspaper articles and books on what I had heard. I interviewed key people. I communicated extensively with the librarians and archivist at Brenau University Library in Gainesville, Georgia, and also the archaeologist and curator at the Fort Bragg Army Base.

Many of the events in this novel are true. Naturally, I changed the names, but the dismemberment, the murders, and the suicides all happened. Lura really attended Brenau College in 1926. The 1926 Brenau College yearbook contains a photograph of Agnes Galloway. Legend has it that when she was a student, she took her own life. Brenau students have reported sightings of Agnes' ghost on the campus for decades.

Some of the characters in the book are fictionalized versions of real people, and others come entirely from my imagination. I hope you enjoyed stepping into Lura's bizarre world as much as I did.

ABOUT THE AUTHOR

Donna Bunting Flake, writer and researcher, lives with her husband Jerry and her black cat Rosey in Wilmington, North Carolina. She is a graduate of the University of North Carolina at Chapel Hill and as a professional librarian has published more than thirty scientific articles.

Flake presents public talks on topics as diverse as technological innovation and global librarianship. She sustains a special affection for the Eastern European country of Moldova and has spearheaded efforts to organize and raise funds for medical libraries there.

Working with stained glass, researching genealogy, supporting amateur theatre, having tea parties with her granddaughters, and attending her beloved Anglican church make her joyful.

The Haunted Life of Lura is Flake's first novel. For more information, please visit www.donnabuntingflake.com.